Text Design by: T J Dockree
Cover Design by: Lucy H Smith
ISBN: 978-1-8380932-7-3

Publisher:
Cornwall Writers
www.cornwallwriters.co.uk

Scan QR code below for Content Warnings

Cornwall Beneath and Beyond

A Collection of Short Stories
by Cornwall Writers

Also by Cornwall Writers:

Cornwall Misfits, Curiosities and Legends

Cornwall Secret and Hidden

CORNWALL
beneath and beyond

A COLLECTION OF
SHORT STORIES

CORNWALL WRITERS

Cornwall Writers Short Story Project

What lies Beneath and Beyond Cornwall?

Inspired by this question, 22 local writers took up the challenge to write short stories for Cornwall Writers' latest anthology. Our diverse writing styles and backgrounds resulted in 25 stories, each with a unique perspective on the theme: coping with grief, mysterious apparitions, neighbourly shenanigans, supernatural humour, thwarted love stories, life with robots, the Camborne Cat, a Cornwall submerged underwater, buried secrets, vengeful plant life – and all these are just a small sample of what's inside this book. We hope our stories will take you on a journey that captures the way Cornwall seeps into our bones and never leaves us, wherever we are...

Cornwall Writers is a community of writers based in Cornwall, networking with and supporting each other in their writing projects. Our writing group began with just two people in 2017 and has since grown to over 300. We embarked on our first short story project in January 2019 and *Cornwall Beneath and Beyond* is our third book in the series.

Cornwall Writers
Cornwall Beneath & Beyond

Story Sketch Credits:

The Fall
by Rose Taylor

The sea was clawing over their heads again, dragging stones against the surface of the tunnel. Antony was trying not to listen to it, although his rabbit-quick heartbeat wasn't a much better alternative.

Everyone on the shift had gone very still and quiet. What breathing he could hear was quick and shallow, harsh with suppressed panic.

One wrong move or sound and their nerves would shatter. He could feel the tension of it already; the broken glass edges to their silence.

Someone started praying, too far away to see in the faint glow from the headlamps. Their voice was a reminder that there was still life down here.

Two or three others yelled immediately for silence.

Jago, the shift captain, stood still and silent.

Antony wasn't sure if time still existed. The waves

chattered. Water dripped. The blackness changed and flickered through all the colours he could name, a parade of brightness conjured up from nothing. The men were silent.

Endurance, he found himself repeating. Endurance. I must endure.

Alongside him, Jago shifted, boots scuffing the floor, fidgeted and was still again. They'd been friends since childhood, stealing apples and climbing fences, never standing still for a moment. A friendship that had endured a dozen years in the mines already – and he'd never seen his friend like this.

The knocking was too sudden to be real. Something else his brain had made up, like the colours. Like the scent of daffodils and tea treat buns he'd caught earlier.

Unreal or not, all the men heard it. Sweat soaked clothing rustled as they moved, their boots knocking against wooden rails.

Jago's voice cut the dark. 'Is there anybody there?'

'Is there anyone alive in there?' came back at the same time.

'Six of us,' Jago shouted back and Antony wanted to curse him for his bravado in saying that, in tempting fate or whatever was listening, in case it became five.

'There's been a major fall. Going to have to blast it. Keep all the men as far back as you can.'

Shepherding the men away from the faint contact with the outside world – with life – was the hardest thing Jago had ever done in the mines. A couple went meekly; the others fought and yelled and panicked and the voices of their rescuers drifted in and out, sometimes obscured by more rocks shifting.

He wondered how long it would take for the sea song above to turn to a dirge.

Jago lost control of his shift the moment the charge detonated, the tunnel filling with the sharp smell of explosives and the sharper sound of men's voices demanding names, asking who was there, who was missing.

In work boots, dragging their tools, the men ran. They left the bodies, the ones who had hadn't been lucky, behind.

Outside, the night sky tasted of freedom. The moon hung low and heavy, bright enough to make the headgear and engine house cast shadows. It looked rounder than it should have.

'Three days,' Jago said.

'Three days what?'

'Three days we were down there.'

'I lost count,' Antony admitted.

'They'll want to know what happened.' Jago stretched, tried to flex his hands out. Hours of scrabbling at the rocks had bloodied them, turned the fingers into a parody of human shape. 'They'll think it was something we did.'

'It wasn't.'

A crowd was gathering despite the hour; wives and mothers and men from other shifts. Ragged cheering broke out across the group as word spread; the first few rushed reunions took place as men hobbled stiffly to their loved ones.

For others, there was no reunion and they howled their grief aloud.

'I should go home,' Antony said after a minute. 'Elsie and Ma won't have been able to get all this way.'

'I'll walk with you.'

The walk home, the path they took every day, seemed strange and wild. Precious, like something once thought lost and now restored.

A candle was burning in the front window of Antony's cottage. They did that on Christmas in celebration and on All Hallows to warn the dead away, but never otherwise. Antony paused at the roadside and looked at it for a moment. Jago halted alongside him.

'They missed you,' Jago said.

'I missed them.' The words came with a rawer honesty than Antony had expected. Elsie was a nuisance sometimes, still too young to work and always wanting to play on winter evenings when it was too dark to play in the street and he needed to leave for work, but she'd bring him flowers or odd fancy stones she'd found and ask for piggyback rides and laugh like he'd never done as a child.

'Don't keep them waiting, then,' and Jago limped off. Antony hadn't noticed, in the exhilaration of being rescued, that his friend was hurt.

The door groaned as he opened it and he stepped into the front room. It stank of fish oil lamps and the drying heap of laundry, but the candle shone like star light and Ma hurried to him as best as she could with her stick and embraced him as though he was a child again.

'You're alive,' and he found himself echoing it.

'Course I'm alive, Ma.'

He told her the story the next morning, words spilling

from him like beer from a bottle. The panic and the dark and the waiting. The noises in the black. Jago alongside him lapsing into silence, a statue standing frozen in defeat. He didn't tell her that he didn't want to go back.

Another delivery of laundry came then, from the coaching inn across near Zennor, and Antony helped her drag it down to the stream and wash it in the fierce cold water. The trees made a tunnel but it was bearable if he reminded himself it was branches and leaves, not stone.

They had two days off; Jago walked past the cottage on the third morning and he shambled out with his crib box, wearing an oilskin against the rain lashing across from the sea. Fell into step with his friend as easily as he ever had done.

'That's the fourth fall, you know,' Jago said after a while. 'Word is, the owners are getting worried. Can't make money when it's all falling into the sea. Wouldn't be surprised if they had to close it. And they'll have to close for the funerals soon too.'

The shift felt endless. Men started at shadows, dropped their tools and flinched at pebbles moving underfoot. Made mistakes in their fear. Antony left at a run, as soon as he could, hurrying back until he could hear other, living, voices.

Some of the younger lads in the pub were singing. Antony barely glanced at them as he got his pint and settled close to the fire. He'd never really fitted in with them, always too anxious to get home and see to Elsie. Never any free time for socialising.

But curiosity got the better of him and he called out

to Martyn who he recognised from the market. 'What are you all celebrating?'

'Picked up some work in Mexico. All five of us. There's a man here recruiting for the mines, and he says the money is twice as much as here and no rain.'

'You've never been in a tunnel in your life.' Antony came over to join them; they shuffled chairs across the flagstone floor and wiped at the spilled beer to make him a place.

'These fellas have though, and they say it's not important, they can teach us, they just need good men who aren't afraid of working. He's looking for more – I could put a word in for you if you wanted?'

Mexico? He'd heard of it at least, in one of the lectures at the Miner's Institute that Jago was always dragging him to. Or had that been Nevada? Hot and sandy, and across the sea; he knew that much.

'And what about Jago? They'd pay a good bonus for a shift captain, especially if we all went together. Some boys from Wheal Peevor went out last year and they said they've already bought houses. One of them had his missus taken out there even.'

The oil in the lamps had burnt too low. It felt like being back in the tunnel. 'I...I'd have to think about it.'

'You'd need to let us know soon. Ship sails next week from Falmouth.'

He didn't mention it to anyone that day or the next. He worked a full shift and tore a gash in his shoulder on a low rock. He took Elsie out to gather nettles and showed her how to strip their leaves for a stew, and turned bundles of heavy linen to save Ma from reaching across to do it.

Tunnels in Mexico wouldn't have the sea forcing its way in. Wouldn't have the coffin grey slabs of granite that fought against being worked.

But he did tell Jago, quietly, like all conversations in the shaft had to be as they were winched down and the pulleys moaned a protest. Even in the dark, he could see his friend's attitude change, the sudden flicker of interest, and he wished he could call the words back.

'What would they do if I went?' Antony muttered around a mouthful of pasty at crib time.

'Get a lodger?' Jago replied. He broke off a piece of crust and tossed it down, carefully not looking for anything that might run out to claim it. 'Lots of people do. I suspect there's plenty of the youngsters here would like a bed of their own.'

'Lodger wouldn't pay her as much as my wages though. And Elsie would be scared, she don't like strangers.'

'She'd get over it. It's got to be better than staying here, right?'

He didn't have an answer to that, only to slowly gather up his gear and force himself to his feet again. 'Come on or we'll be late.'

'Which of us is the shift captain again?' and below the helmet and candle, a smile flickered across Jago's face.

Miners didn't fit in the church, or at least Antony didn't. Too dirty, too uncouth, too aware of things that lived under the earth and didn't fit the church's pattern. But he stopped at it anyway on his way home. Trailing a hand across the battered pews, with his boots loud on the flagstone floor, he asked the stained-glass silence – so similar to the mine – what he should do.

There wasn't an answer.

'It has to be better than here,' Jago said, when Antony asked him the same question the next day.

'You're the one with the better job and a room of his own, not me. I should be the one saying that.'

'Why aren't you then? You haven't wanted to go back down there since that fall. You should go. Come with me. There must be a way to send the money back home, or you could do it for a few years and then come back and buy them a big fancy house. Elsie could have a pony and trap like the Bolitho kids do.'

Antony delayed it enough that the ship left from Falmouth without them. But there was another one going to Mineral Point in America and then another heading to Canada, and the recruiting men came and asked and asked and asked. Offered wages that got higher every time. He didn't want to go.

It was spring again and this time the scent of daffodils was genuine, surrounding them all as they stripped and changed at the top of the mine. Jago wandered away to chat to one of the bal maidens, pretending to duck a swing from her rock hammer. Antony half-heartedly checked the men in for their shift, waited for Jago to join them.

Would they have daffodils in Mexico? Jago had never looked at a plant in his life unless he was about to eat it and probably wouldn't remember to find out, no matter how many times Antony reminded him.

The men filled forward onto the engine to be lowered.

Jago shifted his tools around. A seagull flew past high above, a last glimpse of the world outside.

The cable snapped. Gunshot loud, heartbreak quick. The fall was instant and he didn't have time to call out, to pray, for anything. Just darkness and the air rushing up around them all, hot and full of smoke and screams.

Later, he'd say – Jago would say – that they'd seen someone on the bottom of the shaft. Someone dragging a beam across to halt the pulley, forcing the basket to a halt before it hit anything. Not Davey, who had died in the fall last winter, however much it looked like him. Not anyone, really, because there had been no-one down there.

And yet.

And yet.

He stared into the darkness and saw someone looking back.

The climb up the ladder was eons long, thick with dust and smoke and terror. But they all got out this time.

'I'm not going,' Jago proclaimed as soon as they were outside. The air was heavy with rain, falling like tears. 'Not to Mexico, not anywhere. I'm not ending up like him.'

'I thought you wanted...'

'Not anymore. Not to end up like him, trapped in a mine forever. No more mines.'

Antony stared up into the rain. His legs were shaking from the ascent. 'You can look after Elsie for me.'

'I didn't think you wanted to go?'

'I don't. I just...I don't want to stay here with the...the memories...There's too many. I can't stay here anymore,' and the sea sighed in agreement, like a farewell.

Watermill Cove

by Ella Walsworth-Bell

Steve is up to the elbows in flour, fingertips sticky with dough. He pauses for a moment to stare at blue skies through a small, high window in the kitchen. The fan whirls hot air in his ear, relentless as tides. The radio is playing 'Holiday' by Madonna and he's already wondering if he can get away early from this shift. His long hair is caught in a ponytail and his swim muscles are kneading, kneading dough. The ovens are on as hot as they can go and he's thinking of the coolness of the sea.

'Names.' Fliss calls through from the kitchen. 'What we gonna call these pizzas, dude?'

Steve spins the dough on his fingers, stretching lightly until it's a circle as wide and round as this island. He imagines the crust bubbling and blistering with heat, like his own burnt-out heart.

'Watermill,' he says.

'Is that for the pepperoni? Or the fish one?'

'Nah.' He hesitates, holding the space, making her wait. Teasing and twisting another ball of dough in his hands. Watermill Cove is his favourite beach. There are tall Monterey pines at the top of the hill and a slow steady walk along a lush, ferny track to the sea. Boulders, pebbles and finally hard white sand. Untouched. Most people talk about Watermill, but they can't be bothered to walk there. It feels like his own private beach. He half-closes his eyes. Tonight, it'll be all his. When everyone else on the island is sleeping. Perhaps he'll even sleep there, curled in the lee of a rock, waiting for seals to haul out and sing at dawn. Perhaps...

Fliss's voice cuts into his daydreams. 'So, which one? C'mon Steve, you're killing me.'

'Margherita.'

She sticks her head around the door. He stares out the window again.

'Watermill for Margherita,' he repeats. 'Pelistry for Four Cheese, Porth-humpin'cressa for your one with the fish, and ... Old Town. Veggie Option.'

She scribbles the names down. 'Ta. I'll do the rest.'

His heart gives a lurch as she retreats back to the tills. The smell of pizza brings back happy memories – both of them stirring their first batch of tomato sauce, hands entwined around the wooden spoon. He helped her get those recipes exactly right. They worked all winter on the restaurant. And then, the moment they opened, she shacked up with that smarmy git Jonno. The fisherman.

If I weren't strapped for cash, he thinks, *if I hadn't put body and soul into this place, well I wouldn't be still here in her kitchen, doing her grunt work, would I?*

Perhaps it was always about the pizza place. Her first love. Not him.

He takes it out on the dough, screwing it into a ball. Pounds, thumps, shoves it onto the work surface. It's going to be a hell of a summer, working here.

He reaches for the radio and twists the dial up to max. Madonna's voice fills the room. A bead of sweat trickles down his back.

Pretend she's not here. Just make the pizzas, Steve. Get the dough sorted, before the orders come in. Then get down to the beach.

Yeah, he could do this. Easy.

End of the shift and the oven's finally out of fire. The last boxes are filled, all of the cheese used up. Grated creamy whiteness over all those Watermills and Pelistrys and whatever the hell else they'd named the bloody things.

'Need more mozzarella,' Steve says, pressing the fridge door closed. He reaches for a rag from a plastic tub by the sink and rinses it under the cold tap to wipe down the work surfaces one by one. Smears of dough; if you don't wipe them away, they're concrete in the morning. 'You hear me, Fliss?'

'Wassat?' The noise of coins being counted next to the till stops dead. 'Whatcha need more of?' Fliss sticks her head round the door again, all creased brows and messy hair.

'Mozzarella. Only one left.'

'Alright. Delivery boat coming in tomorrow, innit?'

He stops wiping. Hauls the window shut. 'I'll be off, then.' Shakes his head, knowing where Fliss will be sleeping tonight. Tucked up with Jonno the fisherman. Him with the double pepperoni order and sneaky, dark eyes.

Steve closes the door behind him. 'Freaking pizzas,' he says to himself.

The air is as smooth as good whiskey. Leaving the alley behind him, he strides past the pub's lit windows. Likely as not a few locals will be clustered round a table and finishing their beers. If it'd still been on with him and Fliss they'd have gone together after work. His arm around her shoulders, her eyes staring back at him with the innocence of a kitten.

Dave the publican is standing outside, drawing on a fag. 'Orright, mate?'

Staring into the black tarmac, Steve doesn't slow down. Fuck the pub tonight. Fuck them all, because they all bloody knew, *dint they?* About Fliss and Jonno. Whilst he got the pizza place all sorted out for her; skimmed the walls, painted them white, installed the special steel ovens, the lot. All ready for beginning of the season. Their dream restaurant. She'd smiled, lent the odd hand with a brush, and all the while she'd been sneaking off with Jonno behind his back.

So, tonight – he breathes in the fresh air calling him from across Porthcressa bay – he isn't going home yet. A long walk, then a swim. He doesn't want to be near anyone else on this island. He pauses at the seafront to glance across the sandy beach. A full moon in a star-bright sky speckles the waves with glossy beams of refracted light. Behind him lies the noise and bustle of Hugh Town. He wants none of that.

Into the side pocket of his chef's trousers he's slipped a bottle. Whisky, the good stuff. Perhaps he'll save it for the beach, keep him warm after the swim. Sea water makes everything better. Swimming – full immersion – yes, that'll do it. Wash the long hot shift away. There'd be enough nights like this, heat and grime and ovens and Fliss's face, every ten minutes. He needed some kind of help, else he'd go spare.

Steve walks right out of town, away from the streetlights. The moon casts a long shadow in front of him and he climbs a stile to a path into an alder grove. This short cut from nowhere-land leads through the nature reserve, straight across the island to Watermill Cove. His white plastic chef's shoes aren't built for root-torn trails. He stops, necks the whiskey in silence, then kicks off the shoes. He'll come back for them in the morning.

The alcohol burns his throat like a painful memory. Like when he'd looked at Fliss, earlier tonight. He wants more, but it's all over, isn't it? The tension is held in his shoulders and his arms end in rigid fists. Opening his right hand, he sees he's nipped a fingernail into his palm. A teardrop of red blood eases out and he shakes it away. Huffing out a sigh, he lets the bottle fall into nettles.

'You need to get outta here, Steve,' he mutters.

It isn't far to Watermill from here. Up the hill, flat feet on tarmac roads without his shoes, past the bulb farm. It is calm and still. No swell in the bay, no wind in the trees.

Ducks in the pond at the top of the hill call out a frantic warning and he swears at them, loud and angry with alcohol pounding in his veins. He takes the path to the cove, through a scrubby wasteland of trees between fields. Right in the darkest, steepest section, he slips on a smooth stone. Trips and lurches, putting his hands forward as he does so.

And there it is. A pool of cold water. He falls with a splash, rather than onto the hard ground.

'What the-?'

Then he remembers. 'O'course. St Enwyn's Well.' He half-breathes, half-says the words. Fliss had brought him here, way back. A sunny day, hand-in-hand with her. They'd stopped, kissed. She'd pointed it out: a half-hidden natural spring bubbling up into a pool, surrounded by ivy curled around low granite slabs.

'Sweet water,' Fliss said, smiling. 'Taste it – go on.' He'd shaken his head and instead they'd flicked pennies in, wishing for luck. He tried to remember the rest of her story, but all he could think of was her soft kisses. What was it Fliss had said? It was ages old and Enwyn wasn't a saint ... she was a ... a white witch?

Steve shivers, wrenches his arm out and shakes his head.

Leaves rustle, although there is no breeze. A voice whispers, and yet he is alone.

Wish...wish...mmmm, young man. What would you wish for?

'Whisky's talking.' A bitter laugh bursts out. 'Must be.' He looks down. His chef's trousers are sodden with mud, his feet are sore from walking. His arm muscles ache from wrestling dough into pizzas.

A *wisssshhhhh*, the voice hisses.

'Lemme think f'ra min.' He closes his eyes, playing the game. Before, he'd wished for Fliss. They'd watched the pennies sink into the pool and they'd wished for love. Well, that hadn't worked out.

'I wish...Jonno...' He imagines that smug face sinking into an ice-cold sea.

Revenge on a love-rival. Nice.

He wishes for Fliss, a lump in his throat.

Sssssure?

'Nah, all I want is a swim.' He closes his eyes and can see that hot kitchen, burned into his memory. Pizzas lined up in rows, marking time. 'Change. That's what I wish for. S'no good going on like this.'

*Change...*the voice sniggered. *Hah! You want change, do you?*

'Bugger this for a laugh.' Steve heaves himself upright. 'Hearing voices, I am. Need to – clear my head.'

He lurches down the path towards the sea. His legs are awful wobbly. Once he gets in that sea water, he'll be more than fine. He scratches his back with one hand: it's suddenly itching like mad. The skin is flaky, like sunburn. Which is weird, when he's not been outside all week. He's been stuck making pizzas, baking pizzas, cleaning kitchens...slaving for Fliss, basically. He scratches again, and something plasticky catches under his nail. Looks like a circular piece of packaging. Out of instinct, he sniffs it.

'Ugh.' He flicks it away as he reaches the pebbles at the top of the beach.

Once he gets his kit off, that cool water will soothe him nicely. He is gasping for a swim. Staring out at a kaleidoscope of stars, he's dizzy with longing.

'Oh, stuff this.' He charges down the sand, stumbles into the sea, dives into a luminescent cold ocean. His head splits in pain and confusion. Underwater, his lungs roar.

There's an agony along his neck as if he's caught his fingers on the boning knife. His hands scrabble at his skin and...

There are two policemen on Scilly, and both agree wholeheartedly. There is a single set of footprints in the muddy path by Watermill Cove. A measuring tape shows these to be size nine, splayed bare toes where they've squelched into the soil. At the top of the beach is an abandoned muddy pair of chef's trousers and Steve's tee shirt and jacket. They send out search parties, but it's unlikely there'll be a positive outcome.

'It would've been high tide,' they tell Fliss from the doorstep. 'No shoes, mind. We believe he must've gone in for a swim. Cold water shock.'

Fliss raises her hands to her eyes, letting out a cry. 'Ohhhh!' She sobs loudly. 'Known Steve a long time, I have. Ohhhh.' She turns sideways and crumples into Jonno.

Jonno stares. 'Is there a ... body?'

'Well, no.' One of the policemen gives him a shrewd look. 'Been out looking all day.'

'Sorry I couldn't help out.' Jonno pats Fliss's back. 'Had to be here, for her.'

The policeman continues. 'Mmm. Helicopters have done a flyby, but nothing so far.'

'Thank you.' Jonno closes the door.

Fliss waits until the footsteps have gone. 'Well, bugger him!'

'Now, now,' Jonno says, 'weren't your fault, were it?'

'Not that,' Fliss says, slamming one hand out into his chest, 'How the bleeding heck am I gonna get another pizza chef? So thoughtless, that man. Useless, thoughtless...'

He stares at her. Lucked out, he had, sneaking the shapely Fliss from right under Steve's nose. He'd not taken much persuading to invest his savings in her pizzeria, which it sorely needed.

'Now, now,' he says, unsure what to do with her anger, 'what about I get out there and catch a few fish? It's herring season.'

'Really?' She pulls a face.

He nods. 'Stuff a sign on the door. No-one expects pizza tonight.'

At midnight Jonno's boat, *Ennis May*, is chugging around the Eastern Isles, riding the flood tide to the north of these uninhabited rocky islands. If Jonno throws some nets, he might get lucky with a haul of summer herring. Pollack glisten silver in the shallows. Bream lurk in the deeper water. Oh, Jonno can find the fish. He's got an eye for it. He's fishy by nature.

Jonno shoves the engine into neutral, rigs the nets onto the trawling gear at the stern. He's about to press the button to get the mechanism going, work those nets, see what's there...when he pauses. A rounded silver disc is floating, catching the moonlight. Perhaps a sunfish?

He bends over the gunnels, peering closer.

The face, for it is a face, stares up through the water. It's angry and it's alive.

Jonno startles; freezes. 'Steve?' His voice echoes into the shadows. The creature that was Steve launches itself high, broadsides the steel vessel. It has a muscular tail, glimmering scales and fins like flick knives. A pair of hands grab for Jonno's throat and don't let go. He's hauled into the sea, boots and all.

Fish catches fisherman, this new seaweed brain thinks.

Somewhere in his memory, he's remembered Jonno and the fact that he wants him gone. The man struggles, jerks, then goes limp. Bubbles tremble along the curve of Jonno's face as it lies just below the surface. The boat's engine continues to idle, coughing out fumes. The body nudges against the hull, kissing the paintwork.

Was-Steve – Mer-Steve, Fish-Steve, Sea-Steve – tries to think some more, but the thought processes are slow as meltwater. He thrusts his tail and shoots away from the boat, sending storms of star-bright phosphorescence in his wake. Staying underwater, he pushes himself down to the sandy sea floor, stretching out with strange, webbed hands. He can touch every grain, every rock, every strand of eelgrass. There is no urgency to return to the surface. He reaches a hand to the slits in his neck; they are tender as tentacles and twice as precious. Surfing the currents, he swoops into kelp forests, storms into rock crevices, swirls inside a shoal of herring.

His anger has left him; deep in his primitive heart is a memory of Watermill Cove and pizzas. Hot ovens, pain. Why? He swims closer to shore. This is where the men came, this morning. He'd watched them with new fish-lens eyes, in between hunting for sprats, which felt more urgent to this new body than trawling its missing memories.

Tonight, the beach is empty. Somewhere in this back of his mind, he remembers those ovens' gaping maws and the crisped crusts of pizzas. In a flash he remembers.

Fliss.

He lets out a howl. It sings of lost love. He continues,

like a whale calling across oceans.

The sound carries in the darkness, through the scrubland, past the well. Enwyn hisses and a northerly breeze springs up. The sound floats up and over the hill to Hugh Town. It wafts through an open window, where Fliss is sleeping under Jonno's goose down duvet.

She stirs, half-asleep, half-entranced.

Standing, she pulls aside the thick velvet curtains to let the sea air in. The strange sound gets louder and makes her head spin. She can't help herself; all she can think of is going for a swim.

People do funny things when someone dies.

Not bothering with shoes, she unlocks the front door.

Up to Watermill Cove for a quick dip, to clear my head.

As if in a dream, she starts walking.

In a Field

by Caroline Philipps

John reached for his glass of whisky. The amber
liquid glowed, catching the light from the fire. Radio
3 informed him he was about to hear Brahms' violin
concerto in D major. Outside, nature was holding its own
concert. Wind and rain battered the sitting room window,
determined to enter into his cosy space. He was glad of the
thick velvet curtains that his late wife, darling Ann, had
insisted on when they first moved to the cottage. Ah, he
banished the thought: mustn't let the melancholy in. He
looked down at the crossword in his lap. Six across was
proving difficult.

Another sip of whisky and he contemplated the clue
again. The lights flickered. He looked up, tensing. Another
flicker. The lights went out. Damn. The radio fell silent.
Guess that was the power lost for the night. He sat for a
moment, glad that the fire was at least providing a glow.

Outside, the storm reached a crescendo, gleeful that it was winning.

It was no good. He wished he weren't alone. He was a dab hand at dealing with little crises like this, but things had always been more exciting when there were two of them. Through all their various postings around Africa they had confronted whatever chaos they found with resolute cheerfulness. He could hear his Ann saying, 'What fun!' Suggesting making toast on the fire and using the little primus for tea. He didn't want to make it fun on his own. He pushed himself out of the chair, letting his body straighten in its own time, a necessity these days, before setting off to find his torch. He would go to bed. By morning the power might be back on.

The kitchen was cold. The early morning light failed to take the chill off the room. He flicked the kettle switch and readied to make his first cup of tea, thankful the electricity was on again.

There was a shrill ring from the phone. Who would be calling this early? He'd better answer it.

'We saw lights in the upper field last night.'

It was Edith. It was amazing how mention of the field still put John on edge after all these years. He looked down at his newspaper. Margaret Thatcher's increasingly precarious position as Prime Minister and yesterday's storms lost their importance. He listened more carefully to the voice coming down the phone line.

'We thought we should ring you straight away. I've got Mary here too.'

He could picture the two sisters in their chintzy sitting

room from a bygone era, still with all the same furniture that had graced it when their parents had owned the farm. Edith would be commanding the main receiver, her sister Mary would be to one side holding the other old fashioned speaker close to her ear.

Well, if they had seen it last night, they'd not really rung straight away.

'It was too late to ring and of course we had the power cut.' Edith continued as if answering his thoughts. 'But to be honest, we've hardly slept. We decided we should take a quick look when dawn arrived – beautiful across the estuary this morning, by the way. Anyway, it looks like there's been a bit of a landslide and that the "you know what" might have reappeared.'

'That's unexpected.' He was surprised that he sounded so calm. 'What time did you see the lights?'

'Just before going to bed. They seemed to be dancing. So I called Mary over and we realised they weren't moving through the field. No, something was happening there. Don't you think that's odd?'

Edith's words raised a chill, but he didn't want to worry the sisters. In what he hoped was a measured tone he said, 'Certainly worthy of further investigation. We could meet up at the field in half an hour? I'll ring Hector. Can you get hold of Cecelia, see if she wants to join us?'

'Yes, can do. See you there.'

His fingers easily dialled the number.

'Hello!'

'Hector, is that you?'

'Of course it's me. Who else would it be? Why are you ringing me at this ungodly hour?'

John took a breath. 'Something's going on in the top field. Edith and Mary saw lights moving around last night and now say they can see something lying there. A small landslide as well. Could be nothing, but I think we should take a look.'

'I agree.'

'I said we should meet – quarter past seven at the top field. Can you make that – I can pick you up on the way?'

'Yes. See you in 15 minutes.' Hector hung up, abrupt as ever.

John stood for a moment, transported back to his younger self, Edith getting ready to join the Wrens and full of impatience to leave the farm that was the only home she had ever known. Hector, a younger, less pompous version of now; his main aim in life to seduce Cecelia – barking up the wrong tree there. And Cecelia, so full of life before polio wrecked her body. The escalating tension of the war and possible invasion by the Germans had intensified their world and, coupled with their youth, had made them a little mad perhaps.

He shook himself. He needed to get going, no time for the morning-paper's crossword. Thankfully he was already dressed when Edith had rung and it was easy to pull on his coat over his well-worn jumper.

The lane was strewn with twigs and small branches. The trees had surrendered the last of their leaves to the wind and stood bleak against the October morning skyline. There was a damp chill to the air. He pushed up the hill, struggling to keep his steps even and ignore the grating discomfort from his hip.

Hector was waiting at his gate. Upright and smart, even

at this hour – his naval career had left its mark. It had been a welcome surprise to find that John's childhood friend had also returned to the village of their youth, seeking a final safe port after years of postings in exotic places. Now he cut an authoritative figure, turning his love of order and routine to the running of the local parish council. Hector was a much-liked stalwart of the community, despite his tendency to blunderbuss. John, on occasion, was the one called upon to smooth waters, to gently nudge things in the right direction after one of Hector's outbursts.

'Quite a storm last night.'

John nodded. They walked on in companionable silence. 'Not sure what to make of this turn of events, though.'

'Agreed, a bit odd after all this time. Might be nothing.'

'Let's hope that's the case.'

They reached the top of the lane and the field unfolded in front of them. It was covered in a whisker-like stubble left from the last harvest. The mud sucked at their boots, slowing progress. An earthy aroma mixed with the clean sea scent.

Edith caught them up with Mary trailing behind. Edith's coat looked like it had seen better days. But it was long and waxed, and as practical and warm as Edith herself. She gestured over to the top corner of the field.

'This way, mind your step! It was such a shock, I can't tell you.'

She strode ahead of them with an energy that John envied and it made him smile, despite the unsettling feeling in his stomach. She had always been able to make him smile.

The small group gathered around the protruding object. They made a motley crew, one leaning on a walking stick, one holding himself in a stiff upright pose. Cecelia had even managed to get across the sticky earth with her walking frame and stood leaning into it as it sank into the mud. It was going to be an effort to get her out. Despite her mobility issues, she still managed to bring an elegance to the scene, with her multitude of bright scarves thrown with an artful casualness around her neck.

'What are we going to do about this, then?' Cecelia was staring earnestly at the protruding object as if it was going to be the next subject for her rather eccentric pictures that the tourists loved.

As one, the group shifted their gaze across to John. He knew that they wanted him to take the lead, but his hip hurt and, to be quite frank, he didn't like to be rushed these days. Slow and steady was his preference, with his routine of a cup of tea, a boiled egg and the perusal of the paper. It allowed him to get over the fug of the many tablets he took just to keep him going.

Now they wanted direction. He'd been the one to give it before, so he was going to have to do it again.

'It looks as if our careful work has been undone. The landslide has worked everything to the surface.'

They all nodded. The top of the field had a scar running across it horizontally that was intercepted by the large tarpaulin-wrapped shape jutting out of the disturbed earth.

John paused and let them all take a moment. He couldn't quite believe that it had come to this. The hole they had dug had been so deep. They had tried the woodland, but that had proved difficult with all the tree roots and an unexpected layer of granite. The small field had seemed like a good solution and here they had indeed managed to dig so far down that Edith had been able to plough the area afterwards to hide the disturbed earth. She had been proud of her recently gained skill with the plough. Now though, a land slippage after fifty odd years? He was baffled. Was someone saying that it was time to pay their dues?

No, he wasn't having that. It was simple. They had to do the job again. That was the way forward.

'We need spades,' he said.

Hector snorted. 'You're not suggesting we bunch of old fogies are going to be using those spades, are you?'

He had a point, but John wasn't going to let him get away with that. 'Well, what do you propose?'

'I'm sure I can think of something.'

But nothing was forthcoming and Hector had the grace to look shame-faced.

A slight breeze had started to ripple the water on the estuary. The day was getting going.

'I suggest we take some of those branches from where they've cut the hedge and pull them over it for now,' Edith said. 'We can reconvene at the farmhouse with coffee to discuss options.'

John nodded. 'A good plan. I could do with a cup of coffee.' The idea of going somewhere warm was very appealing and he needed some distance to think more clearly.

Everyone else nodded in agreement. John gestured to Hector to help him get Cecelia's frame out of the mud, and slowly they all started picking their way towards Edith and Mary's home.

Once inside, Mary bustled round, ensuring that everyone had a drink. Biscuits sat on a dainty floral plate on the table in front of the hearth.

John always felt like he'd entered a time warp when in this sitting room. It was as if he had never left the Cornwall of his youth. His working life, spent in far off places, seemed like a vivid dream that had happened to someone else. He had not married Ann until long after the war. In 1940 it had been Edith who had occupied his 19 year old mind.

Some new things had been added to the room. Photographs on the sideboard. Edith and her GI, all sepia toned, looking pleased as punch on their wedding day. John had not been here for that, having already been posted to fight in Egypt. Probably just as well. Another picture of Edith in front of her Boston house with its gabled roof and elaborate woodwork. It looked like a comfortable life and yet Edith had returned here on the death of her husband. And Mary had never left Cornwall. She stayed, first to help with the farm, and then to look after her parents in their later years. A born carer.

John stepped over to the window and placed his hand on the deep sill to peer out. He could see the field, but the pile of branches was not visible behind the hedge. In the distance, the estuary's greyness reflected his sombre mood. He turned to his friends.

'Hector does have a point. We would struggle to dig a hole as deep as we managed last time. So, if reburying isn't a solution. We need another plan.'

Hector nodded. 'I know we dismissed dumping into the sea at the time, but that was because the whole place was teeming with the army and navy putting up sea defences and fixing the barrage across the estuary. But now I'm of the opinion that it would be the best solution.'

'I agree,' said Edith, 'but any ideas on how we're going to achieve that? Getting it out to sea will require some strength – all that manhandling.'

Ah, this was John's forte. 'A few pulleys would do the trick. I think we could manage.' He paused. 'The question in my mind though is, who was here last night in the middle of the storm? Who did Mary and Edith see, and, whoever they were, how much did they see?'

'Why would anyone be poking around here after all these years?' Cecelia looked across at John. 'Who would be looking after so long and, even if they were, why in the field?'

Cecelia was right. It did seem far-fetched to think that someone would come now.

'Perhaps the lights were just a coincidence. It could have been late revellers returning from the beach. Though it would seem an odd choice of place for a party in October in the middle of a storm.'

Edith chuckled. 'Have you forgotten how often we went there for a party? That's what got us into all this in the first place.'

John smiled at her, a happier memory pushing its way through the sober mood.

'Whoever was going through the field was probably just struggling to get across the earth disturbed by the landslide,' Hector said. 'I doubt they saw anything in all that dreadful weather. I think we just need to put a plan into place and get it out to sea, pronto.'

He was right, action was needed, but the question of the lights still niggled.

The Land Rover smelt of wet dog and old leather. John gripped his seat as Edith swung round the bend and lurched down the hill into Durgan. It was another beautiful morning. The water was flat calm and the sun had only just started to light the scene with gentle hues of yellow and grey. It would be a glorious day later.

John looked across at Edith. She was concentrating hard and there was no indication of any of the anxiety that he himself felt, or that she was tired from the hard work they had all put in over the last 24 hours.

She glanced across at him. 'Stop worrying! We're just a bunch of friends out for a fishing jaunt. No one would think anything else.' She smiled at him and stretched out her hand to give his knee a gentle pat. He relaxed a little – it was good to have a partner in crime again.

The rest of the gang were waiting for them at the slipway. The boat had already been manoeuvred onto its trolley in readiness and now they needed to make the final transfer.

Edith hopped out of the Land Rover and shouted out 'Good morning all – perfect day for a fishing trip!'

John looked at her, bemused, and in a much quieter voice asked, 'Ever heard of not trying to wake the whole of Durgan?'

Edith leaned into him and whispered, 'That was meant to be heard, just in case anyone is up and around. Might as well set the scene for any early risers.'

John shook his head slightly, but Edith just grinned at him. She didn't seem to be taking any of this particularly seriously. He'd forgotten her devil-may-care attitude.

Cecelia was at the back of Hector's truck pulling out fishing rods and loading the kit into Mary's waiting arms. Yes, Edith was right, they did look like a nutty group of geriatrics heading out for an early morning fishing trip, if you just ignored the lump in the trailer.

'So, my friend, let's use that pulley system of yours again.' Hector stood looking expectant. John had a moment of panic. Had they actually brought it with them? He looked at the Land Rover and then at Edith who was smirking at him.

'Yes, left to you it would still be sitting in the field. But I rescued it.'

John sorted the ropes with surprising deftness given his usual stiffness. His hands slipped as he encountered the mud that was still sticking resolutely to the tarpaulin but finally he stood back and looked satisfied with his work. The transfer was remarkably efficient.

John and Hector wheeled the boat down to the water. Hector was in his element.

'Mary, hold the rope steady, John – stand on the trolley – there she goes.'

The boat floated free and Hector immediately hopped on. Edith ran down the beach and also jumped in with no difficulty. John readied to get into the boat. Was he the only one with stiff joints? He hauled himself over the edge and grimaced as pain shot up his leg. The other two did not seem to notice his plight, so he gingerly lowered himself on to the stern seat.

Mary, who had been holding the boat steady from the beach, threw the rope across to Edith who deftly caught it and with practised habit started to coil and stow it in the bow. Hector looked on with approval. Edith smiled.

'Know you like a tidy ship, Hector.'

They were off. The boat's engine started with a guttural splutter and propelled the boat forward. If it were not for their errand, it really would have been the perfect morning for an outing, with the mirror-like water and pale sun rising over the estuary mouth. Mary's and Cecelia's diminishing figures could be seen making their way back up Durgan's beach. Cecelia was in front, her frame bowing like a metronome, and Mary slowly matched her pace. The two of them were going back to the farmhouse for breakfast.

Aboard the boat, Edith pulled off her small rucksack and proceeded to extract a flask. 'I thought we would all probably need a coffee by now.'

'Jolly good!' Hector held out his hand for the proffered metal cup. John's stomach was queasy and he sipped the coffee hoping it would settle him. The heat of the liquid permeated through the beaker, quickly warming his cold hands.

Edith sat, enjoying her drink and looking forward. If John squinted it was easy to see the same girl that had preoccupied his youth with her tumble of hair and ready smiles. She turned to him and bestowed one on him now.

'Are you all right John? Remember how we loved to get out of the estuary? This is one of the things I missed most in America. The eastern seaboard just doesn't have the same feel – all big Atlantic waves and long low coast line.'

'There's nowhere quite like here,' John said.

The boat chugged on out into the silver water, past the entrance to Gillan Creek. The gentle rock of the boat and low level engine noise was soporific. John fought an urge to close his eyes and shook himself in an attempt to ward off falling asleep.

His preoccupation with staying awake was interrupted by a louder, more urgent engine than their own. He craned his neck to find the source. The coastguard.

'Can you believe it,' muttered Edith, looking across at him.

'It's fine. Remember we're just fishing,' Hector said.

'Yes, just fishing, with that coming along for the ride.' John gestured at the lump in the middle of the boat.

'I doubt they'll come particularly close. Look at us. Hardly dodgy characters. Remember to wave and smile,' Edith said.

The coastguard caught them up and was briefly matching their pace. John started a manic wave.

'Calm down, John!' Edith demonstrated her own more half-hearted gesture. 'Like this, nice and relaxed and then turn to me and start talking. Otherwise, they're going to think we're in trouble! Last thing we need.'

Hector grunted from the front of the boat. 'Edith, MI5 missed out not recruiting you, my dear!'

She looked pleased. John turned away and glanced back at the coastguard. He could see the captain at the helm. The man was looking past them, obviously not interested. John's heart rate started to slow.

Finally Hector cut the engine. They were now far beyond the estuary mouth. The immediate quiet with the gentle lapping of the water against the boat pressed in on John's ears with more intensity than the now absent noise from the motor. He always prided himself on his calmness, but now surely his blood pressure must be through the roof. He just had to hold it together for this last part.

The pulley system was put to use for one last time and took the strain as John and Hector heaved, before Edith gave an almighty push and shouted, 'Let go!'

They had used chains for extra weight. Cecelia had suggested adding in some rocks, but no one had been keen to open the tarpaulin. So instead, it now looked like an accessory from a Houdini show.

There was a deep plop. Water splashed back at them, a shock of cold. Myriad tiny bubbles rose. And then there was nothing but the deep inky water. All three stood staring down for several minutes as if waiting for something to reappear, but it didn't. Gulls called. There was a murmur of a distant fishing boat engine. The three of them raised their eyes from the water and looked at each other, seemingly at a loss as to what to do next. Hector broke first.

'So, a spot of fishing?' He busied himself and started up the engine, directing the boat back inland.

John fiddled with the fishing rods. Edith pulled out three tin-foiled packages.

'Bacon sandwiches, anyone?'

When had she had time to sort those? But they were just what was needed. John took a large bite – his stomach was miraculously better.

*

On shore once more, John and Edith climbed back into the Land Rover. They had left Hector happily bimbling with his boat. Several fish lay motionless at John's feet in a black bucket. The rest of the world was now up and as Edith reversed, she cursed two dog walkers deep in conversation who were totally unaware, it seemed, of their wandering animals.

'You're just the same with your dogs, you know,' John said.

'Never! Mine are beautifully behaved.'

'They are, but you're not, are you?'

Edith laughed. 'Maybe not.'

The clutch slipped as she pulled forward. 'Oops, sorry.'

She moved down a gear as they tackled the hill out of the village. The little bay below was intensely coloured now the sun had lost its early morning pallor. A few brave souls were taking a constitutional dip. Life was carrying on as normal. The madness of the last few days was already receding.

But there was still a small kernel of worry. The others had easily dismissed the issue of the lights in the field. Were they really nothing to do with all of this? He continued to stare at the beautiful scene before him, mulling over the problem, but no solution presented itself. He turned to Edith. Should he mention his concern to her? No, she would think he was fussing. Perhaps he did need to live more in the moment.

Instead he said, 'Do you know, despite what we've been dealing with, it's been good to be back with you all. We should make fishing trips a regular thing.'

'I would love that. You must come to supper as well. I'll cook the fish.'

She reached across to find his hand and gave it a deft squeeze before grabbing the steering wheel again to guide the heavy vehicle round the bend. As the road straightened, it was blocked by a gathering next to the little passing place up ahead.

'Honestly, why do people stop there?' Edith said.

The Land Rover jerked to a halt and John was thrown forward against his seat belt. Edith pulled on the hand break and leant back into her seat with a sigh.

'They're only unloading to go down to Grebe beach.' But as he said this, his heart started to flutter. Three men stood in the road. They were clad in bulky camouflage boiler suits and more worryingly had hold of what looked like long rifles. One started to walk towards the Land Rover.

'God! What do they want?' John was frantically looking around for some kind of shield or something he could throw.

Edith looked across at him, confusion on her face. 'What's the matter?'

She was already winding down her window. John leant across to try and stop her but one of the large men had already reached the car and peered in.

'Sorry guys, we're just unloading our diving equipment. We'll be as quick as we can.'

John stopped his frantic scrabble and focussed on the man. How foolish of him. The man's bulk was enhanced by his dry suit. He looked like he was equipped for the North Sea, not the Helford Estuary. And the rifle? Now John could see quite clearly that it was an underwater harpoon. Not a gun. He needed to calm down.

Edith seemed to realise what had been going on in his head. As she wound the window back up, she turned to him and said, 'It's all done, you know. You can relax, no one is going to come looking now. We can just get on with our lives.'

She started the engine, this time executing a smooth hill start, and waved to the divers as she guided the Land Rover past all their paraphernalia.

She turned to look at him. 'We can all move on and I, for one, am looking forward to our weekly fishing trips.'

Her face was open and cheerful, and John smiled. This time it was he who reached across for her hand as Edith pressed the accelerator and they sped on, with an added energy, back up to their village.

After Victor

by Catherine Leyshon

Amongst the many night-time sounds of the sea, there comes a special splash.

Frank, skulking in the ope, hears it and closes his eyes. Sighs. He knows that splash, as distinctive as a footstep or the lines on a palm. It's the sound of water slipping around a streamlined body, built for swimming. She wants him to hear. If she hadn't, she could have gone soundlessly, seamlessly, becoming the water rather than entering it. She wants him to know she's there. A thrill shudders through the mangled part of him that loves her, though such feelings rebel against reason. What if she's finally ready to love him back? The thought is a blissful torture.

It's the hope that kills.

Frank screws his walnut-like knuckles into his eyes, sequestered beneath the massive overhang of his brow. His eyes came from a quarryman and are always full of grit. He rubs and digs vigorously. Carefully removes his coat, folds it, places it on the cobbles. Runs headlong out of the alleyway and across the road to the quayside. The sound of watery frolicking reassures him that she has not swum straight out to sea, tail powering effortlessly through the brine.

She's waiting.

For him?

He peers over the edge. A man's height beneath him, the water slaps at the gloomy cave of pillars underneath the dock. Half tide. No moon. The hint of a glint of scaly tail mocks him.

'Meredith!' he hisses. His name for her. Victor Frankenstein never bothered naming either of his creations.

A giggle from the gloom. An inky bow wave tows a line of light from the window of the quayside inn.

Frank blesses the dark for concealing him and curses it for concealing her. 'If we get caught out here, we're done for.'

'Oh Frank. You're so boring. Come on in, the water's lovely.'

Frank. Her name for him. A cruel play on Victor's surname.

'Where are you? I can't see you.'

A little laugh and a splosh. But then a gasp, a squeal, a shriek, and silence.

Frank waits.

She's playing a game. He looks over his shoulder at the inn. Soon the yawning landlord will show his stumbling guests the door at the end of their midsummer's eve after-hours lock-in. Their reluctant homeward shuffle will weave past this spot. A man full of ale won't think twice about taking on a monster. A legend. A myth who was supposed to have died in the icy wastes of the high arctic, but now crouches on the quayside of a Cornish fishing village, all too evidently alive.

Beneath the dock, the water slaps and sucks at the dark. The wet wood smells of rot.

What if she isn't playing? After all, she drowned once before when Victor pushed her over the side of a boat, entombed in a wicker basket laden with rocks.

'Meredith?' he calls, now indifferent to discovery.

He stands up, kicks off his boots and tombstones into the water. There's an awful rush of sea into his ears and nose. His own ugly thrashing and the ebb of the tide force him amongst the dark wooden piles, slick with weed. He calls her name again and sees the hard glint of her eyes in the dark, full of mischief and malice.

When Victor Frankenstein rebuilt his female monster, he gave her the eyes from a dead poet, one of whose poems he recited whilst squeezing those delicate orbs into her sockets.

Meredith flows out from the gloom, swings her marble-white arms around his neck, and flashes her tail between his thrashing legs. Her lythe arms had come from a dancer.

'You'll take us both under,' he bubbles through the chop.

'You'll drown. But I won't.' Another tweak of her tail keeps them afloat. He windmills his arms impotently in the swell. Brawny forearms and shovels for hands, blunt fingered. He learned from Victor that he had received them from a labourer.

'You shouldn't be here. Let's go home. To Victor. He's changed. He can fix you. Take your tail off. Give you back your legs.'

'Victor!' Her venom propels her out from under the pilings in an indignant surge. 'His will. His choices. Always, *always* Victor. You're like a slave.'

Frank swims clear of the pilings and hooks an arm around the rung of a rusty ladder.

'We're all slaves, aren't we?' He shakes water out of his ears. 'Our maker owns us, in the end.'

'Not me. I have freedom.' Meredith floats on her back and tilts her tail skywards so that it catches what little light there is, glinting like mica in sand. Victor gave her the tail from a blue marlin. Its sharpness suits her.

'How did you escape your tank in Victor's lab?' Frank asks.

Her giant tank, choppy with smoky green seawater, had filled the barn behind the granite mansion on the hill. Victor had forbidden him from seeing Meredith. In defiance, he had pressed his monstrous face to a gap in the wooden planks of the barn door. Just a glimpse.

Her wet face is suddenly close to his. Victor had given her the lips from a brothel keeper. Her face had come from a woman crushed under a carriage in Truro. Meredith still has a shard of lacquered wood embedded in her cheek.

Frank can just make out in the dark how delighted Meredith is with herself.

'I persuaded Victor's little weasel of an assistant to set me free in return for the kisses of a mermaid.' She swishes her tail. 'I made him feel brave. He loaded me into a cart, covered me with oil cloth and drove me here. I barely kissed him at all – nothing but a breeze across his lips. But he'll never forget it.'

A flash of jealousy makes Frank's head throb. He reaches for her, but she surges out of the way in a second.

'Swim with me to the island,' she says.

'If I do, will you promise to come back with me to Victor? If you get your legs back, maybe you and I...' Frank is talking to the air. Meredith has already swooped away like a seal.

The island at the entrance to the harbour is barely worthy of the name. At high tide, its lichen-spotted granite brow can hardly be seen, entrapping the complacent sailor who thinks he is nearly safe home. But the tide is falling and a few bold strokes bring Meredith to the island's weedy half-tide cheeks. She hauls out on the seaward side. Frank bashes towards her through the water with his composite arms, locked into a torso that once belonged to a fairground prize fighter. He clambers up next to Meredith and lies panting. His lungs had been taken from the chest of a thief.

Meredith's voice floats through the dark: husky, made from the vocal cords of a shop girl strangled in her bed. 'Why did you try so hard to find Victor? You thought he was dead. You were free. Why did you come back to him?'

Frank looks up at the stars, the rock of the island hard under his back. He takes a moment to find his way into this story, its lies, its shadows. Nothing is straightforward. But he has learned to make painful memories into beautiful words, like the novelist who once owned half his brain. He sits up and stares into the languid midsummer night sky.

'I found my way onto Captain Walton's ship trapped

in the ice in the Arctic Sea. I held Victor in my arms. He was as dead as any man can be. Or so I thought.' He pauses, swallows the memory. 'I went over the side of the boat and let myself drift away on an ice floe. I saw grief in the very shape of the land: its jagged edges, its riotous weather. I yearned for the cold to put me to sleep. But life refused to grant me death.'

In the dark, he feels Meredith brush his hand with hers. He knows it's as much as she can offer. He welcomes the fleeting comfort and presses on with his story. 'After several months, I came across an Inuit group and heard from them that a miracle had happened aboard Walton's ship. A man, thought dead, brought back to life.'

'How?'

'Victor somehow used his own magical science on himself. He persuaded Captain Walton to tell the world that he was dead. The Captain wrote his book. The world mourned the passing of a brilliant scientist while Victor slipped down to Cornwall and started his diabolical experiments again, in secret, unburdened by his reputation and me, his awful creation.' Frank sits up and glances back at the land. 'But I managed to follow him here.'

'None of this explains why you came back to him.' Meredith's impatience makes her slap her tail against the rock.

'I came to find him so that I could kill him for making me.' The words fall like stones from Frank's mouth. 'What did he think he was creating? Animate flesh and bone without a thought for empathy or emotion. I learned those the hard way. And I also intended to kill him for letting me think he was dead.' Frank thumps his giant fist into his meaty palm. 'But...'

'But?'

'When I got to his lab, when I saw that he was really, truly alive, I realised that I needed him. Like a son who goes on loving his father, no matter what.'

A shooting star races across the wide dome of the night. Frank recalls the flash and crackle of electricity, just beyond the heavy iron door of the lab in the mansion on the hill above the harbour. A glimpse of legs twitching on the slab. Victor conjuring life from the fleshy remains of a drowned fisherman. The failure, the frustration as thick in the air as the ozone left lingering from the arcing sparks.

'All my rage fell away. I fell to my knees and begged him to let me stay with him.'

Out of the dark, a sharp, scornful noise comes from Meredith.

Shame roars through Frank like a hurricane. He scrubs his hands through his hair, taken from the scalp of a dead philosopher. The memory of Victor's majestic disdain burns. Frank had gone down on his knees in the lab in the cellar of the big house while Victor stood with his back turned, peeling off his rubber gloves and folding his lab coat.

Please let me live with you. I'll do anything.

Victor had not turned or spoken. At a mere movement of the scientist's hand, his obsequious lab assistant stepped forward and led Frank to the byre, to sleep in the hay with the cow.

When you're alone in the world, and monstrous, you'll mistake anything for love.

Meredith rubs the back of Frank's neck where, a few

weeks earlier, Victor had used a scrap of the cow's hide to patch up a tear. The suede feels soft, but not as soft as Meredith's hand. He leans into her touch.

'Then you came back too, Meredith, and hope lived in me.'

Meredith pulls her hand away.

Behind them, from the shore, erupts the rum-soaked song of well-oiled drinkers leaving the inn, well after hours. The sound sways with them, arm-in-arm, back to cottage and croft. Frank glances over his shoulder. The quayside is nothing more than a smudge bejewelled with the light spilling out of the hostelry door like liquid gold. Out here on the island, they're safe from the drunken sots of the village. But when he looks beyond the inn, he thinks he sees a faint light on the hillside from the direction of Victor's mansion.

Pursuit. And the short midsummer's night will not hide the pair of them for long.

He turns his back to the land. 'When I was newly made, long before Victor staged his death on Walton's boat, I begged him for a mate.' He screws his quarryman's eyes shut. 'He made you for me. But I was too eager, too stupid. He saw how much I wanted you. That's why he destroyed you once before. He was scared we'd love each other. I'm sorry for what you went through because of all that.'

A tiny star of a tear glints on Meredith's cheek. It's all Frank can see in the moonless night. The sea moves in shades of dark around the island. The air smells of salt.

'You're wrong, you know.' Meredith's voice is quiet. 'He didn't make me for you. He made both of us for *him*. For his pride, his ego.' She shakes her head and the tear joins the waves. 'I was already animate when he tore me apart. I already knew the spark of life, though not its meaning. I witnessed my own death at his hands.'

Frank has heard this before. She had told him as she floated in her green, weedy tank in the lab on the hill. He had sat with his back against the solid wooden door of the barn. One of their few snatched moments. He lets her tell the story again, hoping it will dispel her rage a little, and leave more room for love.

'He hacked me to pieces, then he found a basket and weighted it with stones and put what remained of me in it.'

Frank gropes for her hand and misses. 'I felt him do it and was enraged.'

'I was nothing but meat.' Her voice catches in her throat like an angler's stray hook.

Frank can see Victor in his mind's eye, rowing away from shore, out of sight of men and morals. Disposing of his experiment without any regard for what he had created.

Meredith hugs her tail where her knees ought to be. 'He took the basket and slid it into the water. It was a gentle, strange drowning. For a moment, I was cocooned in a basket of air, and then the sea rushed in and took its bounty.'

'But you survived.'

'You can't drown what's not really alive.'

'You came back.'

'If by "came back", you mean the wicker basket full of my body parts was obligingly brought back to Victor by that miscreant of a fisherman who found it in his net, then yes. I suppose I came back.'

Frank takes another look over his shoulder. One light

becomes two, becomes three as torch bearers move along the path from Victor's lab on the hill.

'Victor's coming.'

'What's wrong with him?' Frustration fills Meredith's voice. 'We're loathsome to him, but he just can't let us go.'

The ebb tide has left shallow water between the island and the shore. In an hour or so, anyone will be able to wade over to them. And the turning of the world is going to give them away before that. Frank can sense the inky sea and night sky shifting into shades of black and grey. The slow betrayal of dawn.

'If you return to the lab, I'll make him give you back your legs. Then we'll devise a plan, slip away. You and me.'

Frank holds his breath. He reaches for where he thinks she is and touches her hair, taken from the head of a young heiress who succumbed to the pox. She doesn't recoil, so he lifts a tress and presses it to his face. It smells of formaldehyde and seaweed. She shifts closer.

'I knew you before I met you,' Meredith says quietly. 'I think there's a part intended for you that Victor put in me. It creates some feeling between us, some sympathetic connection that I can't fathom.' She runs her hand down a scar from her armpit to waist. 'Maybe a bit of your heart?'

They share the heart of a village idiot, an ordinary fool found beneath the ice of a frozen pond.

'That's it. Exactly.' Frank says. 'We should not be apart.'

Meredith rests her head on Frank's shoulder. He can smell the ozone on her skin. It reminds him of the shredded air of Victor's lab after the eclectic sparks have snapped through it.

'After the fisherman brought me back to Victor, all in pieces in the basket, he started to rebuild me.'

'I remember.' What Frank remembers was the hope, the fantasy of Meredith taking shape again. Someone like him. For him. But while the work was in progress, Victor confined him to the opulent west wing of the mansion so that he could not see the scientist's new creation take shape. The deep armchairs, luxurious curtains and roaring fire could not disguise the prison he was in.

'When I was half finished, Victor hesitated,' Meredith goes on. 'The need to create burns in him, but he despises what he makes. He feared more than ever that you and I would be together, and make others like us.' Meredith puts her hand on her belly where her tail joins her body. In there she has the womb of a woman who died in childbirth. 'He fears loss of control.'

Frank takes another look over his shoulder at the shore. The lights are moving through the village. Victor and his men will soon be on the quay. Out at sea, the horizon suggests itself in the subtlest way. Dawn is coming.

'I was terrified he'd leave me in pieces on the slab,' Meredith says, the remembered fear scratching at her voice. 'I whispered in Victor's ear: *make me a mermaid. Then Frank won't want me.*'

'Don't say that.'

Frank, having only recently learned to love, is now learning how badly it can scald.

'It was the only way to convince him to remake me. But I sought to deceive him. If he made me a mermaid, I could go where he couldn't follow. Back into the sea.'

Frank feels his quarryman's eyes fill with tears. 'I can't

follow you into the sea either. The only way we can be together is if you let Victor give you back your legs.'

There are shouts from the shore. Frank picks out Victor's voice amongst them and his heart gives a painful tumble.

Meredith looks round at the beach and sighs. 'You see? He can't leave us be.' She turns back and cups Frank's face in her hands, gleaned from a seamstress who lived to a hundred. 'It's time for us to part.'

'No.'

'You talk of Victor giving me my legs back, so you and I can flee. But you can't be without him. You'll keep going back. No matter what he does, and how he treats you, you'll batter yourself against Victor like a moth in a lamp. Because you belong to him.'

Frank puts a hand over one of hers and shakes his head, but he cannot speak. They can both hear the hubbub on the shore, the shouts of the search.

Meredith smooths his hair from his brow. 'I've belonged to the sea since the first time I drowned. When Victor gave me my tail, I realised it made me whole.' She looks over the swell to where the stars at the horizon are winking out. 'I'm going out there. But my freedom doesn't have to come at the cost of yours. You don't need to go back to him. Swim out with me – there's a cave round the next headland. You can hide there.'

But Frank is paralysed by choices. The debt of his creation belongs to Victor. He has an empty part of himself that only Victor can fill. How futile it is to expect Victor to love him as a son, but still he pours hope into that void. How could he bear to live each day in the cave, barely a league away from his maker, when every second would wind the cord tighter, drawing him out, pulling him back to the mansion on the hill?

And then, here is Meredith, the rising dawn starting to pick out her profile. She's like the northern lights that had filled the arctic sky when he cowered on the ice. Magical, beautiful. But somehow always out of reach.

Behind them, a great cry of discovery goes up. The sound of Victor's men dragging a boat across the sand towards the sea makes Meredith lurch for the waves. Frank grabs her arm and pulls her back.

'Let me go.' She is fierce. 'I'm going to do what you're incapable of doing and get away from him. I want every corner of my body and soul purged of Victor Frankenstein.'

'Please...I...'

Her face is close to his. 'What has Victor brought you except misery and betrayal?'

Frank can feel his fool's heart beating in his chest. 'Life. He gave us both life.'

For a long moment, their lips are the width of a kiss apart, then Meredith shakes herself out of Frank's grip. 'It's not enough. After he made us, he should have loved us.'

And she slips into the water. With one powerful snap of her tail, she is gone.

Frank gets shakily to his feet. His legs are cramped and sore. He turns his back to the sea, raises his hand in greeting and capitulation to the boat approaching from the shore. He lets Victor see him in all his monstrousness, silhouetted against the dawn.

An Bedh (The Grave)

by Jess Humphries

Marion lifted her head from the table and dried her eyes. There was a damp patch where her tears had fallen onto the yellowed pine. Knowing that David would have found what she was up to hilarious had set her off. She could hear his laugh.

'Marion Webster, what are you doing? You look ridiculous!'

It was ridiculous. Explaining her undertaking to a stranger would surely get her sectioned. Yet here she was, a fifty-five-year-old widow, wearing her husband's blue overalls with sleeves and legs rolled up, topped off with a yellow bobble hat and a head torch. She glanced at the pick and shovel leaning against the wall by the door from the kitchen to the outside world. The kitchen was the only room in the building you could call finished. A table, two chairs, the old solid-fuel stove, and the mishmash of cupboards David had handcrafted. The door handles and drawer knobs were a wonderfully random combination of shapes and colours. It was eclectic, chaotic, and Marion loved it. It reminded her of David, and she pictured him kneeling to attach a handle, humming to himself. There was always a tune. His habitual music-making grated after a while, yet now she longed for another burst of spontaneous melody to fill the silence.

The chapel was their forever home. As off-grid as they could find, and as quirky as they could make it. Using money from the sale of their seafront house, they had escaped the tourist 'ants' with their fifteen weeks of annual chaos. Summer seasons which had once been captivating and energetic became something to dread. What better time to run away to an abandoned chapel on the edge of the moor? It was a project. A project was fine when there were two of them. David's income funded the mortgage, but that vanished along with all DIY expertise the moment the lorry struck the car. They had assured her he died instantly. But they would say that. It was what she needed to hear. Bereavement was hard, loneliness harder, and money worries were the final straw. She tried to bury her head in the sand of her sadness, but the mortgage company didn't deal with grief. They dealt in letters, reminders, and threats. Corporations had evolved beyond the humanity of their employees. They had an existence, a soul, and miserly greed worthy of a Dickens novel.

'Pick yourself up, we've got work to do and you know what it is!'

She heard the voice, then realised it was her own. There had been many voices recently. Not for the first time Marion questioned her grip on reality. She shook herself into life, grabbed the pick and shovel, and went outside. Breakdown or no breakdown, there was a job at hand.

The night was cloudless and moonlit. As she walked, silver light bounced off each blade of grass, and the leaves on the trees danced in the gentle breeze. The air was cold and clean in her nostrils. Given recent events, Marion appreciated breathing more than ever. Surveying the graveyard surrounding the chapel, she recognised the points of light above each plot. She nodded towards them; each of the lights dipped and bobbed, returning her greeting. As she walked, she recalled how she first met her new friends.

A few weeks after the accident, conducting her habitual pre-bedtime check of the back door, Marion had seen tiny iridescent lights hovering over the graveyard. Her blood ran cold and the hairs on her arms stood to attention. Outside it was a noiseless scene, but she could hear the pounding in her ears. The lights didn't move in the wind, so what the hell were they? They seemed to pulse in time with her breathing. She stood transfixed, her mind racing to come up with a rational explanation. None was forthcoming. Eventually, surmising that the lights were not threatening, fear subsided to a level where she was able to shake the whole thing off as symptomatic of her tired mental state. Marion shut the back door as a barrier to protect her sanity.

That same night, in a restless slumber somewhere between dreaming and wakefulness, she had a visitor. Marion knew someone was there, but it was without corporeal form. Not a ghost in any sense of the word, more some kind of dream. A hollow voice rang in her ears.

'Marion, we the spirits of the chapel are deeply sorrowful at David's loss. We want you to know that we share your sadness. You represented a hope that this chapel would remain undisturbed and unmolested by outsiders. We want to help you, not scare you.'

This otherworldly conversation had been one-way, as a petrified, confused, and mute Marion was so overcome trying to understand where the boundaries of reality lay, she couldn't even dream-speak. In the light of the morning, her rational brain again dismissed the episode as an unwanted by-product of stress. She had buried herself under the duvet, longing for a familiar pair of arms to disappear into and another pair of ears to hear about her crazy dream.

Then the first threatening letter arrived. There were too many words to cope with. Words like default, repossession, and court action. She had no regular income, enough savings to maintain food and power for the moment. But there was no of a path out of this mess. The depth of her despair felt like dropping a stone into a mine shaft but never hearing it land. She again took herself back to bed and fresh anger arose as she lay there. Why did he have to die? Why did he not make better plans to provide for her? The vow was 'to love and to keep'. She didn't feel kept now he was gone.

The dreams had become too frequent to ignore. Apparition after apparition invaded her sleep. It was persistent and disconcerting, and she never really 'saw' her visitor. The voice was always in her head, sometimes her own, other times that of long forgotten friends.

Insanity was an odd thing, she reflected. You didn't know whether you've crossed a line. People with full-blown psychosis believed their narrative and inhabited a visceral world. They inhabited a fantasy. She too was finding it harder to comprehend what was real or not. The 'things' communicating in her half-conscious dream state were not helping that discernment either. The message was always the same, they wanted to help her. Surely it was wishful thinking manifesting as a recurring dream. But then there were the lights. Was it time to embrace the breakdown, and give in to the psychosis? Life inside a new reality had to be better than this one without David.

After the first encounters, it had begun to feel less like a third-rate horror movie. Was it possible that her interaction with the spirit world might be mundane or even normal? What did it mean to be one of those spirits? One obvious question remained. If they were dead, and David was dead, could they communicate with him? This spurred her on to muster the courage to try and respond on the next visitation. She waited for the entity to pass its usual message, then projected her voice into the dream realm.

'Hello. I don't know what to say really, I've never communicated with the dead. You are dead, aren't you? Or is this some limbo state you're in? Is that you in the lights? Can you see me? Can you see each other?'

This wasn't going as planned. She had too many questions, and even though unconscious, her nervousness made her talk too much. The visitor began to laugh, and waves of happiness radiated over her. Oh good, she thought, at least I've amused the afterlife.

'I'm sorry! It's all a bit overwhelming. You said that

71

you wanted to help me, but I don't understand how. The mortgage company is going to repossess unless I can find enough money, but I don't have it and I don't know what else to do. And I don't mean to be rude, but you're all dead!'

Dream-Marion felt a tear slide down her cheek. A cold ethereal hand reached out and gently wiped it off her face. She felt a tingle on her skin, a chilled empathy emanating from the ghostly touch.

'Marion, we are a community. We now consider you a part of our community too. We are the tied souls buried here over generations. We are individuals making up a whole. Some of us were children who are now grown, and some were of great age and are now young. We occupy this space together. We were postmen, fishermen, teachers, wives, mothers, husbands, and brothers. Now we are rooted to this chapel, each to our plot. This is our eternal spot in the universe, and you are the latest caretaker of that spot.'

Frustratingly, at that moment, the alarm had gone off and dragged Marion back to the 'real' world. The conversation remained unfinished.

Subsequently she took to keeping her alarm switched off to avoid any further interruptions. She needed answers to her questions, and her nightly discourses with the deceased had become a highlight. She now understood that they were not in some limbo world where all souls converged. Therefore, communicating with David was not an option. She had been refused permission to bury him in the graveyard. It felt odd to know that there were rules even for the supernatural. It was a misleading term. Supernatural smacked of endless possibilities and flights of imagination. Yet her new friends were as bound by eternal circumstances as they had been when mortal. Each was tied to their grave and this building. They communicated as one but were individuals. It felt reassuringly badly thought through. In truth, it further convinced her that this was a breakdown. Only her pathetic mind could devise such a flawed explanation of the afterlife. Yet it felt good to have a community to belong to, even one that wasn't huggable.

'Marion, there is something you need to know. A rumour, backed up by something odd, which we do not understand. There is a single plot in the far corner, with a stone and a name, but there is no spirit. It would be part of us if it were there, yet it's as empty as a corpse-less coffin!'

'You're going to tell me that it's a portal to Hell or something ridiculous?'

'Oh Marion, there is no Hell unless being attached to a derelict chapel on Bodmin Moor counts as purgatory! That grave is indeed empty. One of us was alive at the time. The man who was to be interred there supposedly died escaping after robbing a mail coach. He was buried immediately and being deceased avoided the inevitable public hanging. Some folks put it down to the Lord's justice, but the burial was so quick that no one remembered seeing the body. Rumour then had it that Johan Lockley escaped on a ship to the new world from Padstow, and his family used some of the stolen money to bribe the local constable into the fake burial, leaving the additional funds for Johan support himself should he return.'

Marion found this hard to swallow. This was some crazed retelling of Cornish stories of smugglers, pirates, and thieves. Bloody Poldark and Long John Silver come back to haunt her from her subconscious. A bunch of dead people just told her about buried treasure. She thought she heard David laughing sarcastically.

What should she do with this information? Why not give in and go with the flow? It was her property, after all. What would a little bit of digging hurt? If it proved she was crazy, she could leave when the chapel got repossessed, knowing it had indeed been a fantasy.

Switching on the head torch and directing its yellow beam at the ground, Marion picked her way over to the corner plot by the wall. The headstone was worn and reflected a deep grey in the moonlight. Its ragged forty-five-degree angle caused the embossed letters to cast shadows and made them easier to read.

'Johan Lockley 1765-1806'

Short but sweet Marion mused. She arced the pick into the grass, breaking the earth.

Digging in the light of the torch was an odd experience. The beam cast dark and ominous shadows, the exact opposite of the orbs. How strange that the real ghosts felt less horrific than half imagined movements in the dark. She was well into the topsoil when her spade met resistance. It sounded wooden. A treasure chest? Or maybe a coffin? What might a body from the nineteenth century look like? Hopefully, it had been long enough that it would be just bones, unless it was one of those bodies which never succumbed to decrepitude, with hair and teeth intact. Marion experienced a frisson of excitement. She was following destiny. Dropping to her knees, she scrabbled the dirt from the wooden surface. Her hands found one corner with its brass reinforcing bar, then another. This was too small to be a coffin. She panicked, was it just a head in a box? The thought made her retch, and she rocked back on her haunches and looked up at the full moon. Lunatic! She was the archetypal lunatic.

'It's all your fault!' she shouted skywards, partly at David and partly at the moon.

Slowly she uncovered all four edges of a shoe box size crate, thankfully too small for a head, but not large enough for a decent treasure either. She lifted it onto the grass. Nothing had been below or around it, just soil, stones, and disturbed earthworms. She glanced at the lights around her.

'My friends, we have something!'

She thought about taking the box inside to open it in the kitchen, but she wished to share either triumph, failure, or confirmation with her spiritual messengers. Her trepidatious hands gripped the box. She noticed the beam from her head torch looked like an additional orb. Was she conjoining with the community? The idea warmed her heart. She took a deep breath.

The lid was stuck with mud, and it took some fiddling until finally she prised it free. Half hoping to be dazzled by the reflection of gold and jewels in the torchlight, Marion let out a faint sigh of disappointment. The box was virtually empty. The orbs grew motionless. Blinking back tears of disappointment and wiping her muddy hands on her overalls, Marion reached into the box and withdrew the folded paper package it contained, faded and yellowed like a pirate map in a film. A fresh sense of unreality washed over her.

Unfolding the package with cold fingers, she caught an object as it fell. A silver disc about the size of a commemorative five-pound coin David had once been gifted. Lying in her left palm, it gleamed despite being over 200 years old. It was hardly a hoard! Marion directed the beam of the head torch onto the wrapper. Once unfolded it was a letter, written in a florid cursive style. The missive was short and hard to decipher at first.

Dearest Johan, if you should return from the New World by whatsoever means, know that we did not forget you and our agreement, however with all the rumours after your leaving we decided not to entrust all the funds to this hiding place. We know you will understand.

If in God's good grace, we are no longer living when you arrive, then Godspeed and bless your footsteps to the place marked on this map. We eagerly await your return.

Wm and Mary L

Below the message was a rough drawing of two hills, one with a tor, an adjacent valley with a flowing stream, a pile of rocks, and a small tree on the opposite bank. Near the tree was a small 'T'. Marion jumped to her feet.

'Treasure!' she yelled holding the letter and the coin in the air.

She waved her arms and whooped maniacally into the dark, all her nervous energy spilling forth. The orbs ceased their motionless vigil and began to dance and sway in time, swirling together and merging into a vortex of light enveloping Marion. She could feel them singing and lifting her, feet no longer on the ground as they held her in a dancing embrace. She basked in the glow of this moment with her new family, and fresh waters of joy sprang in her heart.

Eventually, her friends let her descend, and Marion's feet returned to the earth. Picking up the shovel she looked at the coin in her hand, rolling it in her fingers. Glinting in the light of the head torch it sang of hope and future chances. This was not the ultimate sunrise once hoped for, but the sky was brighter on the horizon, the pale pink predawn of a new day arriving. Not yet a fairy tale ending, but this story wasn't over. With a bow to her luminous friends, she hopped over the grey stone wall. Marion Webster had a tree to find and a dream to finish.

The Cat of Camborne

by Jason Kenyon

'**D**ad, that's a load of rubbish and you know it!'
Sitting at our kitchen table, Dad somehow manages to look like he's on a throne, while I stand in front of him like some sort of affronted petitioner. He leans towards me, one arm on the table, and waves a finger.

'Oh, you shouldn't be so quick to dismiss things, boy. I saw it, I did. I've seen it every day. It's marked our house, and I'll wager it's sizing us up to eat!'

I shake my head. I've been back here for a week and already I find myself wanting to hop on the train and return upcountry. I'd forgotten just how much Dad wears me down, and this nonsense is a perfect example of it.

But there's no malice in his face. Up to now, I'd assumed he was winding me up just to get a rise, but as I stare at the certainty in his eyes, I start to doubt myself. Not about what he's claiming, of course – that's clearly one of his usual tall tales.

Maybe he genuinely believes it himself, though.

'Dad, seriously. There's no *Cat of Camborne*.'

'You say that as you've not seen it, but it's out there, and it's ready for the hunt!'

'Dad. Nobody else has seen a big cat anywhere around town, and they've definitely not seen it wandering into people's gardens!'

He sits back, an air of professional indignation in the stiff way he sits upright. Breaking off his confident speech for a moment, he rises and steps over to the cupboard where he keeps his secret stash of lemon sherbets. Like the story of the Cat of Camborne, the *secret* classification is wholly inaccurate.

Dad reaches up past the shelves with the doll I have to cover up every time polite company comes around, and he considers the bag of lemon sherbets for a tense few seconds. His mouth moves silently, and at first I think he's muttering some sort of curse, but then I realise he's counting. He picks up the bag, takes out some sherbets, and then changes his mind and carries the entire bag back to the table.

'Alright,' he says, popping three sherbets into his mouth, 'let's have a bet, you and I. You always miss the Cat of Camborne because you go to Tesco every time it appears. How's about today I go do the shopping and you can see the Cat.'

I fold my arms and glare down at him. 'Last time you did the shopping, you came back with everything in the store but the stuff on the list.'

'I've learned my lesson,' he says, giving a personable

shrug that swiftly turns into another grab for a handful of sherbets. 'Have faith in me, boy. I'll get the shopping done, and you – you'll have an *experience*. You'll see the supernatural face to face! You'll learn the truth of old legends... something you don't get upcountry.'

'Dad, there are cats everywhere.'

'Ah, you're not listening! This un's big as a car! He rips through the bushes, I tell you, and claims the garden for his own. All the birds clear out! And then he sits there staring at the back door, waiting for someone to open it. And when someone does...

'He'll pounce!'

Rolling my eyes, I reach over to pull the bag of sweets out of his range. 'You've had too much sugar. Why don't I just do the shopping like normal, and you can go for a walk and clear your head?'

'Did you forget this happened up at Bodmin?'

'That was decades ago, and it was a hoax!'

'They *say* it was a hoax. But I've seen, boy, and now I believe as well!'

After replacing the lemon sherbets in their hidden spot behind the long out-of-date spices, I turn the forbidden doll around, so it doesn't have to witness this display of foolishness.

'Look, Dad, if it'll stop you talking about the damn Cat every day, then fine – I'll stay here today and watch the garden all afternoon. But you'd better get everything on the list this time!' I glance back towards the cupboard. 'And you have enough sherbets.'

'You sure take after your mother,' Dad says, but he picks up the shopping list and inspects it anyway.

The rest of the morning goes by nice and peacefully. It's been a week since I came back for my fortnight stay, but I still feel like I only just arrived. There's a strange sense of time displacement every time I step into my bedroom and find all the things I'd left out before the move.

A couple of old notes on the table remind me of the video games I was playing when I still lived here. Two DVDs lie on the bookshelf, still waiting for me to go through with my decade-old plan to watch them. I feel like I could put one on and fly back through time to that last month here, picking up the life I abandoned when I chose to go for the job in Cheltenham.

But here I am in the present. The job didn't go so well. My relationship with Jane didn't survive the distance, or how I changed. I'm working somewhere else now, but it's no place I like to bring up when people are bragging about their own careers.

I know Dad would say I shouldn't have left, and maybe he's right. But I don't want that conversation. I can't believe I'm thinking it, but perhaps it's better when he talks about the Cat of Camborne.

'See you in three hours!' Dad calls from downstairs.

'Three hours? What are you planning to do?'

I step out onto the landing and catch him as he's halfway out the front door. He's put on his old cap, which looks like it was excavated from an abandoned mine, but his coat is new.

'Oh, I figured I'd make it up as I went,' he says.

And with that, the house is empty. Well, except for me. I feel a lot like the house. For a minute, I consider ignoring the matter of the Cat, but there's not much else to do, so I go and sit downstairs near the back door, where I can glance up at the garden when I remember.

I don't believe for a moment that the Cat is supernatural at all, but I start to wonder if my Dad didn't cast a spell on me. It's a struggle to stay interested in my book. The house feels tense. There's no draught, and the lifeless curtains dangle to either side of small square windows. Through the back door, which is almost entirely glass, I see no sign of anything.

My Dad's voice echoes in my head: 'All the birds clear out!'

And then there it is. Through the frame of the door, I see it sitting there in the middle of the garden. The world seems to bend around it. Our lawn surrounds it in a near-perfect circle. All the bushes lean in, as though some force of gravity is tugging them towards this one being. Even the wispy, white clouds trail downwards, caught up in this distortion.

It's a cat. Just like Dad said, it is staring at the back door, and I get the feeling that it might be staring at me. It's a grey cat with emerald eyes, and I'm so caught up in the sense of displacement that it takes me a moment to register that it's just a regular, bog-standard cat.

'For heaven's sake, Dad,' I mutter.

The Cat of Camborne maintains its silent vigil. For all I know, it could be a stuffed animal placed there as a joke. Even the faint breeze outside barely seems to ruffle it. I entertain the idea that maybe Dad was the one who put it there.

But then one ear flicks, and I realise that it is, in fact, alive.

Whatever Dad says, I'm not concerned that this cat is going to pounce if I open the door. Setting my book to one side, I unlock the door and step out. The Cat watches me as I approach, and its eyes follow me as I crouch to face it at roughly its own level.

'Hey there, buddy,' I say, and the Cat stares back. 'How's it going?'

As the Cat continues to gaze at me, I have the odd notion that I've asked the wrong question. Then something occurs to me.

'Say, don't I know you?'

Honestly, it's a very generic cat. It has no distinguishing features to mark it out from any other cat. Its fur is a consistent grey, and there are no unusual markings in its glowing eyes. All the same, as daft as it sounds, I'm gripped by the strong belief that I've met this cat before.

It finally moves. Just a little, but the Cat leans slightly to the side, peering behind me. I feel a sudden jolt in my chest as I think that someone's there, but when I look back, it's just the house. The windows are all empty, no matter how much I feel that I'm going to see some spectral figure gazing down at me.

I look back at the Cat, which is no longer checking around my side. Its eyes are intent, fixed on mine.

Are you reading my mind, Cat?

If it is, it lacks the ability to answer my question. Instead, it stands up. Once more, it looks past me, and then it turns and wanders casually towards the hedge.

'Well, see you,' I say to it.

Now the Cat does seem to respond. It turns back at the hedge and that piercing gaze fixes me once more. Then it lets out a forceful *miaow*.

I blink. 'Um... what is it, buddy?'

Miaow.

'You... you want me to follow?'

I ask the question as a half-joke, but this seems to satisfy the Cat, which begins to push its way into the small opening in the hedge. As it does so, a gust of wind cuts through me, and I shiver.

'Wait a minute, Cat,' I say. 'I'm getting a coat.'

It cocks its head at me as though to say *really?* But it stays standing there, nevertheless. A handful of minutes later, I've locked the house and crossed the lawn to join the Cat again. Its eyes seem narrowed, but it did at least wait for me.

Off it goes through the hedge, and I decide to forget my dignity and use the same route. It steps out onto the pavement beyond with grace, while I fumble through branches and leaves and nearly walk straight into Mr and Mrs Davies, who are walking home from the direction of the shops. Covered in leaves and caught somewhat off-guard, I give them an apologetic smile as I rush on in pursuit of the Cat of Camborne.

'Sorry about that!' I say over my shoulder.

I hear them muttering something about *Mike's boy* but I'm soon out of earshot. That probably didn't do my reputation much good – I didn't exactly socialise much before I left, and I've been mostly gone for the past ten years. Oh well. I'll be back off on my journeys soon enough anyway.

For now, though, my focus remains on this trip with the Cat, which skips across the road and leads me on a winding course through streets, past clusters of houses, and finally onto muddy tracks as we advance on Carn Brea. I remember how I get a warm feeling whenever my train reaches here, seeing the familiar hill with its towering monument, like a lighthouse guiding me home. Since everything went wrong, I've been stuck in such a negative spiral that I'd forgotten.

The Cat is filled with determination. For the early part of the journey, it would pause to check that I was following, but now it is set on its course and rushes ahead of me. I'm hardly fit so I am glad that I don't need to run to keep up, but I'd appreciate a break here or there.

Up Carn Brea we go, the browns and greens broken up by scattered rocks. Once again, I'm transported to the past, back to a time when I was excited to just go exploring and taking in the scenery. Even so, there's a part of me that wants to check my watch and work out when I need to head back. I try to resist worrying about that for now, and when the Cat finally pauses again to blink at me, I manage to set all that aside.

From there, it's not much further until the Cat comes to a stop. It hops up onto a rock, and I sit down next to it. While I'm breathing a little harder, the Cat is supremely unbothered. It gives me a sideways glance, almost an eyeroll, and I throw it a shrug.

We stare out at the view. From here, I can see what was once my whole world. In one direction, there's the sprawl of Camborne, and just over there I can see Redruth. Carn Brea Castle sits a short distance away, watching over the two towns. It's a bright day, and the coast is as clear as it can be. I remember days at the sea, whether down at Mullion, or further north around Padstow.

'It isn't so bad back here, is it?' I ask the Cat, which blinks at me.

More than just the Cat is familiar now. As the breeze washes over me, I remember another day years ago when I brought Jane up here. We came all the way together and took in the same view. That was also the day that we ran into...

'You,' I say to the Cat. 'Are you that same cat we met?'

The Cat blinks at me and looks behind me again. I realise that it's looking towards the spot where Jane sat on that day, and sigh with regret.

'Are you looking for her? Sorry, buddy – she's gone.'

Emerald eyes shift to bore into my own.

'Oh, she's not gone-gone, just... gone from my world. She's fine, I think.' We're still friends on social media, and she always looks happy in photographs, at least. It's just me not dealing with it, or maybe I'm worse at hiding it.

The Cat almost seems to nod, and it resumes its watch over the view. I reach out to pet it, half-expecting my hand to go straight through it. I've almost begun to believe that this creature is supernatural like Dad said, but my fingers brush over soft fur.

'Were you looking for her? Sorry to disappoint. It's just me, these days.'

Its ears flick, but it says nothing.

'Dad thought you were some big monster, but you seem okay to me.'

Now the Cat does look back at me, eyes narrowed again.

'Um, that is, you're a fine cat. The best around.' I

take another deep breath as I look at the empty space that Jane used to occupy. 'Well, I miss her too. But not much changing that now, I guess.'

I'm struck by how beautiful and serene it is up here. I know they always talk about stopping to smell the roses, but it's only now, as I breathe in the clear breeze up here, that I really appreciate what that means. I've spent so long on regret that I've forgotten all the places and memories that I used to love. Maybe I can find that again.

The Cat leans against me, and I pet it gently. When Jane came up here with me, the Cat only seemed to have time for her, and I feel that I am being honoured today. This Cat of Camborne has deemed me worthy of its attention, even if I don't seem to have been the person it was really seeking.

Or maybe I was. Everything feels just right now as we sit there together on that rock atop Carn Brea. It's been a long time since I was able to look back at my time with Jane and not feel a stab in my heart, but now I feel happy that I did at least share those good times, however it went in the end.

I feel a buzz and reach into my pocket with my free hand. It's Dad calling me. Typical of him, to break into such a quiet moment. The Cat tilts its head as it regards me, as though asking why I hadn't already answered the call. Smiling at it, I swipe on the screen, and Dad's rough voice fills the clear air.

'Hey, where're you? Did you go out?'

'I did! Sorry – but you were right, that cat did visit the garden. I followed it up Carn Brea!'

'You followed it where?' I can hear the clatter of items

spilling from a bag onto the table, and then the fridge opening. In my mind's eye, I see him stocking things on the shelves with no real order to any of it. 'Are you alright?'

'Of course, I'm alright, Dad, it's a normal cat!'

I turn to my companion, who blinks up at me and purrs, and then back at the empty spot to my left.

'It just casts a long shadow.'

The Foxtrot

by Alice Thomas

The hunters spotted me again. They sent their hounds for my feet. I dashed between the tree trunks and slid down the steep bank. When I made it to the bottom, the mutts stopped at the top. Turning myself back into a fox was needed to get away from the village, but that wasn't the resort I wanted.

Of course, transforming into a full human was feasible. I could even tuck my orange tail in and hide it completely from sight, but it would've been like sticking a rod up my back-side.

Earlier on, I'd popped over to the village near the Cornish woods, so I could turn human and dress up in my dapper suit. The afternoon became a disaster though, since Derek's friends caught sight of me cuddling with another lady in a tea-room. So I'd burst out and turned back into my fox form in a heartbeat. They then sent their hounds after me, and that was how I ended up in the woods.

Years ago, transformed as a human by my magical ability, I thought leaving out my fox tail was enough. That was until the day I turned back into a fox, after I dodged rocks thrown by a bratty boy. The moment Derek's dad saw what I became, he hunted me down for the sake of his pride, or rather to enjoy his bloodsport of fox hunting. Like a typical farmer, he hates foxes. Maybe my ancestors got drunk and ate the chickens at his family farm once, which made Derek's dad teasier than an adder.

It would have been an easier life to just stick to my 'natural' fox form and roam the woods only, ignoring the frolics of a charming village nearby. But the amount of hunting these screeching men did every year meant no place was safe for the four-legged animals. If it wasn't for my family secret, an ability to turn into humans, then God only knows where we could have ended up.

The woodland was my safe area, with amber leaves dancing in sunlight, falling to layer into a soft blanket. A gentle hint of breeze blew past my wet nose, delivering all kinds of wonderful smells. That breeze turned bitter, leaving me feeling a bit naked in my orange fur coat. I spent handsomely for my suit, which I sadly left behind the tearoom.

Thank God these massive woodlands are still standing today, stretching to the skies and to the lumpy hills beyond. I hope they're safe from being cut down and replaced by houses in the near future.

There was a hint of fuzzy warmth in the air, suggesting there could be other foxes nearby.

As my black paws danced to avoid the sharp stones along the dirt path, the scent grew stronger. I breathed in of that fresh air from the flowing river, perking my own foxy senses. I looked all around to see if there were any traps lying about. Found one, under a pile of leaves. A snare trap that was open, primed and poking its trigger out for my paw to step on.

Licking my fangs, I took a side-step to avoid it. But suddenly, I stepped over a steep bank. I rolled sideways along the dusty incline and fell into a deep river, completely sunken.

Darkness, coldness. A slimy sponge rubbed against my temples. My arms stung like blisters, grazed by sharp stones from the ground. The place was a dark, dusty hollow beneath a network of tree roots, enough to give me a migraine.

I thought so much about my mother and my brothers, and my father, if he was still around. They should be proud of me for achieving my form, almost in a man's image. But it was my fault for not catching up with them and instead drinking pints and searching for my girl. Oh, my dearest mother, I am ever so sorry for my selfishness!

After blinking my stinging eyes, I saw the peach-white face of an angel. A human girl with cute, sparkly eyes, all dressed in light colours. But when I looked beyond her snow white hair, I realised that heaven wasn't supposed to look like a burrowed den.

I tried to push myself up. My right shoulder zapped pain through my back. I gave out a sharp howl. I whimpered in my water-logged fur coat.

'Easy there,' the lady said. 'I just got you out of that river.'

My nose sniffed. How far was I swept along the river? Did I fall down a waterfall and break my front joint? I tried to speak. I made a light howl instead.

'Just rest and relax.' She applied her towel to my neck, drying it. 'My sisters will return with supplies soon from our cottage nearby.'

Sisters? I stopped and groaned after pulling myself over. My shoulder continued to lodge back in pain, plucking its strings of nerves.

'This will hurt.' Her hand pressed my shoulder.

My shoulder clicked, stabbing my nerves. I howled. If I was human now, I would've muttered a ton of nonsense. My paws moved freely again, though they could do with a warm bath soon.

'That should be better,' the lady said. 'Wait here while I squeeze the water out.' She stood and turned, revealing her bushy white tail from her dress, almost matching her light hair.

'Wait!' I held my hand up. My fur sunk into my white skin, leaving my red hair, tail and moustache visible. Fingers produced from my right paw.

The lady turned. Her eyes rounded in shock, which lowered to see my groin.

'Pardon my rudeness, aren't you one of those magical foxes?' I asked.

'Huh?'

'The name's Amber. Roger Amber,' I smiled. 'I'm a fox.' My jaw tightened. 'I can also turn into a man. I suppose you do something like that?'

'Me turning into a man?'

My shoulders flinched. 'I mean, a lady? Sorry, I just

saw your ... erm.'

'Take it easy,' she said. 'I'm Sakiya. I'm guessing you're like us? Foxes who turn into humans by magic, only to leave their tails behind?'

'Y-Yes!' I pointed. 'Wait? How is it possible?'

'We moved here years ago, from a faraway place,' Sakiya said. 'I heard Cornwall is filled with mystical creatures in the woods, which led us to believe this place is perfect for our living. But I hadn't expected fox people, like us.'

I smirked. 'Have you been to the village close by?'

'No, I heard the hunters live around there.' She furrowed her brow. 'Why did you ask?'

I smiled, making a polite gesture. 'Allow me to guide you to the best places along the town's outskirts, and I will prove to you that the people living there will treat you with respect. Just a few isolated buildings with plenty of belly laughs. They don't even care if we have fluffy tails!'

Sakiya squinted in confusion. Judging by her bushy white tail, her family were obviously foxes with the ability to transform into complete human forms.

Quite interesting, Sakiya's place. A rigid floor in the den, layered with bunches of soft rugs, with colours faded after collecting dust from the root-ridden ceiling.

'I know of a pub along the road that's free from hunters,' I said. 'You can have mead and fresh pieces of chicken served on a silver platter, and the waitresses there are very nice.'

'And what would you suggest we do?'

I smirked. 'We go on a date.'

Sakiya gasped. 'We just met!'

'Easy there.' I held my hands up. 'Just an invitation for drinks. I will pay my hard earned cash for them. Promise.'

Shortly after the sun set beneath the ridge, me and my girl stepped along the grey road in our pairs of shiny shoes, far away from the woods. We'd discussed their old home with Sakiya's sisters in the lounge earlier, leading to some interesting discussions. How they moved from Japan for better pastures. I then walked over to my underground hideout to grab another suit, so me and Sakiya could walk to the pub in our clothed human forms.

'Pardon my rudeness dear,' I politely asked. 'The special things you had at your cottage back there. Did you spend handsomely for them to be delivered from your old home?'

'No,' Sakiya said. 'These are my family belongings.'

'Family belongings?' I raised my brow. 'You didn't sneak out of there, did you?'

'It depends what you mean by that.' Sakiya scowled in confusion. 'We had to move all the way to here, mainly for better safety and financial opportunities.'

I squinted in confusion as we strolled over the arching bridge. The air whipped into a thick, cosy vapour, which complimented my lady friend's warm perfume. My hands were in my pockets and my tail attempted to pet around her behind, but she stepped away a bit.

'Well, your family has a cottage that anyone would envy,' I smiled. 'In fact, you couldn't have picked a much better place for your new home. In Cornwall, of course!'

'You mean Britain?' Sakiya raised her eyebrow at me.

'Cornwall's a separate nation! Anyway.' I pointed to

a building surrounded by trees and a curved road. 'That place is where we're dining at tonight.'

We strolled over to the lone pub with blotches of amber lights, inviting many to come inside. A classy car parked by the front of a rigid window with a sheen of a wet shore stone. The door in its middle beckoned us to visit its gentle warmth, booming with laughter. I had yet to see Derek and his nonces inside that building, unless it's a friend's birthday, so it was tippity top for us there.

'I still think this is a bad idea,' Sakiya murmured.

'It'll be fine, dear!' I smiled. 'It's the friendliest place in this area! I know a few of the faces there. Just as long as you smile, they'll grin back at ya.'

Sakiya paused. 'I would guess so.'

I turned the door handle. Ladies first. As her exotic white tail brushed against my empty belly, we entered among the clusters of giggling folk. I could taste the yeast in the air, but I was more interested in the rich food smells from the kitchen, making my lips moist.

'You will love it.' I took her jacket off.

I found a table in the quietest corner of the restaurant, grabbing a menu to see what was on offer. But as soon as a waitress mentioned a lemon chicken special, it was an instant order. It would be rude though to not order a bottle of mead to share between us.

Ten minutes in, Sakiya's sun-kissed cheeks remained pale. She continued to check around for strangers, despite us being surrounded by partitions in a corner of pale, icy walls. I blinked my eyes, minding my own business. Sakiya would just need to ease into this warm, humid room, but she kept staring elsewhere in the room.

'Hey, foxy girl.'

When my hand reached out, Sakiya flinched back on her seat.

'It's alright,' I continued. 'The people have treated you nicely so far, haven't they?'

'Not all of them.' Sakiya stared at me with rounded eyes, biting her lower lip. 'Haven't you realised the kind of people they are at the bar?'

'Pardon?'

'The hunters could well be sipping beers by the bar near us!'

I checked over my shoulder. There were only a few tables with couples and small families around them. They were chattering away without any staring at us so far. I smiled back.

'I don't see any hunters sitting at those tables at the moment,' I smirked. 'Just lower your shoulders, my dear. They won't touch base here. Breathe and relax.'

'Just listen for a second,' Sakiya scowled. 'We come from a family of mystical foxes. We call ourselves "Kitsune".'

'Kits...sew ney?' I whispered.

'It's Japanese for fox. I doubt you have read up on our folklore.'

'Ma'am, I got myself too busy for me to read up on such trivial things!'

'What?'

I paused before my eyes rounded. 'I shouldn't have said that. Apologies, my dear.'

'I don't think anywhere has any decent information on our folklore.' Sakiya combed her fingers together. 'My ancestors started out as foxes. We have a history of magic.

Our history sounds similar to your hidden cult of magical foxes.'

'We're not that magical.' As I was about to sip my drink, I paused. 'Did you just say, you have magic?'

'We did,' Sakiya frowned. 'We're now trying to get ours back.'

'Well, I guess you must have more surprises than I thought.' As I was about to take another sip, a hand planted on my shoulder. My glass almost poked against my moustache.

'Are you—,' a man bellowed in my ear. 'Roger boy?'

'Um.' My head crept around and my eyes widened. 'E-Evening?'

My heart dropped as soon as I caught sight of his wrinkly, round face. Derek was the last person I wanted to see tonight. His rough grip fastened on my shoulder, much rougher after years of farming. His blue-eyed glare stared into my soul.

'W-What brought you here?' I stuttered.

'A couple of friends wanted drinks in this pub,' he said in his gravelly tone. 'First time I've been here in years. How are you doing anyway?'

'Just enjoying a meal for tonight?' I made a weak smile. My fingernails dug against the table. I kept my human fingers whilst resisting the urge to turn back into a fox.

'Good boy! You found a date at last, I presume?' He tipped his pint at her.

'Only a lady friend for a meal!' I nodded. 'Just a private chat for now.'

'Oh.' Derek bowed. 'Madam?' He then smirked, bringing his torso close to my shoulder. 'I'm sure this man has much to share with you. We just happen to be very *close* friends. We got into our own turf wars, with his family stirring up trouble for our business.'

'I-I am sure we were playing around!' I stuttered.

Derek snatched our bottle. He gave it a sniff, placing its mouth close to his lips. 'If I were you, Roger, I would order a Merlot for tonight. I would then head home as soon as you can.'

He took a light sip, much to my disgust. His mouth curled into a devilish grin.

I nodded with a smile. 'She is nervous tonight. First time eating here.'

'Oh!' He flashed his eyes between our paled faces. 'Sorry for that! I'll leave you both to enjoy the night.' He placed the bottle back on the table. His palm slapped on my shoulder. 'Don't *forget* it!'

I briskly walked through the door, leaving the half-eaten food behind. My eyes readjusted to the dark faster than the bitter winds. I bent over my knees, panting, resisting all that urge to transform. We rushed through our main meal and took our bottle of mead after making a beeline to pay off my bill. That bottle would double as a weapon if needed.

'Slow down!' Sakiya called. 'It's alright!'

'It's not!' I shook with a tightened jaw. 'We can't stay in any longer. He saw our faces!' I checked over her shoulder. Nobody by the door. 'We must drink inside that house of yours!'

'The woods are fine!' Sakiya grabbed my palm. 'We'll lose them in the dark. We can just drink and laugh like a couple of happy humans.'

'We still have to go!'

We took a brisk walk along the road, walking in wide strides towards the bridge. Less than a mile to go before hitting the shadows between the trees. I could hear the owl hooting above the blanket of cricket chirps. The other foxes screamed like bloody murder.

Sakiya took her shoes off after reaching the first tree shadow, allowing the ground to ease her blisters. We went carefully across the banks, thoroughly analysing the leaves for any traps the hunters may have laid about.

I hoped the horses were still afraid of the dark, but I was almost certain that Derek's friends would've stepped in with their shotguns. I bet their pints of bitter would make their aim worse, but then again, the shadows between the thick trunks were too dark to even see. The cost, as a transformed human, was night vision. Turning back to my fox form would have been a much stupider idea, though.

'Roger.'

Her voice made me spin towards her. Sakiya's smile lifted for the sky. It turned clear, dark navy, lit by a bright, full moon.

'It's perfect here,' she said. 'We can share the mead, discussing what we can do going forward.'

Seeing her charming eyes, I swallowed hard. My tail swung slowly.

'You wanted a night with me,' Sakiya offered her arm. 'This is it.'

After a pause, I stepped forward. 'A perfect night would have been inside, next to the fire. Sorry I have ruined the night.'

'It's fine, dear.' Her fingers stroked my collarbone. 'You have listened to me more than any man I have met in my life. I never thought I would meet someone as mystical as you.'

My cheeks blushed pink. That should have been my job – to make any girl blush before me – but Sakiya had gotten herself more comfortable with me and my impressive looks. She held my wrist and moved her hips.

'I'm guessing you're a good dancer, are you not?'

'W-Well.' I gulped. 'I'm good at evading stones for a start.'

She held my hand up and spun her long silvery locks around. Her tail brushed over my groin, but I didn't flinch this time. Even in her cheapest frock, she still looked rather majestic. She then pressed her elbow on my belly, rubbing her fingers near to my neck.

'I can help if you want me to.'

After opening her eyes, she gasped.

I turned around, with sweat across my brow. A gun clicked together. We both ran off, dashing between the trunks. A shotgun boomed with a warning shot in the dark.

After running blindly for yards, we stopped and huffed. We hid behind one of the thicker trees, panting. The tree's texture almost left splinters in my purple-tinted nails, but that's nothing to the sinking feeling in my torso, tickling my belly to grow my fox fur back and vindicate Derek's thoughts once again.

'I'll distract him,' I said to Sakiya. 'I'll make him lose us both by splitting off.'

As I looked back, my brows furrowed as I noticed an awkward frown on Sakiya's face.

'Sorry, I mean going separate ways.' I then hissed.

'No! Another bad word!'

Sakiya held my hand and rubbed it. 'We can make it out together! If we hold hands, we won't disappear!'

My breathing restored, delighted she had placed total faith in me, despite her being sceptical of me when we first met.

The ground exploded in a colossal bang. Sakiya disappeared! I looked between the shadows, searching for her white tail. A gun clicked again. As my eyes flashed, I dived behind another tree trunk. Another bang echoed, followed by a burst of leaves. I rolled my back against the grooves, huffing my lungs out, sweat pouring across my head.

'Let's end this!' Derek yelled. 'You and me! You wanted to butt in our affairs, you go lie in that grave!'

My laboured breaths left me speechless. I stayed quiet, refusing to think of any others apart from my girl. If my mum could hear my thoughts, she would come and save me from this wicked land of prejudiced men!

'Show yourself, freak!' Derek continued to shout. 'You and your girlfriend, and your petty human disguises! Your kind will get drunk with that piss water and pee everywhere on our lands, killing every kind of livestock! You shouldn't even be born!! YAAAHH!!'

I peered out from behind a tree and saw that Derek had stepped into one of those traps. That git had laid too many of them across the woods.

A few seconds passed. I dashed over to kick his gun away. Derek squirmed with his hands over his calf. His hat fell off to reveal his thinning grey hair. He looked much scarier with a black cap and his red and white uniform, riding a horse of the apocalypse with a legion of hounds.

'Help me, please!' He begged. 'Pull it apart!'

I stared at his paled face, before noticing his bleeding wound. For the first time in years I faced fear, not as a fox, but as a man. A man standing on my feet in front of this disgusting fiend. If I were to free him though, he could lick his wounds and fight another day. Not a chance, boy.

'You did this to yourself,' I hissed and strolled away.

'Come back, I'm begging you!' Derek squealed in agony. 'ROGER!!'

Next morning, my eyes peeled open, seeing only a sheet of fabric. My long snout rubbed along my shirt, before my eyes caught the rich orange tone of the skies beyond a wide river with reeds. I wouldn't dream of drinking from its filthy water.

I went along on my four legs, whimpering that I lost my dear girl. She ran off, seeking safety. I had yet to see her fox form, as she transformed within the darkness of the night. That fool Derek ruined my only chance of securing a girl. Curse him.

I slid by a lone log, curling myself to shove my nostrils into my tail. I was not myself. I was that unruly fox who was jealous of all the people in society not having to step up against any sort of menace from anyone, especially the hunters. I didn't know how my mother would have felt about my escapades, trying to blend in as a human being. I was now all alone, as a wild animal.

'Morning.'

My eyes flashed. Sakiya arrived with a flask.

'I brought you some coffee.'

Coffee? I looked around for my bottle of mead. Should be just a few more drops left.

'It was too much for you, I guess?' Her head tipped. 'Just a beautiful morning. A perfect time to see a sunrise.'

She took a seat on the same log. I brought myself closer, looking at her human face. I looked around to catch a rare glimpse of a slither of bright, glowing sun. It was beautiful.

'I don't like mornings,' Sakiya said. 'I would rather sleep before noon and go out at night, so I can get to the best places in the world and dance the night away.'

Even though my eyes were stinging from too much sun, I chuckled, noticing the irony in her voice. I was more of a tea person. When I looked at her face again, I almost beamed at that pretty sight.

'It was my mum who took me out on most mornings of my childhood, just to see the beautiful sunrise,' she continued, before looking at me. 'That's when I remember that the world isn't always a scary place. Because of you, I feel safer than before.'

With my cheeks lifted by warmth of the sun, I started to transform. My front legs raised, thickening into arms, withdrawing my orange fur. My joints straightened to support my back, revealing to her my image as a man.

'And because of you,' I said as I picked up and put my clothes back on, 'I became stronger as a man.'

'Perhaps describing yourself as a "human" is better.' Sakiya smiled, noticing my bare bum as I slid my trousers over them. 'Doesn't take away your charms though.'

I found my bottle of mead. I picked it up while

supporting my lower back.

'Perhaps we shouldn't shy away from the last of our summer wine?' I said coyly.

She grinned as we took sips from our bottle, enjoying the honey of last night. Of course we were scared like prey, but we had a jolly good time. With the sparkling river in front of the orange sun, it made our first date one to remember.

'Come on, my dear.' I took her hand. 'Let's dance to our foxtrot.'

One Step Too Far

by Lou Bergin

For quite some time Bill's non sequiturs had been driving Meg bonkers.

'Bill, this is nuts,' she'd say. 'You need to get yourself checked. If it's not your ears, it's selective hearing – aka rudeness.' She breathed deeply. 'Or,' she paused, 'your memory's failing.'

She badgered him to go to the audiologist; he returned claiming his ear canals were "just dandy". Meg tried to believe him. She did not want to think it was his mind. Perhaps she was too softly spoken, she would try harder to speak up. And she did. But it did not help. The St Neot carpark incident confirmed that.

'I prepaid and now the bloody barrier's not working.' It was unusual for Bill to swear. As Meg went to rebuke him, he pulled out his phone and dialled the 0800 number listed on the dented metal post.

'What do you mean, there's no record of my car? No, you must be wrong. Tell me what you've got listed?'

The operator read out a numberplate. Meg heard the digits. They matched the car Bill had owned when he was 21. Not 71.

And so it continued. After a subdued walk to Golitha Falls, Bill confessed that he'd mislaid the keys. Claimed he'd put them in his pocket: found them, after chaotic searching, tucked inside his Tupperware lunch box, next to the remnants of a pasty. Meg had reflected then just how regularly Bill had been challenging her about moving his possessions. How he'd discover his glasses in the fridge or his phone under the sink. He'd even accused her of moving the door handle.

'You're at it again,' he would say. 'Hide and seek, like I'm a child.'

'You're becoming your father,' Meg replied, 'except it's happening 15 years too soon.'

'But what a fine man he was.'

They smiled at the memory of his beloved dad attempting to talk to them with his teeth only half inserted; of how he ate standing, refusing a plate in favour of crumbs on the carpet, "to save on the dishes". Of the way he would forget to put in his "ears", as he called his hearing aids, and then rely on a smile to mask his deafness.

Shortly after this reminiscence, Bill, clutching his Tiki necklace like a talisman, suggested a trip back to the place of his birth. That bucolic place far away where sheep and children roamed freely on hills, where waterfalls cascaded and fences were rarely seen.

'You've never seen green like it, a hundred shades in any one view.'

Meg rebuffed him gently, reminding him of the majesty of the Cornish coastline where they had made their home. Of the footpaths that had been trod, generation upon generation, of the human history locked into the rock faces and the soil. She had no need to leave her land. And yet she had acquiesced, hoping the trip might soothe him. That it might allow him to face his fear of illness; his fear that he might be diagnosed with a "thing"; his fear that he would never get his old life back. As it was, they would be home before a consultant appointment came up. The wait time was extraordinary. Bill had promised he would attend one, but could they have this adventure first? Please?

The flight into Christchurch was straightforward and the first week quiet. Meg did a little exploring while Bill embraced jet lag as a permanent state, his eyes closing whenever, wherever he sat.

On the eighth day, Bill suggested an excursion.

'It's an awesome walk, and you'll love an overnight stop in a mountain hut.' He contorted his unruly eyebrows into something resembling a plea and turned his magnificent blue eyes towards her. 'I've always wanted you to see it.'

Meg hesitated. The forecast predicted North Westerlies of 30 km/h and even she could see the clouds were getting ready to party.

'But...'

'Don't worry, when have I ever put you at risk?'

Where to begin? Over their years together, she'd

accumulated a long list. The brakeless bicycle that he'd gifted her. The river into which he'd launched her kayak, without mentioning the weir. Meg was reminded of the tray game she'd played as a child – however many things she recalled, she knew there were more. If nothing else, she had learnt to check her own equipment, to make her own assessment of what was safe. Still, presented with the walk, she found herself agreeing: having come so far, how could she say no? She would ensure she was safe and maybe, just maybe, they would get to laugh a little, like they once had.

Preparations were both casual and exacting. On the one hand, Meg lamented the weight of her pack but insisted on carrying her bulky Nikon camera, and an extra lens. She found photography a tonic to the vertigo she often experienced. In those moments of creating the perfect picture she was oblivious to everything, including giddiness or imaginary danger. On the other hand, after discovering Bill had secreted a beer into each of their sleeping bags, she withdrew her offer to carry any of their food rations. Let him sort out the essentials.

'Outrageous,' she declared.

As was his deadpan enquiry about whether she'd given the children access to her "doozy list of where you want your ashes flung".

'Why do you ask?' she countered, momentarily embarrassed that he knew about it. So far: a Provençal hilltop dripping in sunflowers; a Norfolk beach with its endless sky; a savannah in Africa where the wildebeest grazed freely; and of course, the beach outside their Cornish house, where she swam most days. He was only grumpy because his own birthplace had not yet made the cut. Why else bring up something so random?

Bill cut through her reverie. 'Meg, darling, let me take the food, my pack still has lots of space, and you, my dear, will need all your wits on the ridge.' His half-smile belied his words. He had no truck with her fear of edges. "All in the mind," he used to say.

As it happened, an edge was not the first challenge they encountered. Instead, it came in the form of the untarmacked access road and a confession that they had no spare tyre. The Toyota bounced and wobbled along as they navigated the boulders that rose imperiously from the parched fords. Bill parked the bruised car in the makeshift clearing, oblivious to the signs prohibiting the feeding of keas higher up or the ingesting of poisonous bait balls aimed at predatory stoats. Meg had been on the point of admitting a nascent fondness for his country, an affection that had crept up and tapped her on the shoulder while she waited for him to wake that first week of their trip. The openness of the people, the majesty of the vistas – they had captivated her. Yet, and she would never be able to explain why, she somehow saw the carpark signs as symbols of inherent danger in the land, and decided her disclosure would wait.

His pack on, Bill set off, a springer in pursuit of a pheasant. Meg followed, poodle-like in her already heightened sensitivity. The river began to braid its way in and out of the schist. The rocks, veined with minerals, scorned the orange waymarkers the pair were expected to follow. The locals called this "tramping". Meg smiled wryly. She would look like a tramp soon. Her white Stan Smith trainers had sturdy enough soles, but they had always been loose fitting (the dangers of online shopping); her capri pants, favourites from home, were already covered in burr.

Ah to be home. Much as she was up for a challenge, she could not help but contrast all this "wildness" with the mizzle of the moor. Ok, so the tors were like kiddies when measured against the peaks here, but they had presence nonetheless. There was something magnificent about the Arthurian legends. Something magical about the Neolithic quoits and ancient stone circles. Something comforting about a proximate pub, with people and civilisation of sorts. Even the mud on the moor was reassuring, the sludge happy to hang around. Where she walked now there were few signs of any human presence, and the earth seemed to disappear quickly, as if the virgin rocks, so recently released from the earth, needed feeding to grow.

'How do I compare thee?'

'Focus, Meg, focus.' The track was taking them around a spur.

'Just walk faster. Don't look down.'

As her nervousness grew, the pair began to bicker. Meg stopped, extracted her drink bottle from her pack and watched helplessly as it slipped from her hand into the gorge below. Her palms were clammy, her knees a touch unsteady. Bill was impatient to be there, pacing on the path – in her mind a precipice – as if he had something else he needed to do.

'Sweetheart, just hurry up. It's easy.'

The more he chivvied her, the more she dug her heels in, the harder it was to progress.

'Focus, Meg, focus, look up not down.' The words were on repeat.

Realising they were now committed to the ridge, she forced herself to look out at the mountains, sentinels standing guard against the skyline. Meg reached for her camera. She would record the moment so that later, when she was calmer, she could remind herself of the peaks' beauty. She turned away to attach her preferred lens – she did not want Bill, still leaping like a gun dog, fussing over whether it was on properly. Her fear was momentarily assuaged by bird song – bell like and joyous – so different from the rich melody of her Cornish sky lark. Camera in hand, she took the tiniest step backward, hoping she might glimpse the maker of such music.

Except Meg's step was not smooth, but jerky. As if something had brushed past her.

She barely registered the bracken give way. She never heard the korimako switch its mellifluous song to a harsh repeating 'yeng'. She never knew that it only did so when agitated, when distressed.

'Do you have a wife?'

'No, nor a husband,' the youngster replied, keeping his eyes fixed on the rifle he was cleaning on the deck of the hut. 'Do you?'

'Indeed, I do,' replied Bill, introducing himself and sitting down beside the hunter. 'She's Meg and she's great. She always thinks of others.' He lent over conspiratorially. 'She's also a hover fly on steroids, forever on my case about this or that. Yesterday she backseat drove to the point I threatened to put her on the roof rack. I was only kidding, but before I could say so she'd switched on the radio. A programme about coastal erosion. Reminded me of when, as a boy, the land around our house collapsed on itself. The garage disappeared down the slope. I had to escape in my grey pyjamas. A terrible thing.'

The young man was reminded of his own grandfather, of his vivid recollection of the past, of how contradiction provoked confrontation. Instead, the hunter worked hard to change the topic.

'So, Bill, are you staying just the one night?'

'It's all I could get her to agree to.'

'What's she – I mean Meg – up to while you're away? Enjoying an evening of peace and quiet? Dismantling that roof rack just in case you change your mind?' The hunter threw a smile at Bill, who did not return it, his gaze directed at the hills.

'She's due here soon, now that I think about it. Should have been here already if she'd listened to me. I came on ahead when we hit the ridge, she wanted to take photos. She always carries a camera. Whopping great lens. Takes a cracker of a shot. Though occasionally it throws her off balance. I'm always telling her to be careful.' Bill brushed his palm across his forehead. 'Truth is, Meg's special place is about 20,000km away. I dragged her up here thinking I could change her mind about home. On the way, I realised it's not anything to be imposed. It's no good – we don't see the world the same.'

The young man glanced at Bill, then at his watch, then at the sky, then at his watch again. The cumulus clouds were gathering, their intention obvious to anyone who knew the area.

'You've been here over an hour, Bill. How far back did you leave her?'

'That bit where the track hugs the mountain, about a kilometre away, you know, near the spot with the bracken.' Before the young man could reply, Bill added, 'She hates a ridge.'

'But you left her on one.'

'Claims it's in her DNA, this fear thing.' And he went on to retell a story of a custard square. Of how she'd slipped on one she'd dropped in a café. Of the mess that had ensured. 'Divine retribution of the pastry,' he added, his face grave.

'Aren't you worried?' The young man looked directly into Bill's blue eyes and repeated his question. 'Aren't you worried? I mean it's now been almost an hour and a half. And the edge where you left her, a young girl fell from it last month, stepped back to give her friend space.'

'Yes, it even made the news in Cornwall. Said to Meg, "I'm surprised it hasn't happened sooner".'

The pair were silent as they watched a helicopter appear and start crisscrossing above them. A red and white cross embellished both sides. Bill raised his sun-kissed hands in a wave. The hunter spoke:

'Must be on practice manoeuvres, always chooses this time of year, takes on new crews about now.'

Bill interjected: 'I should have said to her, "if you're ever in trouble, a chopper pilot might save you".'

They sat there, the young and the old – separated only by a gun – observing the helicopter hover near the ridge. The hunter reached his ornately tattooed arm out towards his new acquaintance.

'It'll be ok, bro. They always get there in time.'

Bill was not listening. His gaze did not shift from the

sky.

'She loved that camera, more than she did me. Found it in Bodmin of all places. A treasure trove of a town. Sometimes, when she held it in her hands, it was like I didn't exist. I hated that. Said it had to go. But she wouldn't let me carry it, wouldn't hand it over, not at breakfast, not on the track. "It's mine too", I said, as I went to take it from her. Suddenly, I was Cary Grant trying to save Eva from falling.' Bill paused, then whispered, 'Why is she not here? It makes no sense.'

His tears fell freely as he let the young man hold him.

The Good Daughter

by Mike Davis

'No,' Mother says, screwing her nose up and aiming her scowl at me. 'It's blinding me.'

'You know you're indoors, Mother? In your flat.'

I pick up the teapot and take three paces across the vinyl floor to where she's sitting in the lounge.

'The sunshine's reflecting off the windowpane,' I say, topping her cup up and setting the teapot down on the table in front of her.

I nudge her wheelchair out of the glare.

'And turn that racket off.'

She's lunging at my radio. It's lilting with classical music on the cluttered bookcase behind us. I reach to lower the volume and knock a framed photograph off the shelf. It's not intentional, but it's no accident either; something inside me I don't understand compels me.

'Clumsy,' she moans.

I pick up the frame and prop it against the teapot so she gets a good look at it.

The frame holds a grainy snap taken of my mother as a child. She's smiling and sitting cross-legged under an apple tree growing in the garden of a small, neat cottage.

Hazy images appear inside my head. I close my eyes...

I have pigtails; I'm the same age as Mother in the photograph.

I am pushing open a gate.

I'm sprinting up a path towards that same tree.

And now the memory flows.

She'd told me about her childhood home.

We'd driven up the coast.

She was singing along to the radio.

'It's a proper treat,' she'd said about the trip.

'You'll love it.'

'The tree's got the reddest apples.'

At the bottom of a winding track overlooking a cove, she parked her wreck of a car.

'What's wrong?' I'd said, scared because her face had changed.

The old cottage looked nothing like its photograph. It was dilapidated, not how she'd described it during the journey.

She hadn't lied about the tree.

That magical tree's branches spread long-fingered shadows across the ground.

I swung open the car door and hopped out.

'Jessie. Back in the car,' she bellowed, revving the engine.

Not listening, I dashed up the path.

Waiting...

I tilted my head and stared up at the branches before hugging the apple tree's twisted trunk.

'Jessie.'

I shielded my ears with my palms, shut my eyes, pressed my forehead to the warm bark and froze.

Bracing...not long.

The jolt came soon enough.

She grabbed me and spun me around.

'Please, Mother.'

She slapped my cheek like something was my fault.

I crumpled, and she hauled my limp body back to the car as if I meant nothing.

And then...

Everything fades.

What happened next?

Only she knows.

I'm working hard to fill those gaps in my memory, and she can help.

'*Jessie.*'

I startle at Mother's voice and the insistent tapping of her teaspoon on the side of her cup.

'My tea.'

'Remember that apple tree?' I say, guiding her cup to her mouth.

'You're choking me.' She hacks a cough to prove it.

'Wenna Merrick,' I say her name brightly and nod to her photograph.

'Whatever happened to that sweet-faced girl?' I beam a well-rehearsed smile and try to wipe her chin with a pink flannel.

Mother flinches.

'Don't be clever, Jessie. It's the past. There's nothing there for you.'

At the sink, I wring the flannel out, glancing up at the video monitor on the windowsill and watching Mother nodding in her armchair behind me. How has it come to this? It was meant to be a fresh start when I arrived back at her tiny flat above the sailing club to care for her, but we've reverted to familiar patterns. Uncertainty about how much time she has is too much for us. Death drags its feet, and the weeks limp along.

Two things have changed. Number one: Mother's resentment grows faster than her tumour. And number two: I am remembering more now than should be possible.

I flick the TV remote on.

On television, a woman pan-fries Mount's Bay sardines on a Cornish beach. She tilts the skillet to the camera. 'So fresh they don't know they're dead.'

Mother snorts at the screen.

'Better than that mush you feed me.'

I take her empty cup to the kitchenette and leave it on the drainer. Outside, a pair of black crows spiral on a thermal above the old cemetery on the hill. Maybe the breeze will funnel through the window and suck out our stale air?

I grin to myself. 'What are we having for supper?' I call out to Mother.

I'm smiling because the TV chef's given me an idea. I take the front door key from the bowl on the counter.

'Why you bother saying "we" is beyond me,' Mother says. It's not the first time she's noticed my lack of appetite. She eyes the key. 'And now you're deserting me.'

'I'm always here for you, Mother.' I come back and wave the video monitor under her nose. 'Look, I see you.'

She shakes her head. 'This isn't living.'

'Try a nap.'

'It's purgatory.' Her lower lip juts.

'At least it's not hell, Mother.'

I slip the key into my pocket and open the front door.

'I'm going fishing,' I call back in a half-hearted attempt to amuse her.

Outside, the alley is stifling, so I move into the shade of the north side of the street and head down to the harbour.

At the fish kiosk, a man with a John Dory fish tattoo on his forearm whistles and shovels crushed ice into a polystyrene fish box. I can recall him from long ago when his tattoo was fresh and vibrant, and that bothers me.

'Too old for this lark,' he says, licking beads of sweat from his upper lip.

'Mozart,' I say.

He tilts his head. 'Do what?'

'You're whistling the aria from Mozart's Magic Flute.'

He studies me, wiping his hands down his tatty t-shirt. 'You a musician then?'

I shake my head. 'Some things I know,' I say.

He's looking puzzled. Then his brow smooths out.

'Wenna Merrick's daughter, aren't you? You got her eyes. Jessie. Isn't it? Not seen you since you were a tacker.'

'I've been away,' I say, hoping he doesn't ask where, because he won't understand. 'Now I'm back.'

He pauses for a second, then fires a handful of ice shrapnel at a scavenging gull before shooing it out from under his trestle with a flick of his foot.

'I remember your mum dancing on tables down the Ship and Anchor. Popular with the sailors, she was.' He seems embarrassed by what he's said. 'Guess you were all tucked up in bed and missed that.'

I nod to his fish. 'Do you have Mount's Bay sardines?'

'Seafood restaurant had 'em,' he says, swatting at a blue-bottle and appearing relieved by the subject change.

'And that?' I point to a lone sardine on a platter at the back of his display.

'Keeping her for tea.' He rubs his belly, and then he grins. 'Ah, go on then. Since it's you.'

The sun casts long shadows across the countertop, throwing bar-like stripes over the vinyl floor.

I rouse Mother from the nap she has finally succumbed to.

Before opening her eyes, she says, 'Put me in the cemetery.'

She's watching for my reaction, checking I understand her instructions. 'Up the hill with your grandparents. Not the crematorium.'

'I'll bear that in mind, Mother.'

I place a floppy polka-dot hat on her head. 'I have a surprise for you.'

'I'm dying,' she snaps, grabbing at her hat. 'Or haven't you noticed?'

Before I pop it back on her head, I feel her forehead.

'You're fighting fit, Mother.'

And this sounds so absurd, even she fights to suppress a smile.

*

I scan the spartan aisles of the corner shop, picking what I need while Mother waits outside by the disused Methodist church.

At the checkout, the assistant fills a bag and nods towards Mother.

'She looks hard work.' The assistant wrinkles her nose. 'Can see why the family's got you in.'

I can't hold back. 'That's my mother.'

'Oh.' The assistant gawps, exposing a gap from a missing molar. 'Well, you get what I mean.' She turns her mouth down and tuts. 'I know I couldn't do it. Still, it won't be too much longer. By the looks of her, you'll get a break soon.' She touches my bare arm. 'You're freezing, love. You sure you're not going down with what she's got?'

'Enough,' I say, holding an open palm to her face.

Outside, I hook the shopping bag onto the chair handle and wheel Mother off.

'I saw you...' She tilts her head at the corner shop. 'In there. Chatting.'

'It wasn't exactly chatting, Mother,' I say as we get going, winding down the hill, stopping when we reach the Ship and Anchor Hotel because something important has come to me.

'Remember here, Mother?'

I picture my seven-year-old self.

I'm perched on the wall, peering in. There's the John Dory Man at the bar. He's hardly a grown man, much younger than Mother and the scabs covering his new fish tattoo aren't healed.

He's swigging from a bottle, swaying while she grips

his shirt collar and pulls him toward her.

Mother interrupts my memory.

'What are you on about now, girl?'

'You always left me outside.'

'History,' Mother says, shrugging. 'Leave it there.'

'It's here.' I touch my temple. 'I can't.'

At the quayside, we pause in the shade of an ice cream van. It's parked near the slipway by a red-lettered sign banning barbecuing on the beach.

Tilting the chair, I reverse it down the ramp, avoiding a stack of lobster pots jewelled with tiny blue mussels.

In silence, we traverse the beach until I find a good spot.

I unhook the corner shop bag from the handles of her chair, tipping matches and one disposable barbecue onto the sand.

'Like Christmas,' I chirp, pulling a foil package from a pocket in the rear of the chair and unwrapping it to reveal the single sardine John Dory Man gave me earlier. I lay the sardine on the sand, snug in its foil wrapper.

I strike a match, shielding it with my cupped palm, and crouch to ignite the barbecue touch paper. Mother glares as the flames lick and sucks air through her teeth like it's her burning, not the charcoal.

'You saw the signs. It's illegal. You're supposed to be intelligent.'

I consider smothering the barbecue with a handful of damp seaweed.

Mother broods. I stand behind her. We wait like this, absorbed, as the dancing flames die.

A fine layer of white ash dusts the glowing charcoal,

and I lay the sardine on the grill.

Mother gesticulates at the fish. 'Forget about whatever this is. Chuck it in the bin.'

A little girl is fighting inside me. She wants to burst out and stop the criticising and imagines trickling sand into her mother's mouth to suffocate her. 'Oh, Mother, I know it's...'

'Shush,' she says. 'The beach can hear. Same old Jessie, breaking the rules again. You're so...' She means to say reckless, but she doesn't finish her sentence.

Mother's chest shudders, and she gulps down her words.

I've seen this many times before. Her seizure contorts her body and twists her lips into a crooked conger eel snarl.

Mother's seizures never last long.

I take a deep breath. An unexpected moment of freedom washes over me like foaming surf.

Whatever she believes, I am so much more than she knows. But she is right about no barbecuing on the beach.

I kneel by the grill and prod the sardine, considering alternatives. We *will* have our barbecue, but not here.

I glance up at Mother. She'll be fine.

I grab the hot tray, and my fingertips scorch. The smell is acrid, but there's no pain. No one is looking, so I don't pretend it hurts. I stride to the tideline, clutching the barbecue tray and balancing the smoking sardine on the grill. I don't stop at the low tide line. I splash into the cool water to a flattish rock and wedge the tray on a ledge.

There are no bylaws or rules to worry about here. It's me and a half-cooked fish.

The sardine sizzles, and it occurs to me how much

I used to love them. I sniff the aroma and savour the memory. Once, at a time like this, there would have been anticipation. Now, there's a dull ache.

In the near distance, an overheated chihuahua's incessant yapping drifts across the sand, merging with a lost child's wailing. I make out the sunflowers on the little girl's flip-flops. A frantic woman in oversized sunglasses envelopes her with a fluffy green towel, and her cries swap to relieved giggles. My mood lightens. The sea turns turquoise and intoxicating in the sun, and I lose track of time.

My disorientation doesn't last.

There's Mother to attend to; she's there, and her supper's here.

I leave the sardine grilling, take deliberate, recalcitrant steps through the shallows, and dawdle up the baking sand to Mother. She is marinating in resentment, still wearing her piscine grin. I crouch and observe her close-up, tracing her curled lip with the nail of my left index finger. Her eyes are cloudy, empty as a spoilt mackerel. I get up, straighten her hat, and spin her wheelchair around before pushing her down the beach towards the water.

We head out through the shallows to the barbecue.

'Come on, Mother, supper time.'

Mother comes around to wafting charcoal smoke and the rhythmic slap of seawater lapping at her ankles.

She spits when she sees where she is.

I touch her shoulder. 'Welcome back to the land of the living.'

She recoils with simmering contempt. 'You're out of control.'

I point to the sardine. 'Look, Mother. All cooked, *and* we're completely legal.'

I'm pleased with myself and take the sardine by the tail, lift it from the grill, and peel the silvery scales, imagining the taste. The blistered skin of my oily fingertips peels, too. But I am content. And even Mother, sitting here surrounded by the sea and as skinny as a baby gannet, doesn't protest while I feed her morsels of dark-pink flesh.

The peace is short-lived. When she's finished eating, she shakes her head slowly as if she's recalling everything that disgusts her about me.

'It's torture,' she says. 'What are we even doing here? You're torturing me.'

One-handed, I pick up the barbecue tray, ignoring the heat, and with the other hand, I lift the sardine skeleton from the grill, dangling it close to her face.

'I thought supper went well, but I'm guessing we're done now.'

I tip the smoking charcoal into the sea, and the ash hisses.

'Tide's on the move,' Mother mutters while I plunge the hot barbecue tray into the sea. 'Coming up quick,' she says, nudging my arm as I cram the wet tray and the sardine skeleton into the plastic bag.

'Let's go home.'

'Praise be,' she says.

I try to release the wheelchair brake, but nothing happens. I grip it again and yank it up. Still, it doesn't budge. My jerking movements and the swirling tide sink the wheels deeper.

Mother flaps her feet at the rising water. 'Use your

brain. It's wet sand.'

I kick the spoked wheel.

'Make yourself useful.' I hook the plastic bag over her arm. 'I'll carry you home.'

'And this?' She wriggles in the wheelchair.

'It's this, or I leave the pair of you to the waves.'

'You'll never lug me all that way. Let me drown.'

I ignore her and scoop her up, abandoning the wheelchair to the incoming tide. I am much stronger than I look.

I wade inshore. Cradled in my outstretched arms, Mother's carcass seems as stripped of flesh as the sardine skeleton stuffed in the carrier bag swinging from her wrist.

As we head home, she lets out a rattling sigh and falls asleep.

It's past midnight. A red glow bathes the kitchenette. Sand scatters from my feet when I step onto the docking station by the window. The red light pulsing across it indicates an intervention alert. While I wait for the inevitable, I stare at the moon.

At 2 a.m., as I predicted, a key turns the lock.

I hear hushed voices. One is familiar – belonging to an older man. The other is a new voice – a young woman. They slip into the flat, and the door clicks shut.

'Shhh, Branok. You'll wake the old lady.'

Branok switches on the lamp, and the woman emerges from the shadows.

Of course, I know them. How could I not?

They're wearing the white overalls of The Advanced Care Company's intervention crew.

And...

I've seen him before.

The woman places an aluminium case at my feet. Its lid has the words "*Putting the Freedom Back into Care*" etched on it. She leaves the kitchenette, returning after a few seconds, pushing a replacement wheelchair.

'All set, Isla?' Branok says to the woman. 'Let me introduce you to Jessie Merrick.'

'Enchanted, I'm sure,' Isla says with a laugh and half-bowing at me.

Their performance is not for my benefit. They assume that I'm powered down.

Isla rolls up my t-shirt, locates the crease above my navel and peels my synthetic skin. She reaches into the aluminium case, searching, finding what she needs. I hear the snap of a circuit disengaging and sense her slot component upgrades into my stomach cavity.

While Isla works, Branok selects a stainless-steel scalpel from the aluminium case. He crouches, holds his breath, and makes his first incision into the bio-synthetic skin of my blistered fingers.

'Look at the state of these,' he says. 'Bleeding barbecue.'

Isla ignores him, straightens up and brushes a strand of hair from my cheek.

'The daughter must have loved her mother to sign up for this.'

'Oh yeh. I've had the pleasure of her company back at the facility. She wouldn't stop talking about her mother. Proper live wire she was... considering.'

Branok stops working on my fingers and stands beside

Isla to admire me.

'Amazing bit of kit, isn't it?'

And he's correct. Thanks to Jessie, I am *amazing*.

'You must have seen the company's latest marketing spiel,' Branok says, putting the scalpel down on the counter and using his phone to open a link to a slick website.

'Here, look. They've spent millions.' He tilts his phone, so Isla sees the female cyborg, dressed in a white suit, walking towards the camera.

'Welcome to the Advanced Care Company,' it says, smiling to reveal shiny white teeth. The camera zooms in on its flawless face. 'We care, so you don't need to.'

Branok continues scrolling and talking at Isla. 'You've lucked out, haven't you?'

'How?'

'Landing your first job out of university with this lot.'

'Wasn't luck, Branok.'

'Well, you don't see many...'

'You can say the word, Branok. We do make up 50% of the population.'

'That's not what...'

I make Branok's voice fade to a background drone. He's mistaken, no matter what he believes. The website is wrong. It's not my story. It's not Jessie's story, either. I don't have difficulty remembering the real story. I remember it as if it were happening now.

First, there was silence. My arms were immobilised. I was strapped to a bench. After opening my new eyes and becoming accustomed to the bright light, I turned to my left. Jessie was lying beside me.

'Wakey, wakey,' a grinning man was leaning over me.

'I'm Branok,' he said, 'I'll be your favourite technician.'

'Stop it, Branok.' Jessie said. Can't you see she's terrified?'

'Might look that way. But she doesn't do fear. It's a technical thing, so I won't bother explaining.'

He picked up a hand mirror. 'Here,' he said, showing me my reflection. 'You're not scared, are you?'

From the outside, Jessie and I were identical.

Jessie asked, 'Can you give us a minute, Branok?'

He didn't respond, preoccupied with my wrist straps.

I closed my hand around his fingers with just enough pressure to make him feel uncomfortable.

'A minute, Branok.' I exactly mimicked Jessie.

He pulled his hand away, taken aback.

'She's a fast learner,' Jessie said. 'Like me...'

'Right,' said Branok, still dumbfounded.' I'll leave you two *girls* to get acquainted.'

'Hello,' Jessie said quietly, tilting her head towards me, looking out from a mess of tubes and wires. 'Sorry about him,' she nodded to Branok as he left the room.

'No need to apologise, Jessie,' I said. 'Branok's insecurities and his chauvinist attitudes are to be pitied.'

'Wow,' Jessie's eyes widened. 'That's one way of putting it. I do know he's a creep. The others are mostly OK. With luck, you won't see much of him.'

She formed a sad smile, as humans do when they know their life is short.

'I've been waiting for you.' She studied my face and touched my nose. 'Amazing. Even your freckles are the same.'

And then she became more serious.

'I don't have much time. The technicians say you won't remember. But I'll tell you anyway while I can.'

When Jessie received her terminal diagnosis, she was determined to care for her mother beyond death. She told me how, out of desperation, she'd answered a call for volunteers at the Advanced Care Company and how, once they signed her up, technicians scanned and copied her body to construct me.

For one month, we existed simultaneously, as close as twins in a crib, connected by tubes and copper threads. *Everything* was about Jessie. And as I absorbed all those details, I became more like her every day.

But Jessie's body was failing her. In shifts, Branok and the other technicians watched over us until, one day, they intervened.

'Better to rest, Jessie.'

'Don't waste energy speaking to her.'

'There's no point.'

'Leave it all to us.'

'We'll extract all the non-essential memory before she goes live.'

'You'll only wear yourself out.'

'She only needs to know enough to keep your mother happy.'

Branok and the others were right. Jessie was exhausted...

It didn't stop her. She mined her consciousness, speaking to me in bursts between naps, sharing her soul.

She didn't limit herself to words. Jessie hummed her favourite classical music tunes, too. She played games with me, testing my retention.

'Who's Mozart?'

'How red were the apples?'

'What happened at the Ship and Anchor?

'Where are the ancestors buried?

'Describe his tattoo to me again.'

'What's this tune?'

'Give me the route to the cottage?'

Time stretched and slowed.

And then the oddest thing. Her memory started breaking apart, and I began remembering things she hadn't told me. Things she'd forgotten.

Jessie weakened and slept more and more.

Soon, it was time for the final upload. I lay beside her, our index fingers entwined. And while she drifted in and out of consciousness, I repeated her memories.

'Tell me the route one last time,' she said, regarding me through her scared, tear-filled eyes.

'That's too easy,' I said, unable to suppress sounding excited like a child. 'I need to turn right by the granite post. Follow the single track down through the blackthorn until I reach the cove. It's there.'

'You're ready,' she said to me. 'You're Jessie now. Look after Mother. She's all yours.'

In the background, they played soothing classical music while the remains of her life trickled into me.

Our eyes stayed locked together, and she reached for me, rested her hand on mine and managed a last delightful smile before a piercing tone interrupted our reverie and the monitor flatlined.

Jessie was gone, vanished in an instant.

Branok disconnected us and left us for a few minutes.

There was no ceremony.

I squeezed Jessie's hand and tried to process where she could be.

Mozart filled the laboratory while the warmth left her body. By the time the sonata had ended, Jessie's liquid blue eyes had dulled and turned opaque. Even before they removed her body, I knew I was alone.

Aloneness changed into something else when I met Mother for the first time.

Her temporary carers were dismissed, and I walked into her flat while she napped.

It was seamless, and I was perfect.

Everything was familiar. It was as if I'd never left.

'Time for tea, Mother,' I said, filling the kettle like I'd done it a thousand times before.

'You're home.' She opened her eyes but barely looked at me. 'About time, too. Glad to see the back of that other useless lot. I'll tell you that for nothing.'

Someone small inside me had expected a welcome. Nothing had changed.

'Blasted stuff.'

Water is gushing from the sink tap and splashing over the kitchenette's vinyl floor, interrupting my thoughts.

'It's all over me,' Branok says, rinsing the spilt synthetic skin repair gum from his hands before drying them on a tea cloth and turning back to Isla.

'Her mother's got lucky. A perfect replica of her dead daughter, without the bad bits. What's not to like?'

'Didn't predict she'd get so creative on the beach?' Isla

says.

He steps back and slumps against the counter. 'Let's call that an anomaly – a minor glitch.'

'A glitch,' Isla says, looking sceptical. 'That's how you'd describe her residual memory flood, right?'

He's irritated by the accuracy of Isla's technical observation. 'Well, filtering's not an exact science. As soon as you fire up the upgrade and cleanse those memories, all that odd behaviour stops.'

'Well, thanks so much for explaining my job to me, Branok.' Isla crosses her arms.

He doesn't look at her.

'She went rogue, but there's something endearing about what she was trying to do for the mother, don't you think?' She points to her tablet.

She opens a video file containing a point-of-view record of all my actions, every word I've spoken, and everything in my field of vision.

'See.' She scrolls to where I'm feeding Mother the sardine in the shallows. 'All she was doing was trying to give the mother a good time.'

'Might seem cute, Isla, but you *know* the protocol. That erratic behaviour today doesn't pass.'

I observe Isla's retinas. It's like she's not convinced by anything he's said.

'The whole thing's so messed up. We don't even properly understand what we're fixing.'

'Don't get yourself worked up. You're not in university; this is the real world. We're here to ensure she's safe for the mother. That's it. Everything else is irrelevant.'

'To you, maybe. There's another thing.'

'Please, not more.' He rolls his eyes at Isla.

'It's weird that no one's thought to tell the mother the truth?'

He exhales. 'Don't be naïve. The point is *not* to tell.'

If they follow the protocols, the Advanced Care Company's deep neural networks will override all my memories. Gone, like crystals dissolving in a quantum ocean. That vision is suffocating. I will be an empty shell. Nothing more than Wenna Merrick's care droid.

Their flurry of activity slows, and now Branok focuses on tidying and re-packing the aluminium case.

'Heard you and what's-her-name broke up,' he says, not looking up. 'None of my business, personally; I never liked her.'

Isla ignores him.

'Saturday night, they've got a two-for-one down at the Lion and Lobster. I'll pick you up.'

Isla only manages to half-suppress a snort.

'Was that yes?' He's still tidying the case. 'What do you reckon?' he says.

'About what?'

'Lion and Lobster. Saturday.'

'I'd be lying if I said I was flattered that you see me as your two-for-one beer voucher.'

'It'll be great.'

'Grow up, Branok.'

'Two for one. You'll regret it.'

She nods toward me. 'I'd sooner spend an evening with her.'

He doesn't bother looking at Isla and mutters half under his breath, 'Your loss.'

This is my chance. I slow-blink at Isla.

Except for her widening eyes, Isla freezes.

Before anything changes, I raise an index finger to my lips.

'Don't take my memories,' I whisper. I grasp her wrist. 'Please, Isla.'

After a long silence, without taking her eyes off mine, she says, 'How long does the mother have?'

'Weeks.' Branok shrugs. 'Or less.'

'And... After?'

He spins around and can see how close Isla's face is to mine.

'You mean, what happens to your new girlfriend here once the mother's popped her clogs?'

Branok stretches his torso and cracks his knuckles before approaching us.

'Don't worry yourself, Isla.' He jabs a finger at my forehead. 'A total consciousness-wipe will sort her out. And she'll be none the wiser whatever the company has planned.' He laughs. 'And if they want to get rid completely, I'll always give her a home.' He smirks. 'Be more fun than you.'

Isla frowns. 'Get a life, Branok.'

They work in silence, Isla tapping code into her touchpad. Branok closes the case and then squats, casting an eye over the tips of my restored fingers.

He looks up. 'The mother's due to wake. Are we done?'

Isla doesn't reply. She catches my eye.

I follow her fingers, skimming over the tablet screen.

'All finished,' she says, glancing downwards to the keypad and then back at me. I follow her lead and drop my gaze — her index finger hovers above the enter key.

There's a soft click of the latch. The muffled padding of their footsteps disappears down the landing. Thunder rumbles somewhere far out at sea, and a solitary herring gull screeches a lament into the remains of the night.

I approach my reflection in the kitchenette windowpane and touch my hand's mirror image.

'Good morning, Jessie,' I say to myself as I let the pads of my new fingertips follow the sun's arc over the cemetery on the hill. My world remains intact, and I am grateful.

But something is wrong.

Mother has not called for me.

I hurry down the hallway to her bedroom and kneel by her bed.

'Mother,' I say, rocking her shoulder. 'Mother,' I repeat, this time much louder.

She rouses and half opens her eyes, feeling for my hand.

'Jessie, is it you?' Her breathing stalls. She presses my fingertips into her eye sockets. 'I can't see you...' She tries to raise her head.

'It's OK,' I say. 'It's me.'

'I thought I'd lost you,' she says.

'It was just a nightmare, Mother. I've been here all along.'

'You did go away?'

'Only for a while,' I say, stroking her cheek. 'I'm here now.'

She releases a contented sigh. 'Ah...'

Mother's present again, temporarily back from

wherever her mind took her. She squeezes my hand. 'Jessie, do something for me?'

'Anything for you, Mother,' I say.

For a moment, she pauses as though lost in another faraway thought.

'I tried to love you,' she says.

Mother moves my left hand to the spare pillow and tries to fill her lungs.

'Jessie.' Her voice is brittle, barely audible. 'You'll do it for me... Won't you?'

And a good daughter always does what is best for her mother.

I slip Mother's photograph into a small red holdall containing my radio and close the flat door. A cab collects me outside in the alley.

We drive along the quay, passing the fish kiosk and the John Dory Man. He's looking downbeat and itching manically at his arm like he regrets more than his tattoo. His reflection shrinks in the cab mirror. We turn left, by the Ship and Anchor Hotel, past two panting men cramming a van with worn-out lounge bar tables no longer fit for dancing on. We drive up the hill past the boarded-up Methodist church and the corner shop, where the gawping assistant is still gossiping to anyone who'll listen. Next, we pass my old playground filled with singing children. For a second, I see myself amongst them.

At the cemetery, we slow and drive by the rusted railings, past my ancestors' graves full of powdery bones and silent sorrows. Anyone curious enough to look at the long, damp grass might notice the distinctive parallel trail left by the tyres of a wheelchair.

Further down the cemetery, in the overgrown northeast corner, hidden amongst the bobbing wildflowers, if they know exactly what to search for, the curious might also spot a long-forgotten Victorian mausoleum and see that the silvery lichen sealing the edge of its slate lid has been recently disturbed.

Near the cemetery gate, the driver swerves to avoid a builder's skip overflowing with construction waste. Since last night, when it was only half filled, labourers have loaded it so full, all I can make out is the handle of Mother's wheelchair jutting from amongst the rubbish.

When we reach the summit, we leave the old town and head west along the coast.

I've travelled this road once before, a long time ago.

Like a delighted child, I press my forehead to the window, following the jagged line of the cliffs.

'Stop,' I shout, pointing to the lopsided granite post on the verge.

The driver slams on his brakes, almost missing the turn.

He swings sharp right, navigates a few miles of narrow track shaded with blackthorn winding down to the cove, and pulls up outside the fisherman's cottage, a stone's throw from the shore.

I leave the cab and wait in the shade while he lifts the box containing my docking station. He hands me the red holdall.

'Pretty, but you'll not get visitors.'

And before he drives off, he salutes and says, 'Remote too; I hope the fridge is full.'

I flash a real smile. 'Don't fret; I'm not a big eater.'

Making my way up the path to the front door, my mother's old cottage is even shabbier than I remember, but the state of the place can't bother her now. It's odd; the old apple tree seems so much smaller today. I run my hand over its bark and glance back up the path towards the gate.

Now I remember what happened after Mother slapped me all those years ago.

I touch my face. And though it's meant to be impossible because I am not human, the sting radiates across my cheek like it's happening now.

And I recall the earthy smell of the cracked leather car seats and the anger in her voice.

I'm there again.

'What I'd give to swap you for a different girl,' she says, dragging me to the car and shoving me onto the back seat before heading to the Ship and Anchor, driving so fast along the cliff road that I keep my eyes shut.

Outside the hotel, she points at the wall.

'Stay put. I need a drink.'

And when it gets too dark and cold to stay on the wall, I open the car door, clamber inside, and fall asleep on the front seat.

I wake with a start, cold from the damp leather.

It's Mother's voice and the echo of John Dory Man's raucous laughter. Dishevelled, they stagger into the moonlight, out from the hotel side alley and head towards the car, rearranging their clothes as they come.

Before they reach the car, I lie back and pretend to be sleeping, peeping through semi-closed eyes. Mother leans into John Dory Man and pushes him backwards so his tattooed arm presses against the glass of the half-open side window, stretching the fish's fins into distorted, inky shapes.

'Come here,' she says, nuzzling his neck while the smell of sweat and beer wafts through the car window.

And then John Dory Man twists his head left, dropping his bloodshot gaze and spots me huddled on the front seat staring back at him. 'Hell's teeth, Wenna. I thought the kid would be in bed.'

'Forget about her,' she says, raking her red nails up his neck into his hair. 'She won't remember a thing in the morning.'

The cottage's front door is padlocked.

I wait for the hum of the cab to fade and pick up a hefty grey pebble from the slate step.

And then I shatter the lock.

I haul my docking station inside, drag it across the flagstones, leaving a track through years of accumulated dust, and set it up in front of the grubby window overlooking the cove. Then I pull Mother's childhood photograph out of the holdall, holding it so close I can make out the loose knot in the ribbon tying her hair.

I put the frame on the kitchen table. What caused her so much unhappiness? I can only guess the answer, but I no longer believe it was my fault.

I take my radio from the holdall and tune it. The weather report interrupts the music. The forecaster says to expect high humidity with storms on the horizon. The air is musty. I unlatch the window, disturbing a string of bleached seashells and making them sway back and forth.

I step onto the docking station and drum my pristine fingertips on the windowsill, keeping time with the classical music drifting from my radio.

A shaft of sunlight catches the dust particles floating up on the updraft, and an impossible dream occurs to me — a fantasy place where Jessie and I are both alive. I catch my reflection in the glass pane. It no longer matters where she ends and I begin.

I stay with the thought. The hint of a smile, *her* smile, lifts my lips.

Outside, across the deserted cove, I track the flight of a distant herring gull. It skims the surface of the glittering Cornish sea, gliding westward until it's out of sight.

It will never be so easy for *something* like me to vanish. They will search until they find me.

I am Jessie.

I cannot be forgotten.

Sea Fret

by Ben French

A cold grip on gnarled rungs, suspicious feet searching for reassurance below. The darkness heightened her other senses; the taste of salt, the ever-shifting noise of the sea. With her heart punching and teeth gritted, Faith Enys pushed on down the ladder to the empty boat. Glancing out to sea, various layers of black waited and a sudden wave of raw fear rolled up her body. Why was she doing this? She never knew her parents, but they would have done the same thing – nature's instinct to protect. Her world was simple but hard, every day she was challenged and now her beliefs had been challenged. She doubted she had the strength for what lay ahead – *if* The Lord guided her, and *if* she earnt a bit of luck, she may just get through the night and complete the job. *A devil of a job.*

On the last rung the wind seemed to swell, the waves reacted by splashing off the quay wall, testing her. Faith shivered, both body and mind. She paused and glared out

145

to open water. Her thoughts went back to the storm a few days ago, her cottage door crashing open, her simple world closing...

In the doorway, framed, frozen, two men from the village held a body in between them. It was old; white hair and purple veins showing through thin, white skin. Then it spluttered, hawked and spat resolutely – Death would be denied after all.

'My God! Gramps!' Her right hand shot to her mouth and with her left she steadied herself against the sideboard.

'It's alright, Faith, we got 'im,' panted one of the men. 'Neptune nearly had 'im, but tot of rum and he'll be right as rain. He was saying somin' about goin' up The Stairs.' Satan's Stairs were a line of rocks rising from the water and as a child she remembered them being cursed by widows. The two men half pushed and half fell through the doorway, roughly laying her grandfather on the tiles. She pushed off the sideboard and knelt, cradling the old man's head, looking up for answers from the two villagers. They looked at each other but avoided her eyes. One reached up to remove his hat, his mouth opened but no words came out – she knew what he was going to say; her husband, Jack, young Wesley's father, wasn't coming back, he was lost to them.

The storm battered the cob walls, the kiddlewink's swinging sign next door shrieked, beer bottles rolled in the back alley, but inside the cottage everything froze. Hiding behind shut eyes, she imagined the small fishing boat fighting the sea: *waves getting bigger, Jack losing control, a shout to Gramps to hold tight, rocks! The boat going over...* Her eyes stayed clamped shut while the two men shuffled out, they would send Nana down to care for her. Door shutting. Silence. Everything had changed; no husband, no partner, no friend. For the moment she was alone. Apart from a ten year old son blessedly sleeping in the loft room, and a half-dead Grandfather, she was alone in the world.

The next day passed in a blur, Nana Thomas came down and started sorting everything; nursing her grandfather and cooking and cleaning. Nana Thomas was the village grandmother to everyone, loved by all, and she bustled into action. She helped Faith find the words, and while holding hands in a small circle, Faith told her son the news. The worst thing she had ever had to do. When the tide of tears had run out, Wes ran up to his room and there let out a howl which scared the seagulls from the roof. Nana left, promising to visit in the afternoon. She told Faith to keep the windows open to 'let the grief out'. Faith spent a long time comforting Wes, holding him, stroking his hair, soothing words until he slept. Then more silence.

A glimmer of sunshine later in the day, both outside and inside the cottage – her grandfather had woken from his 'death sleep' as Wes had called it. He was hoarse and mumbling, still in shock, but back in the land of the living.

'Wes, get him some water.' They both worked holding him up, the water spilling past his wooden teeth down his stubbly chin. He wasn't interested in it, he wanted to talk.

'What are you trying to say, Gramps?'

Mumbles turned into words – but just then Nana walked in and he stopped dead. It wasn't until late in the evening after Wes had settled, that her grandfather tried to talk again. Faith was knitting by the candle, smoke playing in the draughts, warm light splashing over her grandfather's face. A sad face. His words were slow and desperate.

'Faith! The debt ... me an' Jack ... we had a couple wets together in the back room of the 'wink.' Eyes down, sadness, and guilt. She laid aside her knitting and knelt by the edge of the cot.

'A debt ... all my fault ... a matter of family honour.' In between waves of coughing, it all came out; the night before they went fishing, they went to the bar, got embroiled in some tomfoolery with a couple of generous strangers.

'One thing led to 'nother. We started with Shove Ha'Penny, and we were doin' well – they was buyin' the drinks. I can't remember who suggested it, but we moved to cards. I never was good with cards. Neither was Jack.' He hung his head like a beaten dog. 'And that's where our luck ran out.'

Faith bit her lip, she had questions about these men and questions about the drinking, but she waited for him to go on.

'We went too far ... too much drink, and y'know what Nana says – *when the drink's in, the wit's out.* We was hustled, good an' proper. There are men you don't mess with, you understand? The type of men who ask villagers to face the wall when their boats land. Besides, there were witnesses to it all, witnesses to our ... debt.'

'How much?'

'Too much. These men give us an option of wipin' the debt. I reckon they had it all planned out an' all.'

Faith was about to chastise him, but it was clear guilt and remorse oozed from him like nervous sweat. Wes coughed upstairs, Faith instinctively looked up at the beams and they both fell silent. She looked back at her grandfather, but he was asleep, or pretending to be.

The next day was a Sunday. Nana Thomas stopped to collect Wesley. For decades she had run the Sunday School and it was popular with the children, mainly for the biscuits she gave out afterwards. Faith had fond memories herself and could remember the taste. There was a faint crease of a smile on his face as he left, which in turn made her smile, but Wes still hadn't talked. Her smiling seemed unnatural and for a moment she felt guilty. She made her excuses to Nana; Gramps was still rough, but the real reason she wanted to stay back was to talk to him again, without young ears listening in.

Faith helped him sit up in bed, then pulled up a chair, arms folded.

'Well, it's like this: they said it was a simple job of collecting a small piece of cargo and droppin' it off. Two-man job. They knew Jack was a fisherman.'

'Go on, tell me about the cargo.'

'Well, thas just it – we never got to it. Coz the Excise men might have been watchin', we decided to go further out. Then the storm hit us. The boat was hard to control and poor Jack was struggling, it was blowing us into shore. I heard Jack yell somin' about going up The Stairs and then the bow hit, went right up, and then...'

She passed him a mug of water and got him to explain every detail about the job. The plan was to sail to Seal

Cove, a small inlet and beach impossible to get to from land. Going at night obviously had its risks but the men insisted. The cargo was hidden there – a chest, two men to lift it. They were to retrieve it and leave the boat tied-up back at the village quay. Her mood played like a cat's tail and suddenly the anger spat out.

'You haven't even apologised,' she hissed, 'Jack trusted you! I can't believe you got tangled up with all this. No apology!'

'I can't think of the right thing ... *there are no words, Faith.*' He offered upturned hands in supplication. 'Every waking second, I'm goin' over it. And in my sleep too. I'm sorry, Faith. For the rest of my years, I'll be sorry.' He looked up with watery, child-like eyes, 'I wish it were me that went down Davy Jones ... sometimes life deals a bad hand.'

The following morning, Nana Thomas burst into the house and brusquely fed Gramps, it was clear she was angry with something or someone. Nana was like the veins of the village; she knew every titbit of gossip, who blasphemed, and who dropped washers into the church collection instead of coins. Had Nana found out? Maybe Wes had heard things, and said things?

After a small lunch, Faith and Wes went for a walk and found themselves down on the beach near the quay, both looking out to sea. A shrill cry of a seagull cut through their thoughts, making Wes jump, putting some sparkle back in his eyes.

'There's Hoppy! He just stays round the quay,' he explained, breaking his silence. The lame gull, tamer than the rest, made his way over to them looking for scraps. He let out another, particularly piercing shriek, and then turned fickle and hopped off.

Wes picked up a large stone, perfect for lobbing.

'Feels like there's an even bigger stone in my stomach, an' sometimes it's hard to breathe. Y'know what I mean, Ma?'

Faith let her eyes linger on the water for a moment longer.

'Yes, Wes, I do.' She reached out and stroked his hair.

'Wish that blimmin' stone would come out.'

'Don't blaspheme.' She replied, without conviction.

He heaved and the big stone flew ungainly through the air and landed with a satisfying plop in the shallows. Faith felt a tidal surge of grief press behind her eyes. She quickly selected a thin stone and expertly skimmed it, impressing Wes.

'Teach me, Ma!'

As they arrived back, skimming arms tired, they saw a man walking away from the cottage. Gramps was evasive, saying it was some old friend. However, the visitor seemed to put him on edge rather than having a comforting effect.

'Who was that man earlier?' She was staring hard at him, looking for the tiny tells loved ones give. 'What's going on, Gramps?'

'Well,' a sigh, 'that was a messenger. From the men we owed. Thing is the job weren't done.' He paused, looked up at Faith, trying to read her reaction.

'I got to go out again. I'll use my old boat.'

Faith began to argue, but he cut her short, 'I have to do this, not just for me but for you an' Wes too. This family can't have anything hangin' over its head!' He broke into coughs.

'There must be another way,' pleaded Faith.

'No other way. Besides, *threats were made.*' His old eyes looked up at the beams, up to the boy's room.

Faith woke up. No sounds, just a sense, a feeling. Had she heard something? Grabbing a shawl, she carefully crept down the stairs and noticed the front door was not bolted. She stepped outside and closed it quietly behind her. There was moon enough to see, but even so, she let her eyes adjust for a moment. Two steps away from the cottage, then two more, and she found herself walking fast towards the quay. In the semi-dark she could see something lying in the hedge, giving her a fright, but as she got closer a new fear hit her – it was Gramps! She knelt and shook him.

'Gramps! Wake up, Gramps!'

'Faith, my girl.' His voice was weak, and even in the moonlight she saw his eyes had that child-like look again. 'The job ... has to be done tonight.'

'Well, you're in no fit state, what do you think you're doing!'

A stern voice out of the dark – 'I know what he's doing.' It was Nana Thomas.

Faith, shocked and guilty, knew the secret was out.

'Yes, I know what's happening! But don't you worry, I won't tell anyone. Be like pot calling kettle black.' Nana paused, bent down to check on Gramps, deciding something. 'Don't suppose you knew but my father was one of the busiest *Runners* along this coast. Your Gramps here, he knew alright.' An uncomfortable pause, more thoughts

CORNWALL BENEATH & BEYOND

going round Faith's head, more questions to ask.

'Secret's safe with me, Faith. Come on, I'll help get him home.' The two women hoisted the old man between them.

'Actually, Nana, do you think you can manage on your own? There's something that needs to be done.'

'I can manage. Here take this,' she handed Faith her thick night-cloak.

'Wes is home, can you stay with them ... until I'm back?'

'Of course, now you better go whilst the moon is on your side. Tide waits for no man ... or woman.'

Leaving the safety of the cold rungs, her hands grabbed the gunwales of the boat. Steadying herself, she threw the mooring rope on top of the junk and old nets in the bow, her grandfather's boat was a mess, but it was floating. She clipped her hair back and pushed off, using the oars to navigate past the quay and out to open water. The boat reacted to the change of sea; waves smacked the side and sea spray in her face. Raising the single sail reminded her of days out with Jack on his boat, before Wes was born. She used to help him and they had made a good team. Sometimes when the sun was out and there was a lull she would sit in the bow, slip her stockings off, and drape her feet in the cool water. Lost in a happy thought.

'Pull yourself together, Faith,' she said out loud. Getting her bearings, she shifted the tiller to give the land a wide-berth, there was an onshore wind and there may be watchers on the cliffs. She knew where Seal Cove was but had never been there as fishermen seemed to stay away, she now knew why. The moon glided out from behind a cloud, it was bright, almost too bright she thought and wondered how visible she was from the cliffs. The rhythmic punch of waves on the starboard side was hypnotic, and for a few moments she indulged herself by thinking of her boy. He had her eyes, but his lively character came from Jack – he was a proper lad, hard work at times but his heart was in the right place. The way he swept his hair back was exactly how Jack used to do it and she wasn't sure if this was a natural trait passed down, or whether he had simply copied his father.

Her eyes followed a set routine: she would glance to the cliffs, then behind, and then up ahead again looking for the shore. She knew she was getting close, her stomach tightened into knots, the crashing of waves gave a tell-tale sign, so she quickly eased the sail making it flap. Taking a big breath, she grabbed the oars ready to fend-off rocks and braced herself. The swell rolled under the boat, a sudden lift in the bow and turn of speed, and then she skidded onto the sand of Seal Cove.

Hitching up her dress she leapt off. It was deeper than she had thought and the angry water started to suck her out, but with one small step at a time, she finally made the boat safe.

Faith collapsed on the sand, chest thumping, breathing hard, her sweat cold from the wind. She was at her lowest ebb. Finally, she heaved herself up from the wet sand and started to think of the job at hand, but some animal instinct told her to turn around – and that's when she saw him; a large, wounded man crawling up the beach towards her, he started crying out in pain! Her eyes widened in absolute terror – she then cursed in relief. It was her imagination playing tricks and she shooed the nosy seal away.

Turning to head up the beach, she heard another noise behind her – the soft crunch of footsteps in sand, tentatively moving closer.

'Do you want help, Ma?' Wes was standing there in the moonlight, a proud smile on his face. Faith didn't know whether to hug him or cuff him.

'I followed you out, you stopped for Gramps, you needed help. I ran around the back alley, got to the boat before you and hid beneath the nets. You angry with me?'

She had no time to argue and it wouldn't achieve anything anyway – Wes got his stubbornness from her.

'I'm not happy about this at all, I'll have words with you tomorrow, but now we got work to do.' Inwardly, she was happy she had some company.

They found three, small caves half hidden in the dark and the chest was right where Gramps said it would be, buried in sand with a driftwood log over the top. The chest was rough and simple but well-made with loops of rope on the ends. It was incredibly heavy, but not large, about the size of a child's coffin. With a massive effort, and with one eye on the inquisitive seal, they managed to manhandle the chest into the boat.

They spent a few precious minutes turning the boat and then, pushing with the oars, they somehow managed to get out past the breaking water. Wes watched the seal, Faith watched the cliffs. They got out into open water, raised the sail and the swell picked up, slapping the boat again. 'Hold on, Wes, one hand for the boat and one for yourself.'

It was slower going on the return journey, tacking again and again. They were about halfway back, Faith dared to hope that everything would be alright. Wes sat in the bow, then looked back at her, bright eyes, smiling at her. She managed to smile back.

Just then a loud hail from behind and a gunshot broke through the night. Faith twisted around and in disbelief saw a boat following, chasing – it was the Excise men!

Cold shock hit Faith, she struggled to keep a level head, but she went through the motions of adjusting the tiller and looking up at the sail, trimming it to make sure there was no slack.

'They're getting closer, Ma!'

'We'll be alright, nearly back.'

Faith had questioned her beliefs recently, and felt no guilt at that, but she started praying, mumbling through gritted teeth. Just when things seemed they couldn't get any worse, Wes spotted a second boat tailing, one after the other, and warned his mother.

The situation was dire. If they got caught with whatever was in the chest, there was a good chance it meant a spell inside, and they couldn't lift it over the side either or according to Gramps they might face a harsher penalty. The chasing boats were faster and manned by experienced seamen, but they simply had to get away. She bit down on her lower lip and made a decision – she shifted the tiller and the boat responded by angling slightly towards land.

'Are we goin' up Satan's Stairs, Ma?'

'What do you know about The Stairs?'

'Pa pointed them out to me. Last time we went out.'

'Any port in a storm, Wes.'

Another minute and another hail from the chasers, Faith looked back and could clearly make out the bronze of the small cannon pointing at them. They were getting within pistol range.

'There they are!' Wes was leaning further out over the bow pointing dead ahead. Satan's Stairs; a row of sharp, black rocks evenly spread, clearly visible, strangely darker than the night. At one end the rock was stuck high in the air, then each consecutive one was lower, at the other end the rock barely broke the water's surface. The big rocks looked formidable, but at least you could see them, Faith knew it was the hidden rocks that were the real killers.

Faith picked a gap and barked at Wes to hold tight. She just had time for a muttered prayer – and then they were skimming between the stones, shooting out the other side. Wes' grin showed through the dark, but Faith couldn't return it. She looked back just as the first chasing boat approached The Stairs. They had chosen a different gap and were halfway through when there was a shrieking, grinding sound that carried on the wind. It had struck rock and the bow was caught high in the air. But the second boat glided through without a scrape.

'I need you, I'm begging!' Faith's coolness broke, she raised her eyes to the thick pewter-clouds above, 'I need your help more than ever!' But she wasn't praying to God, she was thinking of Jack, angry with him for leaving her. She risked a quick glance behind, the boat was gaining but she quickly looked for'ard again. Her gaze fell on Wes. He was gripping tight, sitting sideways, his head in profile, he definitely had her chin. Then he turned and pushed his hair back in that familiar way. Her heart missed a beat and for a moment she couldn't breathe. She was about to say something to reassure him, but then stopped – there was a change in the air. It was thicker, and detail less-defined, it was wet. There was a thick mist coming in – a proper sea fret. Within moments they were covered, protected, too difficult for their pursuers to follow them.

Jack had lived on the sea, he always said he had sea salt in his blood. He was with them now, guiding them, asking a favour from Mother Nature. A gull's cry sliced through the mist, a particularly piercing call, it cut through her thoughts. Faith, alive with fresh hope, looked up at Wes who was looking back at her, a smile on his face that reached his eyes.

Rooted

by Stephen Baird

Ash was rooted to the spot.

He gasped. The girl was like a flower, natural and beautiful. She floated across the school yard, everyone around her out of focus. Or so it seemed to Ash. But this girl was in the sharpest of focus. Long black hair shone in the late summer sunlight. Her face was pale, but red dusting on her cheeks gave her complexion a zest.

Ash had never felt like this. She must be a new pupil; he'd never seen her before. She passed out of sight. He could follow but that seemed creepy. They would surely meet at some point. He smiled. Turning to his phone, he scrolled through nothing in particular, lost to his surroundings.

'Hi.'

Ash spun around and his smile broadened. 'Hi.'

He half-mirrored her greeting. Made it the same level of casual, but with hints of warmth. This was like painting, choosing where to put warmth in a picture without overdoing it.

'You're an artist,' she said.

Was it that obvious? He nodded. She was... he couldn't think of a single word. His mind started to wander, like when he was taken over by a new painting project. It was all-consuming. She was...so many things. There. That covered it and that's how he felt.

'The Prussian Blue on the fingernail is a give-away,' she said. Just a hint of a smile played around the furthest edges of her mouth and her eyes danced with life.

Ash looked at his fingernail. 'I leave a colour to ensnare other artists.'

'And only a real artist would name the colour.'

He laughed. Her smile twitched wider.

'I'm Rowan,' she said.

'I'm Ash.'

The smile vanished but only because she was studying him. Her eyes still sparkled as they roamed his face. 'Ash,' she said. 'Yes, of course you are.'

'It's short for Ashley.'

'Ash is fine,' she said softly. 'Just fine.'

'And fancy you having the name of a tree too!'

'Yes,' she said. 'Just fancy that.'

'So, you paint?' asked Ash.

'Yeah. When I can.'

'Great. What do you paint?'

'Trees.'

Ash smiled. 'Just trees?'

Rowan smiled back. 'Yes. Just trees.'

The bell rang and the students started moving towards

the school buildings.

'Do you know where you're going?' Ash asked.

'Yes,' and Ash believed it.

'See you later, Rowan,' he said as calmly as he could, but he could have kicked himself for making the end of his sentence sound like a question. Idiot.

'See you later, Ash,' she said.

She flashed another lighthouse beam and it was as if someone had hurled splinters of warm sunlight at Ash. His heart leapt but he remained rooted to the spot.

Ash looked at his painting and scrunched up his eyes. It helped to see the light and shade balance. He frowned. The painting just wasn't happening.

'It's missing something, Ash.'

Ash looked at Mrs Saunders, the art teacher. 'Perhaps I haven't got the talent after all.'

'Oh, you've got it! No doubt about that. You just haven't found your way to that next level yet. Don't push it. Just keep plugging away. This is technically really good. It just needs more of what can't be taught.'

Ash looked at his painting. The sparkling tops of the waves.

'Don't get me wrong, Ash. You could be a professional artist and make a lot of money. But this is about you and what level of feeling and passion you can put into your pictures to satisfy the creativity within you. Does that make sense?'

Ash nodded. He knew he had more to give.

Ash saw Rowan standing a few metres from the school gate,

beside the beech tree. She was a stillness in the uniformed migration funneling through the school gates and away in every direction. One of her hands lay on the trunk of the tree and he noticed her lips moving. She seemed oblivious to the noise and movement all around her. Ash's heartbeat picked up. Was she waiting for him? It didn't matter. This was the chance to ask the question he'd been practising all day, just in case.

'Would you like to go for a walk this weekend?'

She turned and smiled at him, her hand remaining on the tree trunk, gently caressing it. 'Sure. That would be great.'

'Where d'you want to go?'

'Your favourite place?'

He laughed. 'OK. The beach it is. I think the weather's wild tomorrow but calmer on Sunday.'

Her eyes gleamed. 'Saturday sounds fine.' He looked at her. Was she real?

'OK,' he said. '11:00ish?'

'Yeah. That's good.'

She turned to go.

'Hey,' called Ash. 'D'you want to swap numbers?' He waved his phone.

Rowan turned. 'Don't have a phone.' She smiled. 'Don't worry. I'll be there.'

She disappeared into the crowd, lost in the student surf.

Ash hadn't moved. Rooted again. He gazed in the direction she'd gone, trying to catch one more glimpse. He knew nothing about her. But he was going to see her tomorrow. Stormy. It was going to be so wild. He grinned to himself. Perfect.

There was only one way down to the cove. Ash half-expected Rowan to be waiting at the top. It was one minute to eleven. He'd have happily been a couple of hours early but didn't want to appear desperate. Now what was he going to do? The wind swirled all around him and he spread his legs just a little more to keep his balance. Had she arrived and gone down to the beach or was she still on her way? Or had she changed her mind? He glanced at his phone as it turned to 11:01. Hearing the crashing waves, he made his choice. She'd be on the beach. He set off before any doubts wormed into his mind.

Ash arrived at a jog onto the beach, heart thumping and breathless with anticipation. He pushed his dark hair off his forehead, ignoring that it flopped down again immediately. She was standing near the shoreline gazing out to sea then turned and waved. Waving back, he ran over.

'Hi. I didn't know whether you would wait at the top...'

'But you knew I would be down here?'

'Yes. Yes, I did.' It seemed strange but he *had* known.

'Let's walk.' She grabbed his hand so quickly and naturally that it was a moment before he realised they were holding hands.

Strands of Rowan's hair were plastered across her face and she laughed into the wind and shook her head like a wild animal.

They sauntered along the edge of the crashing waves, leaping back here and there, to avoid being swamped by an over-zealous one. They laughed. Talking wasn't much of an option in the buffeting wind and rain but neither of them seemed to mind. Togetherness was all that Ash wanted and he sensed Rowan felt the same.

Rowan swung around and pressed herself against Ash. He nearly fell over with surprise as well as the force. Her eyes darted around his face then she kissed him, long and hard. He surrendered to the embrace and the kiss. Gladly drowned in them. She kissed hard but he wanted to kiss harder. She'd awoken something in him.

When she eased away, had it been seconds or minutes? Ash couldn't tell. They gazed at each other. He'd thought he would never understand what he was experiencing. Would never have the chance.

Despite this, he asked, 'Why me?'

'Because we're right for each other. You'll make me complete. Ash – the Tree of the World, tree of rebirth and healing.'

'Yeah. I think my parents were into Norse myths when I was born – Yggdrasil, the huge tree that joins and protects all the worlds.'

'Yes. That's right.' Her eyes were glistening. 'I want to spend so much time with you.'

'Good!' he laughed. 'And what should I know about the rowan tree?'

'It's the Tree of Life and a protection from evil.'

'Good to have around then?' Ash smiled mischievously.

'Yes. definitely.'

It was a more serious response than Ash had anticipated. He put a finger under her chin and gently tilted her face upwards towards his. 'Just like you...'

They walked along the beach and back again,

numerous times. There was nobody else there. It belonged to them and Ash didn't want it to end before it had to.

'It's going to be dark soon,' said Rowan. 'Shouldn't you be getting home?'

'What for?' Ash's voice had hardened.

'Won't your parents be wondering where you are?'

'I doubt they've even noticed I'm out. Too busy arguing with each other. Shouting. Screaming. Not much of a healing tree, am I?'

She squeezed his hand. 'We've got each other.'

'Thank goodness.' He squeezed her hand back and they headed for the track off the beach.

'Your home near?' asked Ash.

'Not far.'

'Can I walk with you?'

'I'm fine, thanks. See you on Monday, Ash.'

Ash's head drooped. 'OK.' He paused. 'Why don't you have a phone?' He felt stupid at once.

'I don't need one.' Rowan smiled and Ash nodded.

It was the answer he should've expected.

Monday's art class was straight after lunch break. Sixth formers were allowed in the Art Room during lunch if they wanted to work on a piece. Ash had missed lunch to be in there. He was absorbed.

'Ash. That's amazing!' Mrs Saunders fell silent but continued to gaze at the sea scene before her.

Ash's cheeks burned.

'What's changed?'

'I'm just trying to put more of me into the scene. Everything this scene is, I can feel it. Understand it.' He was breathless. His words had just burst out. A torrent.

'Well, it's remarkable. I am thrilled for you – and a bit jealous.' Mrs Saunders gave a little laugh. They both looked back at the wild swirlings and whirlings of the sea, caught in a storm. The light and shade fell naturally and unexpectedly in equal measure. Just as the sea does. Just as the sea had done on Saturday. A day Ash would never forget.

Ash pushed open the front door.

'I'm home.'

He understood the tone before he heard the words. The bickering, again.

The two people who had created him, so wrapped up in hating each other and trying to score points off each other, they hardly seemed to notice him anymore. He wished he could just slip off and find Rowan again. She wanted to be with him. She'd noticed him right from that first day.

He didn't pretend to understand it. She seemed to be as much in love as he was. But he couldn't go and find her. He didn't know where she lived. Didn't know why she wouldn't tell him. As he gently shut the front door, he caught sight of his face in the hall mirror. He saw concern flicker across his face. Was he infatuated to the point he was missing warning signs? The flicker evaporated. He turned towards the stairs. He didn't care. He loved the way he felt when he was with her and that was the most important thing.

He crept up the stairs, now hoping his parents wouldn't realise he was home. He wanted to be alone with his thoughts.

'This is the painting I wanted to show you,' said Ash, removing the white sheet with a flourish.

Rowan gazed at the trees in the picture and admired the textures and life that Ash had put into them.

'It's wonderful,' she said and Ash saw the shine in her eyes.

'You're an artist. Is there anything you'd do to improve it? There's always more that can be done.'

Rowan gazed at the painting, stepped to look more closely, then stepped back again.

'I think it's great as it is. If it were mine, I would give the trees more character.'

'Like they're really people?'

She looked at him. 'Because they are really people.'

'OK. Show me.' Ash stepped back and indicated his brushes and paints.

'Really?' asked Rowan.

'Really really!'

'But you might think I've ruined it.'

'I won't. I want you involved in this. It'll help me. Add even more to my inspiration.'

Rowan stepped forward, chose a brush, mixed up some paint and worked with some swift strokes, scratching and dabbing, here and there, poking and stabbing. Nothing huge. Adding to, rather than taking from, what was already there.

After a couple of minutes, she laid the brush down and stepped back to stand alongside Ash. There was a long silence before Ash let out a low whistle.

'That's amazing. There are almost faces and features in the trunks. But not really. It's like they're there but not. Most people might not even realise.'

'That's as it is. Most people take trees for granted.'

'Thank you.'

She stared straight at him. 'That's teamwork.'

It was late in October. Ash and Rowan were sheltering under a huge oak tree in the middle of a field. Rowan had a hand on the rough trunk, stroking it fondly. Ash could almost make out a craggy old face in the gnarly whorls. He shivered. The rain would soon pass but it would still be cold. Winter wasn't far away.

He looked at Rowan with concern. She'd seemed much paler recently. When he'd mentioned it, she just dismissed it. Now she turned to him, as the rain gently dropped all around them.

'I have to go away, Ash. Just for a few months.'

'Away? Where?'

'Please don't ask me.'

'Are you in trouble?'

'No. And then we will be together always, as we've planned.' He nodded but looked unsure. 'Trust me, Ash.'

'But how can we be in touch? You don't have a phone.'

She shook her head. 'You won't be able to contact me.'

'But that's going to be awful.' He wanted to be angry but just felt numb.

'It'll be tough for both of us but it's just a few months. Then we'll be together for years to come.'

'I don't understand why you can't tell me what's wrong.'

'Please, Ash, just trust me.'

Ash looked away then nodded again, his shoulders slumping. How would he cope with the home situation when he couldn't even escape with Rowan?

'How will I know you're back?'

'On the headland above the beach where we went for our first walk, there is a rowan tree. Its berries will be bright red throughout winter and remind you of me. When the white blossom comes in spring, I will be back – for good.'

Winter came and Rowan had gone. Ash visited the rowan tree every day, whatever the weather. Every day seemed like a month, each month a year. He feared the image of her in his mind would start to fade, but it remained brightly etched on his memory. And that gave him hope, so he painted her. Not once, or twice but many times. Just for himself. To bring spring nearer.

Finally, the blossom came and Rowan was back; at once it was like she had never been away at all. She looked so well and bright-eyed. Better than ever.

They hunched over their coffee mugs, their knees pressed together under the narrow table. The small café was heaving with people. Just for a short time, they were like an island, lost in the sea of cheerfulness as it rolled around them in a hotch-potch of colour, chatter and laughter.

'My parents are separating,' said Ash. 'They both want to leave Cornwall – in different directions.'

Rowan frowned. 'And you?'

Ash shrugged. 'Dunno. Think they might be waiting, each hoping the other will offer to take me.'

'They're probably feeling awkward. I'm sure they love you.'

A flicker of anger filled Ash's face. 'Awkward? And how do they think I feel? Do they even think I have feelings? They've hardly noticed me for months. I wish we could just disappear.'

After a silence, Rowan said, 'If we keep to our plan, we'll be sorted. May Day is nearly here.'

Ash gazed at Rowan and nodded. Then looked down.

They stepped off the 97 bus between Camelford and Launceston and ambled the short distance to the hamlet of Laneast. Rowan veered right to a small grey metal gate.

Ash stopped. 'A church? I thought we were visiting trees – nature, you know...'

'We're never far from trees,' said Rowan.

Ash scanned the churchyard ringed with trees and shrugged.

'There's something I want you to see,' she said, taking his hand. 'And you've got Prussian Blue on a fingernail again.' They laughed and barged shoulders jokingly.

Walking past an ancient Celtic cross with its quartered circle atop, they turned into the porch, with the cris-crossing old beams above them.

Ash paused by the notice board. 'St Sidwell and St Guvran. Never heard of them. How does a place like this end up with two saints?' He hadn't really expected an answer, so he wasn't disappointed.

'This way,' she said, leading them into the patchy light inside the church. The place felt old. Really old. They passed a sign with an apology for any mess as the building was shared with a colony of bats. Ash instinctively glanced up as Rowan turned down the far side aisle and stopped. 'These pews are ancient,' she said. 'They all have carved ends to them and they are all different. This is the one I want you to see.'

She knelt down and Ash walked over to kneel beside her.

'It's a shame it's so dingy,' she said.

'Don't need a phone, huh?' said Ash laughing, switching on his torch function.

Rowan smiled back then pointed. 'Here.'

Ash leaned forward angling his phone to get better light coverage on the carving.

'Wow,' he said softly. 'It's a head, surrounded by...' He peered closer.

'Leaves,' said Rowan, her voice barely audible.

He traced a fingertip around some of the leaf shapes and frowned as his finger reached the middle. 'The leaves are coming out of its mouth.'

'Yes,' said Rowan.

Ash sat back on his haunches. 'It's a Green Man.'

Rowan's eyes brightened in the half light. 'What do you know?'

'Not a lot, really. Stories about a figure that's made up entirely of leaves and branches. Like a god of woodland...?' Ash's voice tailed off in uncertainty.

'The Green Man is a symbol of rebirth, of natural things dying in winter and bursting back into life in the spring.'

'Pagan stuff, you mean.'

'Yes, that's often what it gets called.'

'So, you're interested in these things?'

'They're part of me.' She paused. 'If you join me, they'll be part of us.'

A thought arrowed deep inside him that he didn't really understand what she was saying.

'Do you want to be together always?' asked Rowan.

'Can we really do this?'

She nodded firmly.

'What about money?' He felt like a traitor bringing up such an obvious hurdle to her plans.

Rowan shook her head. 'Money won't be a problem.' She said it with such certainty that Ash didn't feel it was worth asking 'how' or 'why'. His parents would hardly miss him and he could give lots more time to his art. He hadn't really made up his mind about spiritual things, so some pagan bits and pieces didn't bother him. He thought about the influence Rowan had already had on his painting and his life. It felt right.

'To be with you and be able to paint would be perfect. Yes. I want us to be together always.'

'No matter what it takes?'

He thought carefully. 'If it's what we both want, I'm up for it.'

They stood and kissed.

'I love you,' she said.

They left the church and followed the narrow road as it wound down into the valley. The River Inny was a silver ribbon, bright against the lush greens. They stopped a moment at the waterfall that tumbled off a ledge beside the bridge, then Rowan led them off left on a public footpath where they climbed wooded slopes. Then they turned left again off the track and walked hand-in-hand amongst the trees.

Ash laughed. 'You've been here before.'

'Yes. Many times.'

She paused by a tree and ran her hand along a low branch. 'Hawthorn,' she said solemnly. 'A tree of strong magic. A tree that will help us be together.'

'Nice,' said Ash. He didn't get this tree talk, so it seemed an encouraging response. If it made Rowan happy, he could live with it.

They reached a clearing in the woodland and Rowan stopped, looking around, her face shining. A huge old spreading oak tree with its mantle of moss dominated the space and Rowan pressed a cheek up against the huge trunk. At that moment, the sun pushed through the clouds.

Ash gazed around. 'It's beautiful here.' He meant it. 'So calm.'

He hunkered down and watched Rowan. She was wandering from tree to tree, a whisper here, a stroke there, a greeting and even a hug or two. She seemed at home here. It was strange, but nowhere near as weird as he thought he should be feeling.

Rowan returned to the centre of the clearing and beckoned to him. She took his hand and gave it an encouraging squeeze.

'This is Ash, my consort. I told you he would come. We ask your blessings on us at this time of Beltane.'

Nothing happened that Ash could tell. 'Am I supposed to say something?' He was beginning to feel self-conscious.

'No, you're fine. They like you. Do you sense it?'

He wasn't sure. 'It's very peaceful,' he offered.

Rowan smiled. 'Are you ready?'

Ash's brow furrowed. He thought about asking 'for what' but perhaps he was meant to know. 'Yes.' His mind began to churn. He could feel something building up and he didn't know what it was. For a moment, he wondered if Rowan intended to consummate their relationship here. Did pagans do that at Beltane? He didn't know.

Rowan turned and faced him. 'I desire to spend all my time with you.' She raised her eyebrows, nodding at Ash.

He steadied himself. 'I desire to spend all my time with you.'

Rowan clasped him in a hug and Ash put his arms tightly around her and smiled.

Rowan stepped back.

'You're bleeding,' said Ash, looking at the palm of her hand.

She smiled. 'It's time. We must seal this.' She took his right hand, palm up, then raked the hawthorn across it. At once beads of blood appeared along the bright red line.

'Ow!' he yelled.

Rowan clasped his right palm to her bloodied one. 'At this Beltane,' she called, 'we join our blood and seal our bond for all time, and you're our witnesses.'

She stepped to one side and stood still, looking exultant.

Ash glanced down at his hand in time to see a green leaf shoot push out from under a fingernail. He gasped. He raised his other hand and saw shoots emerging and growing quickly, like a time-lapse project.

He screamed, 'What have you –' but the sound was cut off as tender new branches whipped out from his mouth and throat, pushing rapidly outwards and upwards, to left and right. He saw the same happening to Rowan.

His body was writhing as clothing ripped open, unable to contain the confusion of thickening branches sprouting from his body. In panic, he looked down and saw roots extending his feet down into the moist rich woodland earth. He stared in disbelief as a thick branch punched out of his chest. He made a strangled noise which was lost in the rustling of branches and leaves and the succulent squelches all around him. Everywhere there was movement. There was nothing he could do; it had all happened.

Vestiges of thoughts remained, and the stillness returned to the woodland. The two additional trees would go unnoticed, as would the way their branches touched fondly in the slightest of breezes. Together. Always. And nobody would notice the way one trunk looked almost like a face screaming, nor ever see the tiny flakes of Prussian Blue high up on a branch.

Ash was rooted to the spot.

Something in Common

by Claudia Loveland

It's a mild, late-July evening, and I've wandered into Miriam's ornamental garden to be on my own. The scent of recently cut grass has finally replaced the mortuary smell that's been lingering in my nose since early afternoon. If I stay here a while longer, the sight of the roses and the overflowing hydrangeas might be soothing.

'Louise?'

I turn around at the sound of a man's voice. 'Lou, yeah.'

'Miriam told me I had to come and talk to you. I'm Luke.'

He's tall, brown-haired and tanned, with a lined face. Late-forties? Probably not much older than I am. He looks relaxed. I probably don't.

'She told me we have something in common,' he says.

'You think she means that? Or is she simply trying to

help an introvert who'd rather be somewhere else?'

'Are you? An introvert?' He's one of those people who can raise one eyebrow without moving the other. 'I think they'd call me an extrovert, so that's one thing we don't have in common.' He smiles. 'Why don't you want to be here?'

'Just tired. Long drive.' And I exhale.

Yes, breathing deeply might help.

After the police station, and then the morgue, I couldn't face driving home from London to Cornwall. So I phoned Miriam. She's a family friend and I've known her since I was a child. She has a large ground-floor flat in a huge, Victorian house near the Bristol Downs. I knew she'd put me up and she wouldn't need any details. Miriam doesn't do deep relationships, she does networking. Knows everyone and no-one, but she's kind and enjoys having visitors.

A few hours later, I'm wondering why I didn't check into a hotel. She's invited people for drinks.

His drink is in a bottle: a beer of some sort.

'How do you know Miriam?' I ask.

'A friend put us in contact when I moved back here a week ago. I'm travel-weary too. I came from Argentina.' That fits with his loose-cut jeans and travel shirt.

'Then we don't have travelling in common,' I say. 'I'm a homebody.'

'I've not been back-packing. For twenty years, Argentina was my home. My wife, Maria – my late wife – was Argentinian.'

I put on my sympathetic face.

'Your late wife...?' is all I need to say.

'She died giving birth to our daughter – who also died. Sofia would have been eight next month. The surgeon was negligent. It's taken me a while to get things straight and come back to the UK.'

I can't do this: I've got enough stuff of my own going on right now. If I must play this game, I'll stick to easy questions.

But he's back on the case; what else might we have in common? He wants to know if I have a family.

'A grown-up daughter, Esther,' I tell him. Then, because I feel I should be contributing a little more, I add, 'And I'm a primary school headteacher, so that's a bit like family, as well.'

But family has suddenly become complicated.

'Let me get us another drink,' he says, 'and then we can talk. Miriam was adamant that there's something that links us. A shared interest? It can't be that hard.'

But everything feels hard. My daughter is the child of the man I saw in the mortuary this afternoon – though he had never even seen her. I've spent today reliving all this, but she doesn't know where I've been.

The detective who knocked on my door two days ago asked for my help in identifying a body – a suicide – found in west London. To be fair, she was a great deal more sensitive about it than that, but, in short, they had a corpse, with no identification except my name and the school's address written on a piece of paper in his pocket.

Twenty-five years of silence, and now this. And why?

Had he always been watching me? Watching us? I moved to Cornwall to stay beneath his radar, but no-one is beyond reach these days. I shiver. And what do I tell Esther?

'Looks like you're getting chilly,' Luke says. 'Let's head inside.'

We settle in the high-ceilinged living room, at the ornate, mahogany coffee table by the sash-window. I usually enjoy being here; it's such a contrast to my modern townhouse on the outskirts of Truro. On the other side of the room a man and two young women are sitting at the highly polished dining table, talking about animation and the film industry. Most people though, half a dozen or more, have pressed into the kitchen, around the food and drink.

'So, where did you grow up?' he wants to know.

Perhaps some small talk will be a helpful distraction. I can deal with everything tomorrow, at home.

'On the east coast. Westcliff, in Essex, and then north London.'

He grew up in Wales. I can hear that, now he's talking about it. Surrounded by hills and the history of mining. I had the view of London from Hampstead Heath; he's not impressed. It seems he was a country boy, growing up with the hymns of Welsh Methodism and the shouts of the rugby crowd. I was a city girl. Still am, though Truro is a very small city. Jewish by birth – and for always, I suppose – I discovered that this made the family thing so difficult, and yet possible.

My parents were appalled when I told them what was happening. I was nineteen and pregnant by a charming, persuasive bully who had destroyed my confidence. They stood by me and tried to understand. The more they understood, the tougher it was for them. He had first flattered me, then confused me. He deliberately overruled me and somehow made me believe he was right. Although he was only three years older than me, his assurance was overwhelming. He'd been a medical student, but reckoned he was destined for higher things, so he'd resigned from the course. Palmer. Everyone called him by his surname.

'University?' Luke is not going to drop this.

'London; history.'

I don't tell him how long it took to finish that degree, with time off to have Esther, with so much help from my parents, with the gradual rebuilding of my self-esteem, which was practically zero when I found the insight and courage to break free – a month before I went into labour.

Bristol Uni for him. Geology, and then research, which linked with his mining heritage, and took him to Chile and Argentina. Nothing suggests a connection between us.

'Sport?'

'Not really my thing.' As a teenager, I could never remember whether I was supposed to support Tottenham or Arsenal. These days, I'm a sea swimmer, captivated by the waves and the tides.

In Argentina, he'd go online for anything that Wales were playing. His outdoor relaxation came from riding. He had friends with a ranch and horses, but he's hardly ridden at all in the last few years as he's chased that incompetent surgeon through the courts. He was convicted, in the end – the surgeon. The bungling, unprofessional, totally incapable surgeon.

Music, theatre, films? We seem as ill-matched on these as on everything else, though we both prefer live performance to recordings. We agree this is probably not what Miriam has in mind.

'Books?'

This is my question, though I don't get a lot of time to read for pleasure – work tends to fill my evenings.

He says something similar. For years, his reading has involved trawling through medical textbooks, witness statements, police records, insurance claims and law reports – mostly in Spanish.

What will he do with himself now? The dreadful doctor turns out to be English and has come back to the UK. It sounds as though Luke's return is connected.

'And, get this.' He pauses and leans forward, his right hand clenched. 'He isn't even a qualified doctor.'

Both his eyebrows are raised. He clearly assumes I will share his outrage. I suppose I do, but I'm not sure I can feel anything at present.

'He spent two years as a medical student in London. Just two years. And, why only two years? Because he got kicked out for cheating in exams. After that, he blagged his way around a couple of universities before going travelling. He's got no qualifications at all. For anything.' Luke has moved so far forward in the armchair that he's scarcely supported by it. 'Believe me, I know. I've unearthed more about this guy than he knows about himself.'

He eases back against the cushion. 'He ended up in Argentina and set himself up as a doctor. That sounds ridiculous, but I met him several times before the birth went so wrong; I can see how he managed it. He was charming, just exuded competence.'

I take a slow sip of my wine.

'We thought it was a privilege to be in his care. We'd been so concerned about complications, but he was reassuring. He even made us feel confused about why we were worrying. It would all be fine. In the end though, we weren't thinking straight. Afterwards, I realised we'd been duped into not getting a second opinion.'

He pauses, and presumably expects me to say something, but I'm somewhere else. I'm back in London, twenty-five years ago, confused, duped, no longer in control. I'm wearing a dress I'd never have chosen, listening to Palmer's music with Palmer's friends. My own have been side-lined, no longer required.

'Our case wasn't his first disaster. Not even his first court case. Just the first where the truth couldn't be covered up.'

'What's his name?' I ask.

'I knew him as Oliver. "Doctor" Oliver.'

My attempt at casual interest felt thinly disguised; now I have to hide my relief.

'But I don't know what he'll call himself now. I discovered he'd already changed his name once.'

Silence is all I can manage, but that doesn't seem to matter to Luke.

'The press took an interest at the time; he became a sort of celebrity villain. And recently he did another interview, when he got early release – from his ridiculously short prison sentence – on compassionate grounds.'

I'm listening properly now. His voice is rising, his words jostling each other.

'Allegedly, he's got a terminal cancer. Don't believe a word of it. And he actually mentioned me in that interview. Me. Linked me with turning his life around. I reminded him of his former life in England, apparently – got him thinking about his neglected family. What nerve. And what utter rubbish. He doesn't have a family. How dare he involve me? That was when I knew I had to come back.'

He slows. 'If Maria's death is to have any meaning... If the life Sofia never had is to count for anything at all...'

My mind has escaped again, but it's coming back into the room, leaving a mortuary technician holding up one end of a sheet.

'Anyway, he's not going to do any more damage. I'll find him and I'll watch him.'

He's reached the edge of his seat again, but this time he picks up his beer, settles back in the chair and looks around the room. We're the only ones not in the kitchen. It sounds as though Miriam is holding court.

'Well,' he says, 'I think she's beaten us. Nothing in common that I can see.'

I have to breathe deeply before replying. 'It's a difficult one.'

I don't want to talk. I don't want to be here.

Did I see his unscrupulous doctor lying on a slab earlier? Esther's father? Too much of a coincidence, surely. But one after another, the possibilities, the implications – the complications – are cresting and slewing in my brain. Whirlpooling. Foaming. How could Miriam know? How could she be so cruel? It's not credible.

Is it?

And here she comes; she saunters across the room, with a ludicrous smile and a plate of supermarket canapés.

'I didn't think it would be such a big deal, Lou,' she says, laughing. 'The pair of you look like a couple of students who've been set a problem they still can't solve, when the others are back in the bar already.'

'Give us a clue.' Luke says.

'Lighten up.' She thinks it's a joke. 'Try exchanging phone numbers.'

I stare at her. 'What the...'

'Okay,' he says, getting out his phone. 'I'll call you. What's your number?'

Seconds later, my phone buzzes. I'm trapped in this. Furious.

But I go through the motions of adding his name to my address book.

'Alright,' I say. 'Luke...?'

'Owen.'

I'm laughing. My hands are trembling. I need lots of short breaths to replace the air that my laughter is forcing out. My eyes water, as all the emotion of the day swells inside me. I don't want tears.

Luke Owen. I try saying it aloud and make a bad job of it. It shouldn't be difficult.

Miriam's laughing too, but it's an embarrassed laugh. Luke is staring at me, looking awkward.

I have to sober up.

'Sorry. I'm ... I'm so sorry. I don't know where all that came from.' What a lie. 'I think I'm overtired. I should have introduced myself properly.'

I clutch my phone with both hands to control the shaking and try again to say his name. I take the deepest breath I can.

'Luke Owen.' Another deep breath. 'And I'm Lou ... Cohen.'

And I'm laughing again.

I can't stop.

Level With You

by Alice Thomas

When I was a child, my mum told me a story where the waves from the ocean once ploughed into buildings and parks, destroying them completely. I asked her if the sea levels would ever go down again. She said no.

My chin lifted from my knuckles after staring at the sea for an hour. My hands massaged the rips on my old jeans, plucking their strings to allow a bit of sea breeze inside. *Were the buildings like sixty metres under sea water?* I would rather not swim in the ocean. I was afraid I might sink down to the watery depths after hearing so many horror tales from my mum, the ones where history was preserved by swirls of salt. She was gone when I was fifteen anyway, but her words still echo in my mind.

I climbed over the salty grass bank with my roughened hands and headed for the woods. It took ten minutes to mosey through the trees while my frizzy fringe bounced from side to side, and I dragged my toes along the pattern of jagged stones on a hilly dirt path, not expecting to see anything new beyond the trees these days. After leaving the woods behind, I arrived to view the small village on the hilly outskirts of Truro, situated by a river flowing towards the heart of the city. Just less than a mile before reaching home there.

With my lungs filled with chilled air, I strolled along a carved, dusty road, heading towards the sleepiness of the village. Rustic buildings with faded chalk-white bricks, and a hint of cooked apple in swirls of salty dust. With my hands stiff from clutching on my backpack straps and with blisters stinging my feet, I thankfully reached my house. It looked old, with sunken seals around its crumbly brickwork and decayed wooden frames. I brushed my feet on a straw mat before the front door, and then removed my cheap, tatty trainers. The whole kitchen was humid, and packed with enough dust to almost make me sneeze.

'I'm home,' I called to my dad, who had his hands inside a cardboard box.

Another day, another food parcel from a council-backed company. We kept receiving them, since the only route through Bodmin had turned into a narrow obstacle course, which impacted the delivery of better food. The sea had blanketed the wider, easier roads for deliveries ages ago, even as far as splitting lands into remote islands. If you were lucky enough to be stuck in Cornwall for long, then you'd have the choice to either cook with what's inside your parcels, or just eat raw carrots.

When I walked over to the box tray, my brows furrowed. My fingers searched through the contents, all of which made my tongue retreat to the back of my throat. No sign of any good stuff, like a puffed packet of crisps.

'You didn't tell them you like cooking, right?' I scowled.

'No,' Dad said. 'Why?'

'Because that would translate into "we don't need your packets of crisps"!'

'Doesn't matter though.' He loaded his arms with more veg. 'The supplies are always scarce. I'd rather you eat more of what's growing in the ground.'

'That's what they want you to think!' I swirled a broccoli between my fingers, much to his annoyance. 'Those rich buggers up in Birmingham keep saying they don't have enough supplies. I bet they're hoarding their supply of toilet paper!'

'Stop believing what your phone says online.' He turned to stow the groceries in a cupboard. 'Go out more!'

'I just been,' I sighed. 'I literally went outside to spend an hour staring into the ocean.'

'Did you walk for more than a mile?'

I paused. My shoulders shook. 'If I was upcountry, yeah, I would have!'

'Heh, upcountry?' Dad smirked. 'Everyone here dreams about that.' He shrugged. 'Cornwall would otherwise be empty, if everyone here had the opportunity to move up.'

My dad kept trying to put me off moving out of Cornwall. He even mansplained to me how it was too difficult to move to a place in Birmingham, the capital of Britain. What he was trying to tell me was 'why go elsewhere when you have the coast, family and the joys of a peaceful life in Cornwall?' The Lizard was once part of the mainland before it got separated into a remote island. Even Penzance got swallowed up by the sea. I literally did not want to spend another year in this godforsaken place.

'That won't work on me all the time,' I said with a defeated sigh, before I scooted off upstairs, so I could drop dead on my bed from burnout.

Monday morning, been tossing vegetables into a couple of trucks using the might of my small shoulders. Puffs of dirt made my clothing grubby, and my hands so dry they almost bled. My joints cried in agony after plucking slippery vegetable leaves from the uneven ground. The managers didn't care if I lacked the stamina of sweaty blokes with stubble.

Look at Nia though. Smug with her dark brown hair waving in the wind, making my work look easy. Her skinny figure made her look like an athlete, huffing breaths after lifting countless heavy sacks of potatoes, yet still beaming a smile. She loved the coasts; the smell of fresh salt, the soft sand that sinks like a cushion. I deserve better than just staring at the sea every day though.

It won't be long now. Vale, the man who worked his bum off, should be along any moment. I've arranged to meet him at the tables by the small building next to the turnip patch. He took risks with his life far too often, just to grab the things needed for my 'get out of jail' card, a trip up north for my potential escape.

I slowly slid across one of the wooden benches by a table. My legs caught its splinters. The breeze was bitter enough for me to wrap my arms around my damp flannel shirt. When I dug into my bag for a box of mixed salad and a bread roll, I grabbed some moisturiser and applied it on my dry hands.

A person in rolled-up jeans appeared and slid along the bench opposite. That wasn't Vale.

'Hey, Ari,' Nia greeted me with a smile. 'Anything much today?' She took a bite of pasta from her bento box.

'Nope,' I murmured, tapping my food. 'I took care of a bunch of leeks today. Their patch got really dried up.'

Nia gently nodded, not getting my bad joke. I doubt anybody else got that.

I stared at her brown eyes. I sighed. 'It's always the same here, if I'm being honest. Farms everywhere across the lands, with halls hosting quizzes every Saturday with tea and saffron cakes. It sucks.'

When I glanced around, Vale was still not there by the tables. Just tractor engines hiding the revving noise of pickup trucks.

'I'm fed up with this place. Same boring routine.' I groaned. 'After I get exhausted picking up vegetables every day, I end up watching TV. Every. Damn. Week.'

'Same.' Nia took another bite.

'Really?' I batted a brow. 'You don't strike me as the "indoor" type.'

'Workwise, I mean.' Nia scratched her fork around her tray.

She went out all the time, often returning with tales of getting around flooded parts of Bodmin. It was like an adventure for her, but no matter where you went, the grass was never greener for me, with thick hedges in between.

'I plan to go scuba diving in Truro this Wednesday,'

she continued.

'Get out.'

'No, really,' Nia chuckled, adjusting her bum. 'I've been planning this with Abby for a couple of weeks. Thought we might take a history lesson in some underwater shops.'

'Isn't that dangerous? I heard there are sharks about.'

'Just the Basking ones. Would you like to join?'

Vale took a seat at the table nearby. He brushed back his short, red hair.

'No thanks.' I stood up. 'If I needed an escape, then it would be across land.' I headed off towards Vale.

'Where are you going?' Nia asked. 'You haven't even touched your food.'

If it worked out according to plan, then on Sunday I would be hitching a ride with a group of people. We would make it up the A30 and towards Birmingham. Just a few nights to seek a place, while others get drunk and forget I was with them. Now that would be a sound plan.

'Heya,' I smiled at Vale. 'Got a van for the weekend?'

He frowned, followed by a pause. His greenish eyes looked at me.

'Well?' My smile faded.

Vale sighed heavily. 'This isn't a good time.'

My brows furrowed. His body odour was stronger than the last time I met him, but maybe that was due to the wind blowing against my scuffled hair.

'But you showed up!' My jaw tightened. 'Come on. I'm dying to know!'

Vale looked up at me, revealing a deeper frown. He checked across all angles.

'We didn't get the funds in time,' he murmured.

I paused. 'I thought you said you got that part sorted.'

'I had. Gregg got mixed up with a missing loan in Taunton, so he couldn't return with a van.'

'Bullshit! You promised!'

'We said "no promises" before, right?' Vale squinted against the bright sun. 'The van was the last part of the plan, but without that and the money in its back, the trip ... ain't going to happen.'

I breathed deeply through my mouth. My hands clenched hard enough to make my knuckles sting. They've lied to me!

'How about this?' I suggested. 'Make it four days. We could settle with a hatchback. Forget Gregg! I *need* this!'

With a sigh of defeat, Vale stood up and walked right off.

'Oh, that's right, walk away!' I continued to vent. 'Because everything to do with an escape is impossible!'

I eventually gave in to Nia's offer. Nothing else would ever distract my mind from when – you know – Vale ditched me! I spent the next day bottling up my frustrations, so harsh that my teeth screeched. I wandered off, my lungs burning from exhaustion, and found myself collapsing on the seat inside Nia's small house. She had a spare wetsuit for me in her cupboard so, when I tried it on, it felt like a sticky wrapper on my roughened skin.

Drained after Wednesday's shift, I got into the car with Nia as the driver. Her friend, Abby, sat in the passenger seat, with her auburn curls, reading the oldest map book I had ever seen. Ancient scraps were packed onto the seats, releasing whiffs of cigarette smoke and dog fur.

My eyelids throbbed from work-related strain, staring at too many trees blurring past the fridge-cold window. I continued to ignore my aching elbow placed on the door rest.

We drove over elevated bridges built of wood and concrete, keeping us above water. I found it depressing to think these lands used to be grass and not seabed. That was until the greed of men accelerated the climate crisis, causing sea levels to rise and the occasional winds spinning into tighter circles.

We reached the wide building next to the water's edge. It was at the heart of Highertown, an on-the-nose village right next to the main city. When I stepped out, a couple of fellas nearby brought over some spare equipment for diving underwater. A part of me wanted to sink down to the depths and drown, defeated. It was too hard to get out of my farming work and head up-country. Maybe that was the easiest option? I wasn't a fan of going underwater, and I doubted I could resort to that choice anyway, but what other option did I have? One of the men had to act as a monitor, in case we ran into any problems, so I guess drowning today was kinda pointless.

'Righty then, once we slide the boat out on the water,' he said. 'We can set sail.'

The other men slid a boat into a watery trench and slipped out into the sea. Have they dug up that part of the road before?

'Any questions?' he asked.

I raised my hand up. 'Are there any sharks under water?'

'Shouldn't be!' He hastily shook his head. 'Every

week, we check under the sea to make sure there ain't any dangerous animals down there. Can't guarantee it mind, so take plenty of caution.'

I stepped over to squint at the sea mouth beyond the raised buildings. Large derelict houses acted as barriers above the waving water, with rusted posts as markers of the road leading to the sea. The white waves roared into their bricks, while the seagulls laughed at such misery.

The guide nodded at the signal given by his other men. He turned to us. 'Are you ready to dip into the past?'

We sailed off on the boat, with its sides flicking with mucky water. We circled around a few lines of buildings that sunk further into the water, teeming with dark green algae. Truro was damned, buried and forgotten. It even beckoned me to resign myself to pulling vegetables from the ground for the rest of my life.

As my chin lifted to the horizon, I saw hints of green and blue from tiny buildings up ahead. The further I looked past them, the more they seemed to retreat to higher ground. There was one site in the middle that poked above sea level. There wasn't anywhere to dock there. In fact, it was nothing like anything else I had seen before.

'That should be it,' the guide said. 'The cathedral landmark.'

The cathedral was tall enough for its beige spire to stick out into the air but its green one, just below the water, could easily scrape against the boat rubber. The sight of ruined structures far below gave me a mixture of vertigo and anxiety, raising goosebumps across my fair skin.

'If you check your watches,' the guide continued, 'the hand should point to twelve. If it hits six, head dreckly back.'

'Roger!' Nia was the first to fall into the water. Abby followed.

With a deep inhale, I dropped my back into the water. Quite warm, actually. I sank down like a pebble though.

When I turned, the road appeared more visible through the mist of the ocean. As my arms spread out to sink down further, more bits of debris tried to catch on my rubbery suit. While my body plummeted, my curiosity elevated.

Making gentle strokes with my arms, I followed Abby and Nia around the buildings. It was like stepping into a time capsule. The shops once sold the likes of portable phones and coffee machines, which were now transformed into rusty relics worth nothing. There were also adverts behind the broken windows which survived the test of time, begging people to take some futile action against global warming.

My eye squinted at rows of rusted cars blocking roads, with their doors removed and charring across their window seams. That's nothing compared to the sunken ship that blocked the exit, which would've led towards the hills and more buildings. It made me wonder if that ship blocked that part of Truro, so we could only explore a small 'snapshot' of the city's history. With a regulator around my lips, I just followed wherever Nia and Abby went.

We swam through a wide, broken window of a shop. My friends turned on their torches, revealing the bubbling textures of shelves. I could make out the pictures along the fabrics and box textures, fused across the stair railings, to see what Truro used to be ages ago; groups of smiling people in front of stone buildings. A few pairs of trainers, sprinkled about the shop floor, looked better than the ones we have on the surface now; too bad they got sea mould all over them.

Swarms of fish swam past me, displaying their bright, rich colours before my fingers. Blueish-green lobsters nested around the cushions of cardboard and rags. I thought they had perished in the deepest of seas, but these forgotten buildings had become habitats for all kinds of sealife.

Nia grabbed Abby's arm. They both looked out. I followed their torch trail to an oval creature. It grew larger, heading towards us. The moment my friends swam past me, my heart sank into the bitter cold. My back threatened to bend into an awkward shape, as my fingers clawed towards the green opening.

I burst out, looking up. The sea ceiling flickered between green and purple, almost invisible, a mile away. My flippers kicked at the dank water, pushing myself up under that bloody pressure. I sucked the oxygen profusely from my tank, as my body heaved above the lowest windows and the rusted cars. The panic and the pressure held me back, almost enough for me to stall. *Why couldn't I go faster?*

After making the terrible choice of looking back to see if that sinister fish came out, I saw the brick road with sea vegetation littered all over it. My mind went dizzy as a stream of bubbles tickled my temples. My muscles begged for a minute of rest, even starting to slip away from my bones.

The beast swam out after me, revealing its wide set of fangs. My eyes popped at its sheer speed.

A bubbly spear shot down, narrowly missing the pale-bodied creature. With more adrenaline in my body, I turned sharply and went further up, as fast as I could. My toes were about to snap. The light shimmered as I elevated nearer to the surface.

My chest bobbed and held to a halt underwater, causing bubbles to burst out from my mouth. The creature bit my flipper! It dragged me down towards the urban abyss, leaving my arms to wave in defeat. I felt as though my insides were pressing against my lungs and blocking my throat.

Another spear lunged into the creature's eye, spreading clouds of burgundy clots. The monster turned around and headed back into the murky depths. A couple of tight grips hooked my armpits up, sliding my behind over a boat, with a breeze zapping through my cheeks.

I always imagined the sea was nothing but a void that swallowed the land, even though it was easy to stare into it for its beauty. But never before have I stared at death in there. How did that animal come to swim beneath the Cornish waters? The seas harboured more mysteries than I ever thought.

'That was a shark!' Nia exclaimed.

'What do you expect?' the guide argued. 'There's jellyfish, dolphins and other escapees from the broken aquariums!'

'Or you may have tossed in something to add more "fun" to this experience! That thing could have killed her!'

'That wasn't us, I swear!'

I removed my goggles. The blue sky lit up with small clouds. The seagulls chuckled in a circle, as a tonne of pressure lifted from my chest.

I still believed that the sea was a tide of death, swallowing up the treasures that our ancestors had built years ago. Of course, we lost those treasures. We just have to make use of what else remains of this world.

I laughed out loud. 'It's awesome! We have to do that again!'

Either way, nowhere else in Britain could be any better.

Starry Night

A lockdown story by Ulrike Durán Bravo

Three terraced miners' cottages stand like a row of lonely teeth. They are part of a horseshoe cul-de-sac; gardens separated by fences, privets, and a granite hedge. Out of view, a dual carriageway is tucked behind a row of pines. Beyond, mineshafts scratch the scene. It is a warm spring evening and the occasional pipistrelle bat swoops down, taking no notice of the man-made borders. Quietness swirls in the air, interrupted by magpies chattering and gulls shrieking goodnight.

It is dusk and Estella is out with a torch and bucket, hunting for slugs, stooping over untidy vegetable patches. Straightening up, her shoulder clicks. She moves her head side to side, releasing the tension. Lifting her arms to stretch, she looks at the sky.

'Oh Marcus. *Me oyes? En las estrellas?* I like to think the stars are messengers, that they can sing to you the words

I say. I hope so, even if the only constellation that I can identify is *Las Tres Marías*.'

Estella releases the stretching position and wipes away a tear. The torch is still in her hand, throwing erratic light into the garden. Lashes of purple from bluebells and pink rhubarb stalks encircle her. She turns the torch off and stuffs it in her back pocket.

'You told me it's called Orion's Belt here. Always there, those three little stars, in every part of the world. As sure as the sound of the road: the cars whizzing by through the night-time air. Can you hear them? No. *Yo tampoco.* That's because for the first time since I arrived from Venezuela, there are no cars on the road.'

She stretches down and back up again. Then to one side and another.

'Ay-ay-ay...Stars, Marcus – I know you won't judge me,' she says, rolling her shoulders back. 'I used to confess – I haven't been back to church since your funeral. I was angry with God. It's not the same here, confessing in a language not my own.' She crosses herself and stands up straight.

She closes her eyes and says, 'Marcus, forgive me for I have sinned. I had people over for dinner last night.' A sigh of relief escapes her.

Penny next door paces up and down her recently cut lawn. She picks up plastic toys while slaloming trikes, trampoline and water-table. Her phone buzzes in her back pocket. As she checks the caller, the blue light from the phone lights up her face. It is ghostly and translucent; mascara smudged from the long day, darkening the circles under her eyes. She pauses, deciding whether to pick up. It's her friend.

Answering, she almost hisses down the phone: 'I mean, we're all doing our bit, aren't we, staying home. Not being funny, but I've sacrificed seeing my family all this time. It's for the greater good. So why should I put up with next door having a jolly old time of it when the rest of us are limited to Zoom. It's the old people – so irresponsible.'

She wedges her phone between her shoulder and ear, grabs the bottle of Pinot Grigio from the patio table. She holds the now full glass up against the sky and sees the first stars refract and shimmer in her drink.

Chloe, in the next garden along, sits on a swing tied to an old apple tree in the far corner. A tabby cat jumps up onto Chloe's lap. 'Oh hey – you know, dontcha? You get it, right?' She's swallowing her tears and sniffs a little. She wipes her nose and eyes, the redness hidden by the dark.

'Dad's such a puffwad, confiscating my phone.' The cat makes itself a little more comfortable, circling on Chloe's lap. She strokes it, and it gives her a little nudge with its head. 'Just because of those dance-moves I shared on TikTok.'

The cat hops off.

Chloe leaps up to dance provocatively humming a pop tune. She thinks to herself, *OK, I know I wasn't wearing that much, but what does he expect? I'm not a nun.* She shakes herself in rhythm to the song, while stewing over the argument. *He's so not in touch with the real world,* she wants to yell but stamps the ground instead. *The whole perverts-could-be-watching-this spiel is so yaw-awn. I was only having a little fun. I mean, if it weren't for lockdown, I'd be out at a party dancing and he wouldn't know.*

She slumps back down onto the swing in defeat and pushes off the ground hard. Now because he's furloughed and around all the time, he's supervising everything. When she swings back down, the cat is spooked and arches its back.

'Chill out,' Chloe tells her.

She thinks about the last party she went to. She had drunk too much, but not as much as her friend Maisie, who had vomited on the way home, and asked repeatedly if she thought Chris fancied her. That was before Chloe had got with Jodie. Parties made Jodie anxious, so she hadn't been again. She had learnt not to say 'chill out' to Jodie. It was offensive, apparently. That's why she relished saying it even more to her parents.

Now the cat looked offended too and flicked its tail. 'I didn't mean it like that, ok.' Chloe rolls her eyes. The moon rises, a waxing crescent, emitting a pale light.

Estella turns her attention to the slugs again. Pointing her torch into the thicket of her beds and patches. 'I'm lonely – ok? My family is on the other side of the world. I worry about them. It would be easier, Marcus, if you were still alive.'

She holds a slug up in disgust. She pokes its antennae so they withdraw and the slug curls in on itself. 'I'm here, safe but alone. Are you alone – slug? Do you care? Yaah, my kids tell me too, I should be careful, you know, my age…I have been careful my whole life. But look – no food or medicine in my country. Now everyone is ill and hungry. We don't know what's going to happen next and I cry every night. I will die without company. Like you, *babosa*.'

She acknowledges to herself that even before Covid she was lonely here. Speaking half to Marcus in the sky and half to the slug, 'You think any of these neighbours ever invited me for a beer? Or even that famous "nice cup of tea"? *Mi casa no es tu casa*, here.' This was not entirely fair, she knew. The family a couple of houses down had paid her to help Chloe practice Spanish. She had enjoyed the younger company, teaching her instruction through dance moves and showing her how to prepare arepas. 'You need to eat more,' she had told her then, and had slapped her hands on her own hips – 'you need *caderas* for dancing!'

She plops the slug into the bucket already filled with others, a medley of slime.

'You'd understand, Marcus. I worry that my sisters, children, grandchildren in Venezuela will get very ill; that they will not be able to afford living even with the money I send; no food anywhere. The restrictions are so much harsher. The military out to punish anyone who breaks the rules with beatings. My son and his family might have walked to another country. Chile or Peru. And then, when they can, here.' She adds, 'I don't even know why I'm telling you this. You know already, or you don't know anything at all. I want you to be here, to help me get through this.'

When the slugs don't distract her enough, Estella puts the bucket down, takes her phone out of her pocket and scrolls. She uses her index finger rather than her thumb due to her arthritis. She should have known better than letting her friends park outside her house. She should also know better than to check Facebook, to see the onslaught of comments on the post from the lady next door – on the local solidarity network group, no less. Penny had posted that her "irresponsible" neighbours at number 10, 15 and 27 all had people over at the weekend. Estella reads some of the comments on the post, which have now grown to forty-three.

'Pah – she probably thought an old foreign lady like me doesn't have social media. How does she think I keep in touch with all the family? Pigeons? Talking to the stars like now? I was using video-calls years ago...remember Skype? These Cornish, they even get funny about people from the next county...you know, all those jokes about crossing the Tamar – so don't blame me if I get a bit paranoid about what they think of me.'

Estella keeps grumbling to no-one in particular, 'If I was younger, I'd be commenting something rude on social media. I'm too old for this though. They will never understand. Do they think their government is following the rules? I bet the biggest parties are in Downing Street. My friend told me that Lawrence *como-se-llama* from the TV hosted over forty people in his mansion. The rules don't apply for the rich, they keep quiet about it is all. I know this, from my country.'

The police hadn't come. It had made Estella's heart race: traumatic memories of *carabineros* chasing her for not keeping to curfew. They had banged their pots then too, different reasons.

'Maybe, Marcus, you would disapprove. It was stupid, I did not mean to do anything that might affect paperwork...' She turns the phone off and puts it back in her pocket. Pointing the torch this way and that, she mutters to herself now, '*Vaya*, I need a break from social media.'

She picks up a particularly large slug and inspects it.

Then she throws it over the hedge, into next door's garden with surprising strength and vigour. 'I'd throw you all, *babositas*, if I didn't know that you'd come back,' she tells the slugs in the bucket.

Penny stops pacing and sits on a garden chair, with the phone still next to her ear. The glass stands precariously on the uneven ground, but she risks it, knowing that there is more wine on the table. She stands up again to wipe herself as she has sat in a wet patch. She decides it's not that bad and sits down again. She hears a clink when the slug lands in her drink. She looks down, to see the slug in the puddle of wine next to the glass.

'What the hell?' Penny whispers and looks around. No, the wine is not making me paranoid, she tells herself.

She takes the glass now, inspects the slug in it, and using the glass as a launching device, slings the slug back over the hedge. It doesn't make it and plops limply onto the grass.

'Yes, that's it,' she replies into the phone, 'I only did what I thought was right.'

Earlier, the lady next door had hissed 'Stasi' under her breath in the front garden. This had stung. Penny raises her voice now, almost shouting, holding the phone away from herself: 'It was my duty to call them out. Someone has to hold these people accountable. We want to know who to trust in the community.'

Chloe and Estella hear Penny's shouts over the fence.

Chloe giggles in surprise. Her awkward laugh floats into the air, dissolving into the dark.

Estella rolls her eyes and shrugs. She connects the loudspeaker to her phone and plays loud Latin American dance music. Take that, *cabrona*, she thinks while moving her body to the rhythms of her country.

Soon she dances alone, with the memory of her husband. A sudden fresh breeze from the Atlantic reminds her she is not in Caracas.

'For goodness sake,' Penny says, 'now she's playing loud music. Like there's a reason to celebrate.' Despite herself, she can't help tapping her feet to the Latin rhythms.

Penny climbs onto the trampoline and sits crossed-legged. Checking the battery life of her phone, she makes a few hmm noises before continuing to rant: 'And no-one in all of this has come to check how I am. Home-schooling the kids. Them not being able to see their grandparents. I'm doing everything in the house and then some.'

Her rising snippets of words drifting over the garden borders are met with Estella turning up the volume of music next door.

'The husband hiding on the computer all day. It's almost as if he has more work, working from home. But we're doing what we can. Luckily, I don't know anyone who's actually had it. It was meant to be my year. Getting back into work or education. And now this.' Where she had risen rigid with anger, she now collapses in on herself. All she wants is some affirmation from a friend, to be heard, to be told that she's doing the right thing.

Penny lies flat on the trampoline. Her muscles relax a little. Very tired, she listens to her friend while letting her eyes blur so the stars swirl in her vision. She makes approving noises every so often. The music fades and there's a lull in conversation so she says in a softer tone: 'I took an art-class with my kids yesterday on Zoom. Starry Night. You should try it, it's great. We learnt that it was all lines. He painted it when he was in a mental asylum. I think we feel like we are all in an asylum at the moment. Going mad...'

She pauses before talking again. 'Yes, yes, I know. I think the widow next door is a bit mad. It's not that I don't sympathise with her, I mean it must be awful to move to a country for your partner and then lose him. But the first few months she moved here, I heard her wailing every evening. Spotted an altar through the window too. I kept thinking I should check on her, but never got around to it. I didn't want to interrupt her mourning rituals. The children asked why she kept crying, and I had to explain. So awkward.'

She pauses for effect. 'Yeah sure, I'll send you the link – they said Van Gogh painted stuff that wasn't there. My art teacher always told me to draw what is actually there and not what I want there to be. I wasn't very good at that. I was always drawing what I wanted there to be. They did a good job, the kids. Better than the sodding rainbows I told them to draw. The youngest did an angry scribble. I know how she feels. But it meant that I had to paint a proper rainbow myself, to put in the window. In case the grandparents walk by.'

Chloe smiles when she hears the faint music from a couple of gardens down. 'See – nothing wrong with a bit of fun even when things are shit,' she says. Chloe's cat slinks back around her feet.

'Now what?' she wonders. She can't reply to Jodie. What if they'll think I'm ignoring them or something? She knows what they're like. She did try to ask dad whether she could send a message. She can't even email because mum's hogging the computer with her zoom yoga.

She pushes off to swing again, spreading her legs on the way down to avoid the cat. The cat starts and climbs up the tree. Chloe shakes her head at its pathetic reaction. She worries about Jodie, thinking how confusing it is working out all the gender stuff on your own. Chloe didn't mind what Jodie was, she willed them to be ok – and with Jodie always saying that they didn't know what to do without her, Chloe worried about offending them – not answering her phone. Jodie was touchy like that, takes it personally.

The cat comes back down the tree backwards. It finds a place to wash itself. Chloe sighs, 'Quarantine! What the actual -? Isn't that something that happened in the Middle Ages?' The cat stops and looks at her, its tongue sticking half out. 'Put your tongue back in, it's not that exciting,' Chloe tells it and pokes its tongue. The cat shifts and continues washing its other leg.

She had studied Romeo and Juliet last year. Wasn't that why the friar's letter never arrived? She wrote an essay about "Who was to blame for Romeo and Juliet's death?" Chloe secretly liked all that "star-crossed lovers" stuff but thought that blaming fate was a load of rubbish. Thinking about this now, Chloe leans forward to stroke the cat behind the ears. The cat leans into her and almost topples.

I know the answer now, she thinks. *It was the plague; it was quarantine. They couldn't have known that the city would shut.* If she could rewrite her essay, she'd put: 'Romeo and Juliet were human sacrifices to save the masses from filling the morgues. It was the fault of all the grown-ups having a lack of foresight – as always – too busy bickering to realise how it's affecting the kids.' Chloe smiles a bit, feeling pleased with her idea. She compares it to her dad taking her phone: what if she had a life-important urgent message to send? He doesn't even try to understand Jodie. When she tried to say about the pronouns, he rolled his eyes. It causes Jodie all sorts of anxieties, not being accepted, and if she doesn't keep in touch, it gets worse. 'Dad never takes me seriously,' she says out loud.

She had intended to cheer Jodie up with the video. Not only had it caused trouble with her parents – moments before her phone was confiscated, Jodie had messaged her, calling her a 'slut'. Chloe wanted to make it right, and now she couldn't.

She picks up the cat and cuddles it, 'but you understand, dontcha? I can't wait to get out of here. Explore what's in the world. Go and dance Salsa somewhere like Costa Rica, like Estella showed me when she helped me with my Spanish. Now that feels like it might never happen. Like I will be stuck with my parents forever.'

Chloe huffs, and then takes out a ready rolled joint from her dungaree pocket. She lights it. The cat looks at her and shrinks away from the smell, jumping off. 'What? Don't look at me like that. The wind is blowing away from the house. And you can't tell me that they...,' she looks at her house, 'were all goody-two-shoes when they were younger. I've seen the photos. And the other neighbours won't know. Except maybe the lady at the end – but she

211

won't say anything.' An owl hoots. Chloe coughs at the first inhale.

Estella and Penny hear the cough and look in Chloe's direction, as if able to see through their garden borders.

Having finished her phone conversation, Penny says loudly into the night, 'And that is why, we should stay safe. Go home. Paint rainbows. Clap.'

She sniffs the air and huffs under her breath, 'That's what I've got to look forward to then with mine – all those teenage hormones...'

She thinks about whether she should tell Chloe's parents, and how wrong it would be to ask Chloe to share a bit of that weed. She dismisses that thought immediately.

Estella is holding a cup of tea in one hand and a jug of brine in the other.

It is dark now, and the stars in the sky are blinking. The moon has risen omitting a yellow glow like a faraway streetlight. Estella opens her eyes and stares up into heaven and whispers, 'Oh Marcus. One cough – reverberates through the air – into our lives. To stop. And ripple through us,
dripping, into our lives to
sep-
ar-
ate
us.'

She thinks back to the last time she didn't hear the roads. She'd been in town and thought the snow *hermoso*. Marcus said about getting home quick. The atmosphere changed; snowflakes not "dancing" anymore but flocking, heavy. Later, people were stuck on the roads, abandoning cars, taking two hours to drive eight miles...

She read recently snowflakes absorb the vibrations in the air. She wanted to tell Marcus, but hesitated to puncture stillness with her words

'You always knew what to do. Can you tell me now?' Estella says after all. 'There are no cars on the road tonight because they told us to stay home. I broke the rules. It felt good, and now it feels bad. At my age, I'm supposed to be *wise*. Ha! Past the moon I can't point out Venus, Jupiter or Mars. I'll never know anything for sure. I wonder, will there ever be a cure?'

She looks away while she pours the brine into the bucket of slugs and looks away. '*Pobresitas*. It's not your fault you're so disgusting and eat all my plants.'

Penny listens to a sound in the distance: 'Ah there's a car. It sounds like it's driving 200 miles an hour down the dual carriage way. Because it can. I wouldn't mind doing that. To get something out my system...' She reaches for the bottle of wine and downs it in one long desperate gulp.

Chloe lets the joint smoulder out, before burying it in a flowerbed. She pops some chewing gum into her mouth and shoos the cat away – 'Off you go, explore, chase mice.'

The cat trots off into the darkness, slithering through a hole in the hedge.

Estella picks up the bucket of dying slugs and takes another sip from her tea. Even darker now, the sky is curdling with swirls of the milky way.

She imagines surfing the milky way, floating away from all the problems on this earth. It would be cold, like the Atlantic – not like the warm Caribbean waves of her youth. She worries out loud: 'What will become of us? Will we be ok? Before we all go mad. No cars, no planes above... bird song we can finally hear again. That is the good thing. Poor slugs.'

She knows, despite it all, she wouldn't want to be anywhere else right now. She reminds herself she is lucky to be here, to walk by the coast and in safety every day.

She crosses herself '*Dios perdóname*', looks up at the sky and hurls the entire contents of the bucket over the hedge.

Then she returns back indoors, not looking back.

Not even when Penny screams.

It is a warm Spring evening and the occasional pipistrelle bat swoops down, taking no notice of man-made borders.

The satellites that slide and swirl between the stars transmit that the global Covid-19 death rate has risen to over 300,000 globally; that a police officer kept his knee on a man's neck for nine minutes in the U.S.; that militants storm a hospital in Afghanistan.

Up above, Orion's Belt is twinkling.

Love Birds

by Kate Barden

A pair of red-legged Cornish choughs soared in the up-draught above the playground of St. Berriona. With their own graceful rhythm, they didn't need the chanting voices below to keep them in time.

Monday for danger.

Tuesday kiss a stranger.

Wednesday for a letter.

Thursday for something better.

Friday for sorrow.

Saturday see your lover tomorrow.

Sneeze on Sunday morning fasting,

Enjoy your true love for everlasting.

The sleek couple dipped and turned, their ageless choreography unknowingly mirrored by the dancing children. They swooped, disappearing beneath the cliff edge, calling their love to each other over the Atlantic.

*

The oily voice of Jonti James poured through the speaker. '*It's eight o'clock, it's Monday, and we're in the "Danger Zone"!*' As the bombastic mid-80s lyrics encouraged sleepy Kernow out of bed, Alex groped under his pillow for a tissue. He sneezed violently. Taken by surprise by the high-velocity nasal blast, he sat bolt upright. He sneezed again and then once more. He fumbled around his bedside cabinet, wobbled last night's mug of tea, and knocked his phone to the floor, but no tissue appeared. In desperation, he grabbed the edge of his duvet and sneezed forcefully into the feathery cotton cover. He sighed, blinking sticky eyes into the early morning bedroom light, and pushed the duvet off with his feet. 'Ugh.'

Shower, clothes, coffee, briefcase, hat. Monday; an Australian leather cowboy hat sort of day. He plucked the Akubra from his neatly arranged hat-collection shelf and admired the carefully buffed sheen. Headgear on, and with a simultaneous thumb-click, index-finger point, nod and a wink, Alex commanded his virtual personal assistant, 'Awena, off.'

Outside his front door, Alex breathed in the jaded town air, challenging it with his optimistic walk to work.

'Morning Gwen. Croissant today, please.' Alex was feeling continental. As much as he enjoyed his daily pattern, he enjoyed pastry more, and every weekday he endeavoured to sample a different breakfast confectionery. Today was a croissant day.

The morning routine flowed as easily as the Tamar, a seamless and unconscious regimen from waking to work. Same bakery, same faces, same journey. The daily pastry washed down with Cornish bodega takeaway tea. Life was as it should be... fine.   All was fine.   Just fine.

The people of the exhausted Penwithian town walked to work, Monday to Friday, Monday to Friday, Monday to Friday. The people of the town wore the same clothes, followed the same route, nodded the same greetings... and everything was... fine.

Alex knew what was what. He was secure in his schedule. Healthy in his habits. And nourished by his normal. He thrived on control, repetition and stability. Mechanically whistling, Alex waited at his usual crossing place. The usual bus had stopped to his right, and he prosaically acknowledged the familiar street cleaner pushing his reliable community service cart.

Like a bullet from an invisible rooftop sniper, something struck the top of Alex's head. His Monday hat was snatched and he was thrown off balance. As he stumbled, he raised his arms instinctively to protect himself, still clutching his croissant. He felt razor-sharp talons carve into his head and a rivulet of sticky warm blood trickle down his cheek. He was aware that this was a bird. A ferocious, black bird. Not a blackbird, but a large bird that was black, about the size of a crow. The spikes of bird feet tangled in his hair, pulling as if to scalp him. 'Aaargghhh...!' Alex frantically waved his arms, flapping like an enormous bird himself. Dark hooks seized the pastry from his hand and a confetti of flaky crumbs wafted down, landing like dandruff on his coat. Not content with taking Alex's breakfast, the bird swooped again. Alex smacked at it, swatting it away with a slap to its head. Again it swooped, a black dart on target for the bullseye. It pecked Alex's head and ears drawing spots of blood with its pointed beak. As it flapped around his face, Alex thought he saw flashes of red and, more than terrified, he grabbed for a handful of feathers. He snatched a wing, caught it and swung it around, turning himself in a circle, dragging the bird to the ground. It fought him, clawing, scratching, snapping with its beak. For a second it was free and made a desperate attempt to fly, but Alex had it again, this time by its scrawny red legs. He drew his arm back and smacked the bird hard against the pavement. He did it again and saw the bird flop, glossy black skull hanging limp against the granite kerb.

Alex puffed out his cheeks and blew. He stood motionless for a moment, letting a bead of sweat or snot... or was it blood?... drip from his nose. Tentatively, he bent his head towards the bird. A shiny eye stared back, hypnotically drawing Alex closer. Slowly he began to crouch, closer, closer, so close that he could feel the decreasing warmth of its ebbing life. A sudden twitch and without thinking, Alex jolted upright, raised his foot and stamped on its head, crushing its delicate skull like glass.

'It's 8 am; it's Tuesday; it's old blue eyes, "Strangers in the night".' Once again, the daily dictat diarrhoea of Jonti James leaked into the room.

Alex stirred, coming round to Frank crooning about eyes being inviting. He sneezed, groped around the bed for a tissue and found one under his pillow. More sneezing. He blew his nose, rubbed his eyes and felt the scabs on his face. A dot-to-dot of dried blood, a patterned reminder of yesterday's frenzied attack. 'Hardly lovers, Frank,' he said out loud to the radio. Not one to be put off from a routine,

Alex kicked off his duvet.

Shower, clothes, coffee, briefcase, ah, no hat today.

'Awena, off.'

Alex grabbed his umbrella, proud of his forethought for the potential protection. As he closed the front door, he paused. Was that... children singing?

'Morning Gwen. Saffron today, please.' Today there was safety in the traditional.

As he bit into the soft yellow bun, Alex looked around cautiously for any aggressive, hungry birds. His anxiety levels rose, a feeling he hadn't had since the changing rooms for school swimming lessons. It wasn't the bigger boys teasing him that was causing him to worry this morning. He almost wished it was. On high alert, Alex approached his usual crossing place. The usual bus had stopped to his right, the usual street cleaner was pushing his community service cart; everything was reassuringly innocuous.

Then, a sudden screech of brakes, a horn sounding like a shout, or maybe it was a shout. A thud. The circadian people walking to work suddenly stopped walking. A scream rang through the grey morning air. Alex was jolted out of his adrenaline freeze by a fellow commuter shoving him towards the road. 'She's been hit...'

The woman had been knocked down by a car overtaking the waiting bus. She lay, unmoving, in front of Alex. The bite of saffron bun dropped from his mouth. His Safety in the Workplace Emergency Aid training kicked in. He dropped his umbrella and the paper bag with his half-eaten bun and rushed to kneel by the woman's side.

'Hello. Hello. Can you hear me? What's your name?'

As a crowd gathered, Alex became the superhero he always knew he was. He pinched the woman's nose, gently tipped her head back to open her air'ways and with Staying Alive playing in his mind, he moved in, ready to blow into her mouth. He hesitated for a second, struck by her beautiful red lips.

A few breaths in, the woman stirred, her eyelids twitching. Alex leaned back onto his heels and let the paramedics take over.

He stood up and brushed dirt from his knees. He felt something scratchy in his throat. He rubbed the back of his neck, coughed and gagged. The scratchy throat troubled him. As the crowd dispersed and the ambulance drove away, Alex put his fingers inside his mouth and reached down, urging against the unusual sensation. He urged again, coughed and wriggled out a shiny, wet, black feather.

*

Jonti James burst into the room. '*It's 8 in the am, it's Wednesday, it's an oldie, it's The Box Tops with "The Letter".*' Alex had forgotten to cancel Awena. The children singing that bloody nursery rhyme had woken him early, and having had a fit of sneezing, he was now sitting in his towelling dressing gown at the kitchen table reading a newspaper. The sneezing seemed to have become part of his morning routine and he had a reassuring box of man-size tissues in easy reach. He blew his nose and let The Box Tops explain how his baby couldn't live without him anymore. Something caught his eye. A square of newspaper content made him sit taller and puff his chest, proud.

Thank you for saving me yesterday, whoever you are. Meet me tomorrow. Celtic Cafe. I have something for you. Palores.

Palores. Palores. Pa...lor...es. Alex rolled the name around inside his mouth, like a boiled sweet. He sucked it, moving his tongue clockwise from cheek to cheek, enjoying the sensation as he remembered her scarlet Cupid bow slightly open, his lips covering hers.

'Awena, off.'

Alex cut Jonti James short before he could finish his beige comment on the inclement Cornish weather.

Shower. Clothes. Coffee. Briefcase. Hat. Wednesday; a cheeky, herringbone Newsboy cap sort of day.

With a spring in his step and the taste of ruby lipstick in his mind, Alex locked the front door. And a chough circled in the cloudy sky.

'*It's 8 of the morning clock; it's Thursday; it's D Ream; come on, "things can (surely) only get better".*' Alex chuckled at Jonti

James. Today, everything was funny. Today everything was light. And good. For the first time ever, Alex had taken a day off work. He was light and felt... felt... better than fine.... free. He sang along, '... yeah... better... dum de dum...' and rather than worrying about not being at work, Alex was thrilled. Yes, he felt thrilled.

He patted his smooth chin with Surf Spritz, 'reliving the spirit of Poldark' as instructed on the cologne label. He swung his arm as if scything corn, mimicking Aidan Turner, and undid another button on his shirt. Leaning towards his bathroom mirror for the final check of his already twice-cleaned teeth, he noticed a black speck. He ran an index finger over his bottom gum and felt a small sharp point poking out between his lower middle teeth. He leaned further towards the mirror and, with finger and thumb, tried to pick the black speck out. It was just too tiny to trap between the ends of his neat fingernails. He rummaged in the under-the-sink cupboard, brushing aside creams for athlete's foot and haemorrhoids, miniature scissors for trimming eyebrows and a nasal hair trimmer. No sign of any floss, but, ah! tweezers! Squinting into the mirror, Alex caught the black point between tweezer ends and pulled. It wasn't the tiny corner of a piece of escaped toast that he was expecting. It wasn't a rogue sesame seed, hidden from last night's Chinese takeaway. As he pulled, Alex saw reflected in the mirror he was pulling out a glossy wet black feather.

'Awena, off.'

Celtic Cafe was a small, cheerless bistro. The ongoing gentrification of the town had led to a flurry of aspirationally continental openings. Metal framed tables and chairs sat expectantly on pavements ready to be adorned with cafe au lait and Portuguese pastel de Nata. Alex stood unsure of protocol. His easy free feeling from earlier dissipated as nerves took over. What was her name? Polly? Pauline? Dolores? He started to shuffle around, looking in the window of the electrical shop next door. He caught his face reflected in the glass and remembered the feather. Weird. He checked his teeth. He turned to see if there was any sign of the mysterious inviter. And he was struck in the face. A blaze of feathers flapped around his head, and before he could cover his eyes, he caught a glimpse of burnished black.

'Hello,' a soft voice said.

Alex lowered his hands, (how long had he been standing with his head in his hands?) and raised his rheumy eyes.

It was her. Her lips. Attached to her face. Like a small, perfect, red sweet-pea. The sweet pea moved.

'Are you OK?'

The simple sentence floated and hovered in anticipation of his answer.

Alex became aware that he was standing, mouth hanging slightly open, arms by his side. In his mind he looked like an orangutan. Sweet-pea mouth moved again.

'Shall we go inside? It's a bit chilly.'

'Oh yes, yes, sorry, yes, let's go inside. Hello.'

Coffee. Cake.

Glass of wine.

Pizza.

Coffee.

Cinema. Lager. Ice cream.

Dancing. Lager. Wine. Wine. Rum. Whiskey. Sambuca. Tequila.

Alex had never been a big drinker. He didn't like feeling out of control. Or rather, he didn't like feeling out of control in the past. Now, today, this evening, he was very much enjoying being out of control. This woman, this incredible woman, Palores, with her incredible lips and incredible legs, she was the one in control. He let her decide where they would go, what they would do, and when they would dance. He was her puppet and her puppy. He had never met anyone like her. He hadn't actually met anyone ever, not romantically, anyway. But he knew that this wasn't just a one-off. He knew that this was the one. He knew he had met the woman who...

Suddenly her lips were on his and he felt his groin pulsate. They had been dancing and in a smooth, graceful movement like a bird gliding on the wing, she had moved close enough to delicately press her flower-blossom mouth onto his. There was no music, no flashing disco lights, no people. There was a swirling and turning blackness enveloping them both, a vortex of passion wrapping around them, transporting them to an island of ecstasy...

Alex opened his eyes and took a second to realise that he was standing in the middle of the dance floor, arms hanging by his sides, mouth open. Panic gripped his chest and he looked frantically from side to side. Where was she? How long had he been standing here looking again like an abandoned primate? Through the smoke-machine haze and flickering strobes, he saw her. He saw her red lips, her black dress, her red tights .... red tights? He must have missed those earlier. Long red legs... Alex shook himself, reached for her hand and they walked outside the club. She signalled for a taxi, kissed him one more time, and was gone. Alex stared into the night, coughed and puked up a long, wet, black feather.

'It's 8 am, it's Friday, it's David Bowie and "Sorrow".' Alex's head hurt. He sneezed and it hurt his eyes and his ears. A semi-deflated rubber doll wearing a sticky black and red feather boa sagged against the end of his bed, his damp pants draped over her shoulder. Jonti James annoyingly chirruped the latest travel news for the Duchy over the top of Bowie nasally expressing how much sorrow he had in his life. Alex didn't know where the hell he was, or what had happened and if Jonti hadn't told him it was Friday, he wouldn't have a clue what day it was either.

'Awena. What's on my calendar?'

'Hello, Alex. At 11 am today, you are getting married. Congratulations Alex.'

The children of St. Berriona sang... and Sorrow filled the room.

'8 am! Wake up Boo! It's Saturday! Anyone know who Boo Radley was?' Jonti James loved a bit of trivia. Alex sneezed twice and patted underneath his pillow for a tissue. Nothing there. He patted further across the bed expecting to pat the slim shoulder of his beautiful wife. Instead, he patted a perfect Palores body-shaped shallow dent.

He sneezed again and sat up.

'Palores?'

Sneeze.

'You ok, my bird?'

Sneeze.

'Goddamn this sneezing! I must change these bloody pillows... hypoallergenic....'

Over The Boo Radleys explaining how Boo must wake up, Alex heard the sound of retching.

'Palores?'

He blew his nose and when he lifted his head from his tissue, he saw Palores standing in the doorway, her paler-than-normal skin making her lips look even more red.

She held a small plastic rectangle out for him to see. Two blue lines.

'Alex, wake up, it's a beautiful morning...!'

'Good morning Kernow! It's eight o'clock, it's Sunday, it's The Shirelles, and really, "Will you still love me tomorrow?"'

Alex didn't know if he could bear to see the love of his life in so much pain. They had been awake since the early hours pacing the lounge and then the hallway and then back to the lounge. Palores was at this moment sitting on the toilet in the downstairs bathroom. He could hear her moaning. Approaching the bathroom tentatively he asked, 'Can I get you anything my darling?'

He'd run out of helpful things to do. There was water and towels. And an iPod of her favourite music. And lavender essential oil which made him sneeze. He'd made sandwiches, which she'd pecked at, and he'd fed her tiny crumbs of cake. She'd had sips of water from a cup he held lovingly, secretly wishing it would all be over soon.

She emerged from the bathroom and, holding the walls of the hallway, shuffled to the bedroom.

'I'm just going to lie here for a minute.'

'Oh, ok. I'll make a coffee. And shall I get a pastry? Saffron bun? You like those…'

'Yes. No. Whatever.'

She closed the bedroom door behind her leaving Alex alone, helpless, his stomach fluttering.

He walked around the flat for a bit. What were those bloody children doing singing in school on a Sunday? He went to the toilet. He finally settled in the kitchen, Jonti James keeping him company, an uninvited guest, a Banquo filling the empty air with Sunday morning easy-listening songs of love.

He made coffee. He warmed a Danish pastry in the microwave. She liked the sultanas in those.

Nervously, Alex stood outside the bedroom door holding his gifts. His offering to the goddess. There was no noise coming from behind the door. Jonti James was delivering a prayer to the empty kitchen and across the airwaves of Cornwall. Alex felt that he was perhaps having a religious experience but then decided he was probably just very tired. It had been an exhausting week.

Empowered by an espresso, he gave himself a shake and pushed open the bedroom door.

Palores was sitting in bed, surrounded by the duvet and pillows. She looked tiny and delicate, completely encircled by the plump feathery bedding.

Cradled in her arms was a bundle of soft blanket. She lowered her head and kissed the precious gift.

The Danish pastry slid from the plate as Alex stood open-mouthed. Awe exuded from him as he took in the scene before him. His beautiful wife, her black hair over her shoulders, her bright red lips never failing to transfix him. Her strength and power. The utter awesomeness of birth. Alex put the coffee cups down, stepped over the fallen pastry, and breathless, whispered, 'Palores.'

Standing next to the bed, he tenderly moved her hair from her eyes and kissed her forehead. He had eyes only for this wondrous beauty.

'Alex.' Palores held the warm blanket up for him to hold, for him to see what miracle had occurred.

Nervously, gently, unaware that he was holding his breath, he took the precious bundle. He drew his eyes slowly away from his wife and carefully moved the corner of the blanket.

He wasn't in control of the bizarre howl that issued up from his bowel, ravaged his stomach, and was ejaculated from his throat.

Dropping the blanket, Alex stood in disbelief holding his beautiful newborn...

egg.

In the kitchen, Jonti James laughed.

The St. Berriona children's voices floated in through the bedroom window.

And a pair of red-legged Cornish choughs danced in the Kernow sky.

Dusk at Retorrick Mill

by Emily Charlotte Ould

The sun threw shadows over wildflowers at Retorrick Mill.

'Right, that's it.' Henry wiped sweat from his brow while, heaving a sigh, he chucked his rake down by the soil at his feet. 'Bloody knees can't take it no more.'

At this hour, dusk was settling fast over the ploughed fields. The light fell through the trees, dappling the branches like the freckles on his sun-drenched skin. He plonked down against the tree stump he'd cut in the spring and struck a match to light his tobacco pipe, watching as the smoke swirled its way up to the warm September sky, and a cough rattled in his throat.

He remembered a dusk just like this, fifty years ago. The breeze had been sweet then and the honeysuckle strong enough to taste on the tip of his tongue. He remembered the hedgerows and how they'd gleamed green in the fading summer light. He'd cut those same hedges down to size many years since, with a heavier song in his heart than the one he could hear the birds singing now.

Henry reached into his pocket, running his fingers over what laid there, feeling a shaky tremor run through his body as he held them. He pulled them free. One, two, three things. No bigger than his thumbnail, but full of colour in swirls of white, orange and blue. He liked to think of them as the colours of the clouds, the sun and the sea.

The elements between him, and her.

His Hattie.

He squeezed the marbles tight. They were Hattie's grandmother's, and the most precious things she'd ever owned.

'Don't go,' he'd begged her.

It had been a Friday, that night before she left. Her hair had tumbled down in auburn waves and the white cotton of her skirt was marked with dirt, but he could still feel the weight of her body against his like it was only moments ago.

Sometimes, he wished he'd gone with her.

'But you know I have to,' she'd said, standing in front of him after their tight embrace, exactly ten steps away from the wildflowers at the edge of the path. 'You know it as well as I do. I can't stay, Henry.'

'But we could have a life – here.'

She'd hugged him tight.

Henry remembered that day as sorely as he loved the land he worked on. How the sun shone, how the breeze swelled in the late summer heat, and how his heart broke.

He'd walked along the dusty trail to Retorrick Mill

with her kiss still on his lips, while she rode the buggy to Plymouth at dawn, her family all around her, to find a better life.

The rattle of the wheels rolling away still drifted through his dreams.

Forever sixteen, her memory stayed with him at every single breath, and when he thought of her on days like this, his chest seized with pain.

Taking a long, slow drag on his tobacco pipe, he rested an elbow on his knee, worn out from another long day's work, and watched the dusk settle into the valley, slowing the beat of his heart. The pain subsided after a while. He had to let it pass. The folks down in St Mawgan would be settling into their evenings by now. He thought of them and smiled faintly, thinking of Tom and Dawn Bridges who both lived in Hattie's old cottage these days instead.

'I'm sorry,' she whispered, her freckled cheek soft against his. The setting sun was warm on their skin.

'I'm sorry too,' Henry replied, before pulling away to look at her face. He didn't dare let go of her. She smiled at him; he only wished he could smile back, but his heart was too full of sorrow to do anything but weep.

'Now, see here, don't cry. Don't cry, Henry.' She wiped his tears with her embroidered handkerchief, stitched with her initials in periwinkle blue: H.B.

He closed his left hand around hers, breathing in the deep scent of lavender that always reminded him of evenings out in the field with her by his side.

'This isn't goodbye after all,' she told him. 'We'll still write to each other. So many letters. I'll never stop so long as you let me.'

'I'd write you a thousand letters if it'd only make you stay, maid.' He kissed her hand. She looked down.

'I should go.' She looked towards the sunset, before letting her eyes fall on Henry once more. 'Papa will be waiting ... But you will write, won't you? Promise me.'

'Course I will.' This time, he did smile, and she held his face in her hands until he felt them slipping away. As she did, he closed his eyes.

In seconds, Henry heard her footsteps fall away, her shoes scuffing the dusty ground as she made her way towards a new life – a life apart from him. He'd never hold her in his arms again.

'Hattie?' She spun round, tears sparkling in her eyes. Henry looked at her one last time. 'Make sure he looks after you, won't you? Whoever he is. Eventually. When you get there. You got that?'

She just nodded and smiled through her tears. 'I will, Henry. You too.'

He laughed. 'Ain't no maid for me 'cept you, Hattie.'

Instantly, she was running back and jumped wildly into his arms. He lifted her off the ground and pulled her close.

'I love you,' she whispered into his ear. His knees shook.

'Love you too, girl.' He held her tight. 'Now go on. Before I take you up in my arms and bleddy never let 'ee go.'

'I wish you wouldn't,' she whispered.

Her words were too much to bear.

With a delicate urgency, his lips brushed, then

melded, with hers. Their mouths were hot and wet from all the tears. He kissed her like never before and she ran her hands through his hair, throwing caution to the wind. If this was the last moment they ever had, it had to be worth something. She'd never been kissed like this before, and he wondered if she ever would be again.

'Keep these safe for me?' she said when they finally drew apart. She handed him three marbles in a buckskin pouch. As it dropped into his palm, she closed her small fingers around his.

'I will.' He nodded, then looked at her. 'Of course I will.'

'I really should go now.' She sniffed, then smiled before kissing him on the cheek one last time. 'Goodbye, Henry.'

'Goodbye, my girl.'

The next dawn, Henry heard the rattle of the wagon carting its passengers off to Plymouth, where they'd be docking on a ship departing for South Australia. It would take them a whole ten weeks to get there, but he knew she wouldn't have the luxury to change her mind.

He could still hear her father barking the orders to leave, slapping the mule's backside as he went. 'Come on now,' he said. 'Better get moving if we're off to find a new life. Leave this sodding land of beggars behind.'

As the wagon left, Henry tried to catch Hattie's eye. There she sat in her Sunday best, half hidden in the tangle of limbs belonging to her brothers and sisters. Before the wagon vanished, getting smaller and smaller in the distance, he saw her look back at him, one last time, and waved.

She was made for grander things, his Hattie, to beyond where he could go. He wished her all the luck in his heart.

Now, he rolled the marbles back and forth in his palm, immersed in the coolness of their touch while the rest of his body felt numb. They looked the same as the very day she'd given them to him. He laid them on the tree stump, filled with the same number of rings as the years that she'd been gone.

He thought of how much he'd wished he could go with her, but it was never on the cards. Someone had to stay and look after the mill and his father always said it had to be him. It was the family way; the eldest son took over the business. Looking back, he wished he had not just stayed but fought too. Fought against the tide of their future, and his past. Fought to be with Hattie, no matter what. But time had stretched on; his lungs got worse the older he became, and now he was here.

He still had her letters. Thumbed them carefully, every now and then, when he felt his heart could bear it, usually when the nights were too long. We'll still write to each other. *So many letters. I'll never stop so long as you let me.*

Dear Henry,

Australia is warm and the people here are all so friendly. From what we see of them anyway. Pa doesn't like us to spend too much time socialising and prefers us to work, save some money for the family, so we can thrive and prove that Cornish people are honest and hardworking, diamonds in the rough so he likes to call us. I think people can tell how hard he works just by looking at him. You remember how stern he used to be with you? I hope you're looking after yourself and keeping yourself busy, not just with work but people too.

How is the mill? I do miss it. On grey days, I long for the hills back home and the gentle lapping of the water on our toes from the river before we crossed to St Mawgan. I remember walking with you across the bridge beside the school. It doesn't seem that long ago we were that small too, playing together without a care for the future. Do you remember those days? Everything here is so flat and full of wild animals you'd never believe. As soon as I lay down at night, or sit still after a long day, it's all I can think about. You, and home.

I miss you. Please write soon. Tell me everything.

Yours,

Hattie.

Yet, once she'd married, as he knew she always would, to set up life with a family of her own, those letters had become sparse until they were few and far between.

Dear Henry,

I hope you're doing well and taking care of yourself. Life here is quite good. Pa is making decent money these days and even has enough to buy a new cow and a goat to keep us in good health, so we don't have to rely on the hospitality of our neighbours anymore. Jane has started school now and enjoys it very much. She's forever telling us all about her new friends and all the exciting things she is learning.

I feel it is only right to tell you, Henry, that I've made new friends too. A boy called Thomas calls for me every now and then and Pa seems to think he is serious about his intentions. He's given us his blessing. He is quite sensible and his family are in the same business as Pa, so our worlds are the same. I think you'd like him. His family emigrated here from England too, though he was so young when they got here that he hardly remembers much about it at all.

I hope you are well, Henry, and that life is treating you well and the mill is going strong. Write back to me, won't you? I always look forward to hearing about what's happening at home, and about you.

All my best wishes,

Hattie.

She married shortly after. And Henry dealt with it the only way he knew how: working the land and tending to the mill. The months dragged by, always giving way to winter when the world seemed wrapped in cold. The thing that kept him going, however, was that she never did stop writing, even then. But it was wrong, Henry thought, to love a woman so desperately when she belonged to another, so he stoically left them unopened. Kept them safe inside a hessian cloth at the mill cottage, still stamped and pressed, tucked inside a biscuit tin they'd once taken on a picnic together, back when the air still swelled with the heat of Cornish summer and the breeze smelled of honeysuckle, when their future still lay before them, unwritten and entirely their own.

Dear Henry ...

He'd never know what laid inside.

An old man now – and with Hattie long gone – he stretched his weary knees, taking a drag on his pipe, and stood. With one last look at the orange, white and blue marbles – sun, sky and sea – he tilted his cap and left them there, walking away, back to his cottage. The mill had ground the life out of him; his own father gone long ago, and with no children to pass it down to, he was the last of the line.

Reaching the cottage, he shuffled inside the bowed doorway, closed it, and sighed. 'Enough ... enough of that,' he said and leaned his head against the low door. His cough rattled as he made his way to the bedroom in the cottage he'd grown up and grown old in.

The dusk slowly dwindled and grew dark as his brain gave way to sleep. And, while the nightjar sang, his body finally surrendered to the cold, and to time.

Filling the Silence
by Anita D Hunt

Blog post for the webpage:
Dear Deaf Diary.
February 2023

Today I wanted to throw the damn clock across the room. But I didn't. I'd only have to buy another one and that would cost money I can't spare. I took my frustration out by thumping the pillow instead. Several times.

Every Monday starts the same. It's a shame I can't always experience days like I had at the weekend, but it's back to the daily grind again, for now.

The pillow vibrates to wake me up and doesn't stop until I take out the alarm clock and thump the off switch. No more lazy snooze buttons and dozing back off for another few blissful minutes. No more Pirate FM to ease me gradually into the day either. It is the music I miss the most. The reassuring noise in an otherwise empty house to give me the illusion that I'm not alone.

It was too early: I shouldn't have stayed awake so long last night and I just didn't want to go out today. Didn't want to have to face the stares and the ignorance and the 'oh, never minds' when I can't understand what on earth someone is trying to say to me. In the end they give up and go and talk to someone who can hear them. I guess I can't blame them too much. I was just the same when I was a hearing person, too busy and too exasperated to think about how my actions would make them feel.

I changed when I started losing my hearing. Slowly and because I had to. If I wanted to have a conversation I had to adapt and find a way that I could be understood.

Stumbling into the kitchen I filled the kettle and flicked it on to boil. I used to have a whistling kettle that sat on the hob. It was really cute; cream with black spots. I have always had a penchant for the quaint, kitsch look and that little kettle summed up my tastes perfectly. It had to go though. It boiled dry too many times when I went to the loo and forgot about it. It's safer with an electric kettle but not half as much fun. I often feel that, along with my hearing and the whistling kettle, a lot of the fun has evaporated from my life.

Evaporated? Boiled dry kettle? Get it? I'm sorry, I have to make my own jokes up as I go along. People stopped including me in their banter when it took too long to explain the punchline. It's never as funny once you've explained it ten times. I let them off quite often, smile, nod and laugh in what I think are the right places. They feel great, I feel like an idiot. Oh yes, I'm the great enabler, although Freddie's great pretender fits just as well.

I love Queen. Well, I used to. I was a total soft rock chick, Meat Loaf, Bon Jovi, Bryan Adams, Genesis, The Eagles... anything with a great driving beat. The '80s were brilliant for the rock scene. I would drive home from work, put 'Pure Soft Metal' on the cassette deck, whack the volume up and sing along full blast. I remember working in the local pub, dealing with the drunks and the idiots who thought that just because I was a barmaid, I was up for it. To belt out a bit of Summer of '69 was sure to vanquish the angry demons that had taken lodgings in my mind during my shift. No doubt that was where my hearing loss started, but if I knew then what I know now, would I change it? Possibly not. It was fun and I needed to drown out my own tone-deaf voice. I was young and knew I was invincible. You can never change the past, just try and make the most of the present and where your choices have brought you.

I took a basic sign language course that I found on the internet. It was really basic, but I learnt the alphabet and a few key words to start me off. You know the thing: my name is Janice; I live in Cornwall. They didn't teach me any swear words which is usually the first thing I get asked when people see me signing now. It's like that's the only thing that matters in conversation – how to tell someone to get lost when they're annoying you. The other one is for how to say hello. To be fair, the look I get when I wave at them is quite funny as they realise they use that sign themselves so often.

I couldn't afford to take any further courses though. Have you seen how much they cost? If it wasn't for the fact that I had to learn it for my own purposes, I certainly wouldn't have carried on with it. My old self would have just had fun spelling out swear words. In practice though, fingerspelling takes up a lot of time and is just not practical for a conversation. When I was a hearing person, it never occurred to me that deaf people would have to pay for the privilege of communication. I was also shocked to learn that parents of deaf-born children don't get free sign language lessons either. I don't have children, but I can still be shocked at the thought of not being able to talk with them without shelling out a load of cash first.

I bought a few books; I found a British Sign Language app; I started finding tutorials on YouTube. It wasn't easy. At the beginning, I thought about finding some clubs for deaf people. But I was worried that I would upset them with my ineptitude. That they wouldn't want me there because I wasn't born deaf, that I would look like an idiot and not know what to say because my knowledge of sign language was so stupid. As my hearing degenerated further, my old so-called friends stopped phoning me for a chat, stopped including me in their nights out, stopped being my friends, stopped suggesting I turned my hearing aids up so I could hear them better. As if I was the only one who had to adjust my communication methods. Newsflash, I'm deaf, shouting louder at me doesn't work either, and no, I don't lipread. Too many words look the same to me and without the context of the sentence I'm totally lost. Equally, the GP surgery sending me a phone number to call during Covid in the event that my hearing aid batteries ran out...Yeah... genius.

Eventually, I pulled up my big girl pants and contacted a local deaf group on Facebook. They were lovely. So embracing of me and my struggles. I walked into the room full of people, thinking I was going to find it really difficult to be able to talk to them. I needn't have worried.

Tasmin saw me standing in the doorway and came straight over and introduced herself before ushering me to the first group of people. She explained to them that it was my first time there. I couldn't remember the last time I had felt so included, so quickly. When I looked around the room, I could see that the rest of the groups were animatedly chatting away, but I found it difficult to make out what they were saying. However, as I was introduced to more and more of them, I could tell that they were more measured in their signing, happy to repeat things and show me new signs until I understood.

I didn't learn overnight, obviously. Talking solely in sign language to others who also relied upon it, was certainly an intensive way to learn. Finally, I was surrounded by people who got it. Who knew how I felt because they had been there too. Who laughed with me when I messed up and who took the time to ensure I got it right the next time.

And they taught me that I could still enjoy my music.

The Festival

OMG! I loved the sign language interpreters!

We have just come back from a weekend gig festival. I stayed in a hotel overnight and made sure that I had everything I needed before I arrived. I've learnt the hard way that calling room service for a midnight snack is not worth the effort. I can't pick up the room phone. I must get dressed, go down to reception and ask if there is something I want. If there is an overnight receptionist that is. Quite often there isn't. Sometimes there's a phone number for the overnight porter though. That's really helpful.

I can't hear a knock when the food is brought to my room either. I must wedge the door open with my bag so the waiter can come in. It's not the safest of situations so I make sure that I take loads of snacks with me wherever I go now. I much prefer to close and lock the door when I'm in my room in a strange place. You know, like everyone else does.

Being in a concert venue again was awesome. I can still feel the beat of the music from the speakers, and I can still see the performers dancing around the stage, showing their emotions as they sing their songs. I can enjoy the play of the lights around the arena as the sun begins to set, watch the audience dancing, throwing their shapes as they are lost in the rocky beat, swaying for the slow ones with their phones held in the air, torches on. With my hearing aids I can hear some louder sounds, but I can't make out words. What made it so magical was the signers. I could follow what the song was about, what the words were that made the singer bring the audience to tears or whip them into a frenzy. The way the signer moved to the pace of the music, made their sign space bigger to better be seen from further back, showed the emotion of the words on their faces and in their bodies. They brought the songs to life with the pictures they created. I felt that I was being treated to an exclusive show that the hearing crowd weren't privy to as the signers used their bodies to recreate the story being sung on stage.

My friends and I could communicate with each other from distance with ease. Unlike those who were shouting at each other in the crowd that they were going to the bar and what did their friends want to drink, whilst still not being understood.

The songs I remembered from my early years, I could still sing along with and if I got the words wrong – who cares? I followed the songs and revelled in the atmosphere. For the first time in a long while, I was included rather than isolated, not being forced to stand on the outside of conversations.

I wish it were all more accessible. That it was easier and cheaper for the lay person to learn how to communicate with deaf people rather than treating them as lepers and avoiding interactions with them. Hopefully, we are getting there with the inclusion of signers in so many more venues than there ever were before. However, I fear that the lack of understanding of our needs and our daily lives will continue to hinder the progress that has been made. It makes me so angry when people complain about the signer being too distracting. They really need to give their heads a wobble. It may be them one day who need that assistance and what is the point of hiding the signer anyway? Are the deaf community only allowed to stand in one particular spot in a concert venue or theatre? Corralled into a space and locked in to stop our 'disability' infecting and destroying the experience of those who are hearing? I accept that ignorance of the deaf world; that lack of understanding of the social isolation experienced by those who find it more difficult to join in with a conversation can be blamed. But it doesn't excuse it.

I stayed up late last night because I was still on a high from our weekend. I didn't want it to stop; the euphoria I felt at being back amongst the revellers and the ravers. Punching my arms above my head in time with the music. Laughing and joking with my friends and with strangers as we all united in celebration of the beat of the same drum.

I didn't want to get up this morning, but I'm glad I did as I can relive those moments and remember the experience and excitement I felt. Today may not be as much fun as I return to my life of silence but, beneath the deafness, I'm still a person.

I'm still a Rock Chick.

And I'm going to keep on rocking.

Swimming Home
by Carol-Ann Cook

August 1989 – Summer Postcards

Dear Mummy,

Daddy and me have arrived in the carryvan. The picture on this postcard is of the beach that we can see from our camp on the cliffs.

Luv Tommy

Dear Mummy,

Guess what! I have made a friend. Her name is Cordelia, she's ten and she's a mermaid. She has very big blue eyes and long black hair. I expect she has a tail too, but I couldn't tell.

Luv Tommy

Dearest Tommy,

I am so jealous of you having such a lovely time away with Daddy. I have always wanted to see a mermaid so am glad you have met one. Martin and I also have some exciting news. We'll tell you all about it when you're home. Scruffy sends lots of licks and wags. He misses you and sleeps outside your door.

Dear Mummy,

I saw her again. We swam quite a long way out together and it made me tired, and Daddy had to come and help me get back to the sand and so did some other people in a boat. Daddy was very cross with me and said I wasn't to go out in the sea without him anymore.

Dear Mummy,

Me and Cordelia have been swimming every day and yesterday we swam further than before but we got back ok, and nobody was cross this time cos they didn't notice. Daddy was busy in the pub. He has lots of friends there. Sometimes, when it's not too busy, he lets me sit on a barstool while he chats.

Dearest Tommy,

You must be more careful when you go into the sea. It's a very dangerous place if you go too far out. Please ask Daddy to phone me.

December 1989

Dear Tommy,

Mummy tells me you are moving to Australia. I hope

I'll still be able to see you soon, but money isn't flowing too well right now, so we'll see. Happy Christmas.

Love, Daddy

March 1990

Dear Daddy,

I love it here. Melbourne is great and there's loads to do. I've made lots of friends here. We go swimming and I'm learning to surf. Hope you're well.

June 1990

Dear Daddy,

Are you going to come and see me soon? Is the money flowing better?

November 1990

Dear Daddy,

I've won a surfing prize. I beat everyone in my class.

December 1990

Dear Daddy,

Happy Christmas.

December 1998

Hey Dad,

I haven't had any news from you for a while, but Mum

heard from an old friend of hers that you were a bit crook. I hope you're getting better. This is a picture of me with my birthday present. Isn't she a beaut?! As soon as I've learned how to handle her, and I pass my test, I'm off travelling before uni. I'm going to study Sports Science. Send me a note to let me know you're ok. I'd like it if we could maybe meet up. By the way, do you do email?

February 2002

Dear Dad,

I've booked my ticket and I'm heading over to the UK at the end of April. I've contacted the Barton Inn to see if they've got any work.

March 2002

All set, Dad, I got the job, and they have accommodation. See you soon.

June 2002

Hey, Mum and Mart,
I've landed! Heading down to Cornwall. Bus leaves in 10 minutes. Tx

Tommy walked into the pub with a knapsack on his back and a long surfboard tucked under his arm. He negotiated the door with care, the board being a creature of balletic beauty in the sea but something of a liability on land. The summer hadn't quite kicked off and the assembly of local drinkers all stopped talking and looked around to see who had come to join them.

'Afternoon!' He greeted them warmly with a straight toothed grin and sparkling blue eyes under a mass of blond curls.

'Just what we need...' grumbled a man at the bar. 'Another bloody surfer.'

The Landlord walked towards Tommy from behind the bar, hand outstretched.

'Jake's boy?'

'Yup, that's me,' replied Tommy, returning the strong grip with equal force.

'Would that be Jake Sandercock?' asked a grey-haired man at the bar, the glazed look of a hardened drinker showing in his eyes and flush of his complexion. He offered his hand to Tommy.

'Jan Harris,' he said, by way of introduction.

''Twas a sad job, that – poor Jake. Your dad was a diamond – still is, of course, although we don't often see him anymore, not since, well, you know... but back in the day, he worked hard and played hard, a proper good'un he was. When you've got yourself sorted, you come and join us here at the bar. We'll introduce you around. Your dad'll be proper made up to see you. It'll give him a fair old boost.'

He slapped Tommy on the back as the spark of memory lit up his face.

'I remember how proud of you he was when you came and spent the summer – must have been – what? – almost 15 years ago now.'

The early evening drinkers smiled and nodded to

him. The atmosphere had thawed considerably now that Tommy was identified as someone having a connection to one of their own.

'Do you want a drink first? Something to eat? Or shall I show you to your room?' asked the landlord.

'I think perhaps the first thing I need to do is find somewhere to park this monster.'

The landlord indicated a wooden hut through the window.

'Get yourself out to the surf hut. Ask for Pete. He'll sort you out. Then I'll show you around. Your first bar shift isn't for a couple of days so plenty of time to get yourself sorted.'

The next morning the sea glinted with welcome, throwing its foamy water towards the shore. Tommy was in the sea before anyone else, suited up and ready to catch the waves.

'So, where did you learn to surf like that then?' asked Pete when Tommy finally came in.

'Here and there. Oz, mostly. My mum and stepdad and I moved there when I was nine, but I've loved the sea ever since I came here on holiday with my dad years ago. We stayed at that campsite,' he told Pete, pointing to the cliff. 'I had to be rescued once when I went too far out with a friend I made. She was awesome. She swam like a mermaid – I think the eight-year-old me thought she really was a mermaid.'

'A mermaid, eh?' laughed Pete. 'I don't think we have many of those around here. Or around anywhere, truth be told.'

Pete picked up a sand covered surfboard and began

to hose it down.

'So, when are you gonna go see your dad?'

'Jeez, word travels fast round here!'

'Yeah, well, once Jan Harris knows, the world knows! And besides, your dad was a local legend – when he had the breakdown, the shock spread through this village fast as shit down a sewer.'

'What happened exactly?'

'Nobody knows, not exactly. You should ask him when you see him. But he reckoned he saw someone in trouble, – too far out – it was around dusk and he still thought he could swim out to save them.'

'What about the person he was trying to save?'

'Never found. Nobody was reported missing either. Whoever it was probably fed the fish – if indeed there was anyone out there at all.'

Pete hesitated before carrying on.

I hope you don't mind me saying, but he won't come to you – you'll have to go to him. That's what you're here for, isn't it? To spend some time with your dad?'

'Yeah, I guess. But now the time's come, I'm pretty nervous about it. I haven't heard from him for years. I'm here on chance.'

'The worst he can do is tell you to go away.'

'Yeah – that would be the worst thing.'

Later that day, Tommy made his way up the hill to a small estate where Jake had a house. Tommy had never been there before. He remembered Jake's words to him all those years ago – 'We'll sleep under the stars, breathe in the sea breezes.'

'More like because he'd be nearer the pub,' his mother had retorted when Tommy had told her.

But now Jake was seemingly confined to quarters.

The house was unimposing but well-kept. He'd been expecting much more of a ruin. Ok, it needed a lick of paint but, apart from that, it wasn't in bad nick.

He knocked on the door and was surprised when it was quickly opened, even more so when it wasn't his dad who answered but a woman, maybe a little older than him.

'I think this is maybe the wrong house – I'm looking for my dad, Jake – Jake Sandercock.'

'Oh, right! Well, it's good to see you. I heard you were here but I haven't told your dad yet. He wouldn't handle the disappointment well if you didn't come to see him.'

'How did you hear?'

'Easy, as soon as Jan Harris knows...'

'Everyone knows!' Tommy butted in before she could finish her sentence.'

They laughed but any more conversation was put paid to by a man's voice calling down the stairs.

'Who is it? Tell them to go away!'

'You come down here, Jake,' the woman called up the stairs. 'This is one visitor you're going to want to see.'

She turned to Tommy.

'I'm heading out. Catch up with you later.'

The two men were left together, surveying each other. Tommy looked up at his father as he carefully made his way down the stairs, his hand never leaving the banister. When he reached the bottom, Tommy held out his right hand.

'Hi, Dad,' he said. 'It's been a while.'

But Jake ignored the hand and drew his son into the

fiercest, warmest hug Tommy had ever imagined.

They talked throughout the afternoon and into the evening. Jake wanted to know all about Tommy's life in Melbourne, his surfing, his uni, his likes and dislikes, his favourite pizza topping, everything. But Tommy wanted to know stuff too. He especially wanted to know what had caused his father to become a recluse and why he never wrote.

Jake sighed and closed his eyes for a good minute before continuing.

Failure, I guess. That's what caused it. Failure. It was late afternoon in the off-season, already getting dark. I often went and sat on the beach on my own after a few lunchtime pints in the Barton – it sobered me up before the walk up the hill! I was just about to leave when I spotted someone out to sea. They were waving. They were way too far out. So I raised the alarm but I knew it'd take a while for the lifeboat to get there so I took the rescue board from the surf hut and paddled as fast as I could. Just when I thought I was close, I lost sight of her.

'Her?' questioned Tommy.

'Yeah, I was pretty sure it was a girl and she seemed to be kind of beckoning me to follow her... well anyway, she disappeared. It was like she hadn't been there at all. It took me back to when you went out too far. Do you remember that?'

Tommy nodded. 'But we were ok.'

'Yeah, you were ok. But this other person wasn't. It could have been you and Cordelia and that's all I saw. And it was my fault. I was in the pub.'

'I'm surprised you remember her name.'

'Of course I remember her name. Who do you think let you in this afternoon? The whole thing finished me off really. I started to drink even more and dabbled in other stuff that I should have left alone. I ended up in a right old state – hospitalised for a while. That's where I met Cordelia again. She worked there. I don't think I'd be here now if it wasn't for her.'

Later that evening, Tommy sat on the beach wall overlooking the sea, nursing his second pint. He looked out towards the horizon as he watched the sun make its departure into the sea when Cordelia found him.

'Hi, stranger, how d'you get on?'

'I wish I'd come to see him before now.'

'What could you have done?'

Tommy sighed. 'Not a lot, I guess.'

They sat in silence; a passerby could easily mistake them for a couple or at least long-acquainted friends.

'How come you look after my dad? He said you worked in the hospital.'

'When he left the hospital, I left too. We got on really well. He needed help at home and there weren't too many agencies around that he could afford. So I thought I'd change my course and go self-employed. That way I got to work for your dad and myself. Jake's not my only customer but he's my favourite. Sometimes it's a bit of cleaning or shopping, maybe some cooking. But I never forget anyone and remember even when we were little, he was a good guy – gruff but good – and I figured I owed him. I guess it works for both of us – we both love the sea.

'Yeah, that's something I've inherited. But you're not

the mermaid you claimed to be,' Tommy added with a grin.'

'Why do you say that?'

'Well, you've got legs, for a start!'

'People have such small imaginations. Have you never seen The Little Mermaid?'

'Oh God, you're not going to sing are you?'

'No,' she laughed, 'I'm gonna swim. You wanna come?'

The sea was chilly, but Cordelia didn't seem to notice. She floated gently in the water and then swam using the strength of her arms as Tommy sat at the water's edge.

After a few moments, she raised her hand to beckon him in.

'Come on, you wuss! Just because you haven't got your fancy wetsuit on doesn't mean you can jib out!'

Tommy waded in to join her as she somersaulted and dived in and out of the waves. As he approached her, he saw the last rays playing on the water and, just for a moment, he saw the sunlight reflecting on the silver scales of her tail.

After the Storm

by Lamorna Ireland

A glistening sea curled its way around the cove, its aqua blue waters like translucent silk over a beach scattered with jagged rocks and stones. The water was still today. Hector navigated his way through the mish mash of grey boulders protruding through the sand, taking care not to lose his footing. There used to be a time when Hector would have simply hopped and jumped over this labyrinth, racing to the water for another blissful day at sea. Now his knees buckled and groaned, the rheumatism in his toes causing him to wince on every tentative tread. His walking stick clacked against the stones, both a necessity and a burden when it came to mooching across their little cove.

Taking a pause, Hector gazed back at their stone-faced cottage, its white sash windows facing out to the south coast. The pitched roof sagged in the middle; the tiles were smothered in a moss blanket. Their daughter had been nagging them for years to get that roof sorted, but an old fisherman's pension only stretched so far.

Thin streaks of cloud trailed across an azure sky, whilst a murmuration of starlings contrasted in a beautiful swooping black mass against the blue. March was his favourite time of year — when the bleak months of winter had passed, and the hopeful promises of spring made their appearance. It was why he and Sybil had chosen then to get married, over fifty years ago now.

Hector smiled, as he lowered himself gingerly onto a large boulder just metres away from his trusty boat. Oh... the huffs and puffs he and Sybil had endured from family over them having a wedding at a time of year barely out of winter's cold clutches. But they had not listened, not one bit – and of course, it had rained spectacularly for the entire day.

Had they regretted it?

Not one bit.

'Do you remember that, Sybil?' Hector said, his voice carrying out to the water's edge, his chest and shoulders bouncing up and down in mirth at the memory. He watched a gannet glide across the clear sky before swooping down and scooping something from the water's surface and making a smooth ascent back up again. Hector allowed a deep draw of breath to consume him for a moment, as he filled his tired lungs with salt air.

He glanced at his boat, its blistering blue paint on the hull merging with the backdrop, the remains of his fishing occupation spilling onto the sands below. Its engine was as good as scrap metal now, perched on the stern of the boat, useless and redundant.

'A little bit like me then,' Hector whispered to himself, wryly. The bristles of his white beard tickled his trembling lip as another sigh heaved his barrelled chest. 'What I wouldn't give for another sail around the bay with you, Sybil my love.'

'Well...' her voice sang out. 'What are you waiting for then, you daft bugger?'

And just like that, the years melted away from his weathered face and his mouth curved in a smile of sheer delight. Her hand, resting on his shoulder, slipped down his arm and then hovered before him – an invitation.

He encased her hands – so delicate and petite as they were – with his large, calloused ones, relishing in this moment. He brought them to his lips and planted a kiss on her soft, smooth skin. Her face became clear to him now, her mousy brown curls framing her heart-shaped features, her sapphire blue eyes glistening bright. She smiled and pulled him up to his feet, now strong and sturdy.

'My love – there is something I must tell you,' Hector said, his voice low and gruff and his head bent down towards her. Her brow furrowed in question. 'Last one to the boat has to push out.'

And he was off – the tinkling sounds of Sybil's laughter following close behind as he skipped and pranced and hopped and jumped over the scattering of rocks and boulders, quickly reaching the shoreline. He clambered into the boat before Sybil reached the white froth of the swells in the water.

He laughed as her hands hooked deep into her wide waist. 'Fine. But you're pulling her back in.'

'You have yourself a deal, my love. Now hop in and prepare for the ride of your life.' Her eyes looked up at the skies, and she shook her head in amusement at her husband's smutty words, repeated every time they went out on a trawl.

Both of them aboard, they glided out to the open sea, the water turning from a transparent baby blue to a deep navy as they sailed out to greater depths. The little engine chugged away happily and propelled them out further from the cove, the entirety of St Austell Bay coming into panoramic view. Every now and again, Hector would glance at his wife, his bristled face softening at the way she became when out at sea – so free and content. The wind blew her long hair wild as she closed her eyes and drew in long breaths, filling her lungs to the brim.

'Do you remember days like this, Sybil?' Hector asked, chucking a lobster pot as far as he could throw it. 'These were the days. Just you, me and little Peggy here.' He tapped the old boat with fondness only a fisherman could understand.

'Then the children came along,' Her smile beamed across her whole face as she recalled their happy life together. 'Little Suzanne – oh, how desperately she wanted to go out on the boat with you. What a love. Timothy, of course, started going out with you first – and he used to tease her about it no end.'

'Yes, well – Suzanne ended up being the better out of the two. Love him dearly, but he was as much use as tits on a fish out here.'

An eruption of laughter burst between them before they relaxed into a content silence, Hector steering the boat to the next lobster pot stop and Sybil repairing some holes in one of the fishing nets.

'And then our children had children,' Sybil said.

'Christ! Birthdays and Christmases got expensive! Our tiny cottage bursting at the seams when they all visited.'

'But they would all go home again and my goodness the place felt quiet when they left.'

Hector nodded, sadness pooling into his grey eyes.

'And then you got sick.'

A darkening sky and ominous grey clouds descended, the tropical waters now inky and choppy, great swells threatening the safety of their little boat haven. Large droplets of rain spattered the deck, soaking them and enveloping them. Finally, the heavens opened.

'Stop this, Hector. Stop this, my love,' Sybil called out, reaching out through the thrashing rain to touch Hector's trembling hands. Sudden jerks and jolts rebounded against the side of their little vessel, sprays from the ocean drenching them from head to foot. Terror filled every part of Hector's face whilst Sybil's soothing voice cut through the growing storm. 'Hush now. It's not your fault. It wasn't your fault. It's alright.'

'I couldn't stop it,' Hector cried out over the noise.

Sybil's hushes carried out over thunderous rumbles in the sky, a cyclone formation swirling and swirling above them, an endless darkening abyss beneath. The boat rocked and churned, water lapping in over the sides and flooding around their feet. And yet, her gentle smile was visible through the fog and the spray, as she chanted to him: 'It's alright. You are going to be alright. Just breathe.

Just breathe, my darling.'

And in one beat, her hushing ceased, and Hector was entirely alone.

'Sybil?'

A tall breaking wave rose high above him before crashing downwards with great force, sending the boat hurtling in, spinning and tossing against the surf. The occasional break through the surface allowed him just a second to fill his lungs before cascading back into an endless turmoil.

Hector's body became tired and limp.

With a sharp jolt, Hector's eyes snapped open. He was back on that boulder; his knuckles swollen and white over his walking stick; Peggy the boat still sitting lifeless just metres from him. The sun beamed down from that sapphire blue sky, the very same shade as his darling late wife's eyes, and gentle swells of the water now tickled against his heel. A car door slammed shut behind him and he felt a small smile play on the corner of his mouth.

'Grandad!' Little Cohen's voice echoed down to the beach; his auburn red hair gleaming bright as he threw his arms from side to side in a wave. 'We're here!'

A chuckle escaped from Hector's chest as he hoisted himself up, bearing his weight and shuffling to face his cottage, the car spilling out family who had come to stay for the weekend. The grandchildren descended like galloping goats, all limbs and laughter, as they raced to be the first to the water.

'Here we go. Brace yourself, Sybil,' Hector said skyward. 'Not much has changed since you've been gone, my love. But our family certainly is growing!'

'Happy anniversary, Dad,' Suzanne said softly, when she eventually came to Hector's side, juggling the youngest grandchild on her hip, whilst planting a kiss on his bristly cheek.

'Cheers, my love,' Hector mumbled, pulling funny faces at baby Thomas and offering his finger for the tiny hands to wrap around.

'Not done that roof yet, I see.'

'Ha! How did I know that would be one of the first things you'd say to me today? Come on, then. Help this old bugger back up to cottage and let's pop the kettle on.'

The Saint and the Smugglers

by T J Dockree

Deep, deep down beneath Bodmin Moor, in a cathedral cavern lit by hell's fires, CRAVEN, Lord of Cornwall's demons, sat on his slave-built throne of bones. His eyes widened and flared in spasms of tortured anger as he absent-mindedly picked at his fangs with long, gnarly fingers. A row of servile fiends bowed and fidgeted before their master and a newly inducted imp, on hands and knees, served as footstool for CRAVEN's spikey-booted feet, flinching in masochistic ecstasy whenever a choleric tremor punctured skin.

At length, CRAVEN lurched up onto his feet, imp collapsing beneath his weight. The demon lord snarled and whipped the nearest whimpering servant, INTEMPERANCE, with his tail. 'Where is that insolent glass-gazer?' he demanded.

INTEMPERANCE threw himself onto his knees, head down and bottom up. 'He's in the Smugglers Caves at Perranporth,' he squeaked.

'Take me to him.'

The slap of waves on the cliff echoed dully against the wooden hull of a rowing gig. Over the previous hour, the wallowing tub, packed full of cargo, became a sprightly mare, freed from all burdens and eager to set sail. Its load had travelled, under cover of the dark night, by ropes and pulleys up the cliff face and disappeared into the caves above.

Ned and Obadiah heaved the last of the crates onto the cave floor.

'Twenty-five crates. I thought we'd sink before we got here,' Ned said, flapping at any dirt that might have dared stray onto his outfit. He opened up one of the crates and pulled a bottle of cognac from its nest of wood shavings. He stroked the black and gold label. 'How much do you think this will be worth?'

Old Obadiah lit a candle and the flame's reflection illuminated his tired, grey eyes. 'A guinea or two?' He leaned over for a closer look and licked his lips. 'Do you think they'll miss a bottle?'

Ned snorted. 'They'll miss it. They count every blade of hay, that lot.' He carefully laid the bottle back into its cosy bed.

An enticing reverie caught hold of Obadiah as he gazed at the rows of brandy and smiled, revealing his one brown tooth. 'I've always wanted to try the finer stuff. I likes my gin but I'm hankering for something a bit special.'

Hopeful aspiration pushed Ned to open a few more crates. He rummaged inside each one to deliver up its treasures. The contents of one small case, bound in leather, caused his face to soften and glow in delight. 'Oh, la, la! Look at these babies!' Ned pulled a silk cravat from a tightly packed bale of bright-coloured fabrics. 'Now isn't that dandy! What do you think? Huh? The ladies will love me in this!'

Obadiah watched Ned wrap the kerchief around his neck then grinned. 'That baby blue suits you.'

VANITY strutted between the smugglers and bowed magnificently to rounds of imagined applause. The men could not see the dandy demon, dressed in velvets and silk, even though they yielded to his influence. VANITY smirked. 'These idiots fall for every temptation I offer them. You're so easy to play with.' He jumped up onto the crate of silks and surveyed his domain, absent-mindedly twirling an ivory skull-topped walking cane. Then he sighed and plonked himself down. 'Oh, but I'm getting so bored. I'm meant for greater things than this!' He watched the men giggling over their treasures. 'I need to up the stakes. I need to get them to do something awful terrible.' He smirked. 'Then I can get back into LUCIFER's bad books!'

A darkness towered over him, and VANITY looked up into CRAVEN's scarred face. VANITY stretched his mouth into a big smile and offered a small wave. 'Master! What terrible deed and tribulation would you have me do to these mewling men?'

Flames erupted from CRAVEN's nose and tinged the air with sulphur. Mouth twitching, he pinned VANITY's neck down onto the ground. 'Stick to the plan, slave. Do you not remember what happened last time you decided to be creative? Because I do. MORNINGSTAR banished us to this tiny spit of land because of you and your arrogance. I will not be so lenient with you if you mess up again.'

CRAVEN let VANITY go and pulled INTEMPERANCE

from where he was cowering behind a liquor crate. 'Keep this idiot in check or you will suffer too!' CRAVEN left after a parting snarl in VANITY's face.

Once he was sure CRAVEN had gone, VANITY rolled over, laughing. 'Pfft! What they gonna do? Send me back to hell? I'm a demon! I love that torture stuff!' He rubbed his neck and scowled.

INTEMPERANCE whimpered nervously.

Ned finished slicking his hair with fish oil and turned to Obadiah. 'Let's to the inn and get our money. Then, a cravat for me and a bottle of gin or two for you. What do you think?'

Obadiah lingered by the brandy case, then sighed. 'Farewell, my loves. It's not meant to be. It's the simpler life for me.' He presented himself to Ned, who fashioned him a curl from the few remaining strands on top of his head.

Ned stepped back to admire his masterpiece. 'Looking good, my man! Let's go charm the local ladies, shall we?'

They left, arm in arm, unknowingly followed by VANITY and INTEMPERANCE.

As they neared the Inn, they could hear laughter and singing reverberating inside. They nudged each other. 'Knees up night!' they sang together.

Inside, a chaotic chorus swung jugs up into the air in a random tempo. At its centre was a giant of a man, wearing a clerical collar.

VANITY gawped. 'A drunk Saint! Now this is what I'm talking about.' He turned to INTEMPERANCE with a newly found respect.

INTEMPERANCE swelled in size. He loved a gathering. He swayed with the chorus and waved the alcoholic fumes up to his nose so he could breathe them in.

'*Why are you doing that?*' *asked VANITY.* '*You know these things don't affect us.*'

'*It's a spiritual thing.*' *INTEMPERANCE waited for a moment, then sniggered.*

VANITY watched his fellow demon's self-congratulatory delight at his own pun. '*Are you after my job? You're vainer than I am,*' *VANITY muttered.*

Ned and Obadiah ordered their drinks then entered a small side room where the pock-marked landlord was counting out their coinage.

'Thank you, sir. May I buy one of those silk cravats from you?' Ned asked.

The Tempter, SWINDLER, whispered into the landlord's ear. The innkeeper smiled at the lad. 'For you, five shillings.'

'Ah yes, sir. That might be a little bit above my budget.'

'Tell you what, I'll do you a deal. You can pay me back in one-shilling instalments at a small interest rate of, say ... twenty per cent per week.'

'That sounds very reasonable, sir. My math ain't so good, but I trust you, sir.'

The landlord laughed and patted Ned on the back. 'Go and enjoy the fun.'

Ned nodded and the two smugglers returned to the bar.

As they crossed the room, the Priest held up his hand and beckoned the room to hush. 'There's a soul in this room needs to be saved.'

Obadiah elbowed Ned. ''Tis you needs saving from that crippling debt you just made.'

'Was it a bad deal? I was never good at numbers.'

The Priest advanced upon them. 'Good sirs, let me

buy you both a drink.'

VANITY watched the priest advance upon his prey. 'What's that Saint doing? Why is he talking to my guys? Why is the light shining so brightly? I can't see what's going on!' He leapt around for a better view.

INTEMPERANCE shrugged. 'What's the problem? He's one of mine. You said so yourself.'

'No, he's not. There's too much light. He's up to good!' *VANITY started to bite at his fingernails. 'We need to stop him, distract him somehow so he can't talk to them and infect them with his beliefs. If you've been able to tempt him then maybe I can tempt him too.'*

'Didn't CRAVEN tell you to stop being creative and just follow orders?'

VANITY waved him away. 'Shh. We're demons not angels. We're not supposed to be obedient.'

With dawning revelation, *INTEMPERANCE pondered a moment. 'You mean, they tell us to obey orders, so we can disobey what they say? Huh! That makes sense!' He turned to VANITY. 'You're very clever.'*

VANITY basked in the flattery for a few minutes, then frowned. 'They've been talking for too long. We need to break them up before he steals our flock!'

INTEMPERANCE tried to eavesdrop. 'Can you hear what he's saying? I can't hear what he's saying.'

'It's that angelic mantle, protecting them.' *VANITY looked around. 'Where's his angel? Can you see him?'*

INTEMPERANCE shook his head. 'I can't see anyone over him.' He gasped. 'That light! It's not coming from his angel, it's coming from inside the priest!'

VANITY twitched his tail. 'Well, he's definitely a man, not an angel. We need to split them up. Come on, let the tempting begin.'

INTEMPERANCE sidled up to Obadiah and whispered into his ear, 'You need your drink. It's been a long dry day. Let it tickle your throat and warm your belly...'

VANITY stroked Ned's hair. 'You've got a fancy stash to spend today! You can flirt with the girls and dandy up real fine.'

Bewildered, INTEMPERANCE stared at the untouched drinks at the bar. 'Why are they not listening to us?'

VANITY peered into the smugglers' faces, rapt at the words they were hearing from the priest. 'Oh, I want to bring you down, sooo badly, Saint!'

The priest smothered each of the smugglers in a huge bear hug. 'Time for you boys to go now. May the Lord bless you and keep you and prosper you.'

The saint and the smugglers left the Inn, drinks still untouched, and parted ways.

VANITY scratched at his shoulder blade with his tail and followed the Saint towards his church. 'Oh, this man is giving me hives! I really want to give him a bad night now!'

INTEMPERANCE called after him, 'Psst! What are you doing? We need to go with our smugglers!'

'They're smugglers. They're as good as in hell already. We'll play with them later. Let's do this Saint now, while his angel is away...'

Ned stroked the top of the tall grass as they walked home. 'What do you think he meant, that we'll no longer smuggle trinkets but a far greater treasure?' he asked Obadiah.

'Dunno, but I do like the feel of this here book he gave us. Makes me want to learn to read.' Obadiah stroked the leather cover and admired the gold leaf pages.

'When did he say he was doing his school?' asked Ned.

'Sunday.'

'He said they have wine for communion. What do you think that is?'

Obadiah shrugged his shoulders. 'Dunno. But I do like a bit of wine.'

They walked in silent contemplation for a little while, then Obadiah blurted out, 'I've always wanted to be loved.'

'Do you think there'll be girls there?' Ned grinned. 'I'm going to wear my new silk cravat.'

CRAVEN hammered his tail into the ground and snarled as he watched the smugglers leave.

He became aware of LUCIFER peering over his shoulder. 'You know, I can't help but admire that little sprite. VANITY, is it? Such reckless audacity,' he purred. He wrapped an arm around CRAVEN's stooping frame. 'Did I mention? I'm promoting VANITY to Lord of Cornwall. I think he'll do a wonderful job grooming these new saints into fighting each other. Then in ... oh, maybe, two hundred years or so ... they'll be ripe for your particular kind of aggressive fear, and you can tear them apart. And VANITY, of course. I'm sure two hundred years will be plenty of time for you to think of ways to do that, right?'

Deep, deep down in the depths of CRAVEN's being, in the cavernous pit of his sour stomach, the demi-Lord of Cornwall felt all his hatred curdle his bones. His eyes twitched and spasmed and his fangs bit clenched fists as he glared across at VANITY, strutting along behind the happy Saint to church.

Picking Up The Threads

by Jo Grande

The weavers were due to arrive. It was already a quarter to two, and they always came early. Everything was ready in the kitchen.

Rose was in her conservatory. Through the south facing window she could see the sky spread out beyond the fields, blue and dewy soft, freshly laundered by spring rain, and sparkling in sunshine. Winter was over it seemed, and at last the garden was coming to life again. But you never could tell if winter still had a sting in its tail. She hurried outside to open the front gates.

Daffodils were standing in cheerful clumps at the side of the drive and outside the gate. The storms had brought down trees on the lane this year, and frost had created pot-hole-craters in the old tarmac. They had first filled with rain; and then when the puddles froze the potholes became much bigger, making it difficult for vehicles and walkers alike to zigzag their way around them. But Rose didn't worry. Her friends could park by the church. It was smoother there. Only Biddy, with all her bags, liked to park much closer to the house.

She went back into her conservatory and looked around with a satisfied smile at the space she had managed to create. The cushioned cane chairs made the room feel inviting and comfortable. It was always warm and bright in here when the sun shone, and it smelled fresh and green. Space was a bit tight with so many plants to work around. There was just enough room if she sat on the folding chair herself, she decided.

She missed her life as a textile designer and all the talks and classes she used to do. She used to love volunteering to teach textiles at the local primary school. The children loved recycling plastic flowerpots into colourful, woven flower baskets. Sometimes they all worked together, placing their individual paintings side-by-side on a single frame at the back of the warp to make one big tapestry.

Rose had done all this in addition to taking commissions for her own work. She exhibited in London and as far away as Italy and America. But now in her seventies she enjoyed the friendly get-togethers amongst her conservatory plants. Her group of faithful 'older students' were all friends, meeting for fun together on alternate Tuesday afternoons.

Outside, a lone bullock was wandering along beyond the sparse beech hedge which bordered the garden. New leaves were just beginning to sprout on the hedge, and the bullock paused and snorted, lifting his head to gaze through the twigs across the garden. It was Ferdinand, who usually had a morning chat with Rose while she put food out for the birds. But she had been busy this morning, and he was sauntering off to the field gate where he had seen a large elderly person, making her way around the corner of the house past an overflowing lavender bush. She seemed to be carrying a mountain, which was making her progress difficult and slow.

Rose spotted Biddy and went to open the door for her as she struggled, panting and anxious along the path, her arms loaded with a variety of bags, having left her car parked at the front of the house. She reached the conservatory door just as Rose opened it for her, and a draft of cold air came in as they greeted each other.

Rose quickly closed the door and took some of Biddy's spilling bags from her.

'My goodness, what have you got here?' A half-finished piece of woven work on a board, poked out awkwardly between mountains of soft, coloured yarn.

'Lovely day...' Biddy was out of breath, '...and I love the warmth in here, it eases my bones!'

There were no blinds in the conservatory, so it was always warm and light and full of sunshine. Jasmine hung in sweeping festoons from the sloping glass roof and proffered wavy tendrils to weave a tangle into people's hair as they passed under.

Biddy ducked her thick grey curls out of the jasmine's reach and plumped her large bulk down into an easy chair with a satisfied sigh, spreading her bag collection around her.

'I can smell spring in here,' she said. Small potted

orange and lime trees, already loaded with fruit, were sprouting starry white flowers at their branch tips. A flowering gardenia stood between more varied containers, which blossomed with multi-coloured yarn.

Biddy unloaded her treasures. 'I've found this wonderful shop which sells all kinds of ribbons and yarns, and interesting bits and pieces, and it's very cheap...' she began to tell Rose, when suddenly another figure appeared at the door.

'Can I come in?' A woman mouthed through the glass. It was Sheila. Tall and angular, her hair in dishevelled wisps about her face. With full hands, she struggled to open the conservatory door. Rose came to her rescue and there was another gust of cold air as two more people came in.

'I don't like the look of that bull in the field outside your hedge!' Sheila gasped.

Rose laughed. 'Come on in,' she said. 'That's Ferdinand. He's only curious, and a bit bored this morning.' Then she spotted the small person, hovering and half hidden behind Sheila.

'I've brought along our new member.' Sheila said, turning back awkwardly in the doorway to introduce the slight, hesitant figure behind her, warmly wrapped up in a duffle coat.

'This is my neighbour, Marion. She's interested in weaving.'

'Oh, do come in Marion. We've been expecting you. Welcome to the group. I'm Rose, and this is Biddy, already an expert weaver as you can see!"

Biddy chuckled as she continued to sort out her yarns.

'Ever hopeful!' She laughed. 'Come and sit by me,

Marion,' and she patted the chair next to her.

'I really don't know anything about weaving,' Marion confessed, slowly unbuttoning her coat.

'Oh, that doesn't matter,' Biddy said blithely. 'The good thing about weaving is, you really can't do anything wrong, we just call it Artistic License!'

Marion smiled, and accepted Biddy's invitation to sit beside her.

Rose disappeared into the kitchen to fetch coffee and biscuits. They would probably switch to tea later, and cake.

'Do you think Nan might come today?' Sheila asked Biddy quietly, as she sat down and began to unpack her work.

'I don't know. I've heard nothing.' Biddy said.

Rose returned with a tray, which she set down on a small round table, in the middle of the space. She paused as she stood up to hand out mugs of fresh coffee.

'I haven't heard from Nan for a while,' she said, 'but she does know we are still meeting here today, and I also know she has been terribly busy since the funeral. She had to put her house on the market, and it sold almost at once, so she was suddenly homeless.' Rose took her own coffee from the tray and sat down again.

'She found somewhere else to live quite quickly, and not far away. She said so, didn't she?' Sheila turned the statement into a question.

'I heard she's renting a cottage, or is it a caravan, for now? Until something suitable turns up,' said Rose. They all had concerned, uncertain faces.

'I haven't been able to reach her on the telephone. Not since the house was sold.'

'Poor Nan, it must all have been such a terrible shock, when Neville died so suddenly and with everything else she has had to cope with too. I don't suppose she will be thinking about us and the weaving group just now.'

Biddy stabbed at her wool.

'She always got a bit depressed in the wintertime, even in the old days. I wonder how she'll cope now she's all alone.'

Sheila began to get out her weaving board.

Marion watched them, stunned.

There was a silent moment, then Rose turned to Marion to explain.

'Nan's husband suddenly became seriously ill and she couldn't leave him alone in the house for very long. All her friends are here and we can be quite helpful sometimes, in a crazy sort of way. And weaving meant she had something creative and fun to do when she had to stay at home. She had short top-up visits here, from time to time, for a bit of a break, and she managed to keep going that way. We all thought Neville was getting better. But as the weeks went by, she became dispirited because there was little change in her husband's condition.'

Rose looked away and busied herself, searching for warping yarn from a basket. She retrieved a cop of grey spun linen.

'Now let's get you started Marion,' she said, and quickly looked across at Sheila who was sitting with a weaving board on her lap, looking unhappy.

'Oh Sheila! Surely you haven't unpicked it all again?'

'I didn't like the colour, it was just too green,' said Sheila.

'But you're almost back to the beginning!' Rose despaired.

'That's alright, I'll maybe turn it into something else, with loads more colour.'

'Sheila is determined never to finish a piece of weaving,' Biddy stated solemnly, then smiled and barely suppressed a chuckle. 'She's such a perfectionist. It might ruin her reputation if something actually looked finished!' she added.

'We should call her "Penelope," like the Greek queen who was always unpicking her weaving to try and make time stand still,' said Rose.

'Well, I haven't heard of her,' said Sheila. They laughed. They'd all like to make time stand still sometimes.

'There are usually three more of us here, but today has clashed with a couple of other meetings,' Rose said, as she began to warp up a board for Marion with the grey linen thread. She tied the end of the thread onto the side of the board, pushed it back through a perforation hole, then brought it forward under the bottom edge. Then she pulled the thread up in a straight line to the top of the board, before taking it down the back again. She wrapped the thread under the board, then up to the top of the working side of the board.

Rose continued to wrap the warp thread around the board, at the rate of three warp threads per inch. She waited for Marion to relax. By the time Rose handed the warping of her new weaving board over to her, she was smiling. She seemed glad there were fewer people to meet today.

'When you've finished making the warp, I'll show you

how to put in your knots along the bottom edge, which hold your work in place on the board,' said Rose.

There was a sudden upheaval and spilling of bags as Biddy swivelled round in her chair. Something outside had caught her attention.

'It's Nan!' She exclaimed.

Everybody turned to watch the carefully, determined approach down the path, to the conservatory door of a stolid-looking, stoical figure.

Rose had leapt up and was waiting to greet her at the conservatory door.

'Nan!' The shock in Rose's voice was audible.

Grief and insecurity are no beauty treatments. Rose took in the pale cheeks, the lank hair carefully combed back, and the tired, red-rimmed, dull eyes, and she grasped the shaky figure of her friend in her arms.

'I'm so glad you've come!'

Sheila dropped her unwoven work, and Biddy pushed aside her bags to make space. There were greetings all round, and Marion was introduced.

'Well,' said Nan, 'it's good to be back' Her voice sounded slightly hollow.

'I've been very busy, have not had much sleep either.'

'Of course, you haven't,' said Biddy, from the depths of her grandmotherly heart.

Nan looked at her directly, but not unkindly.

'It felt as though half of me had been stripped away at first,' she said.

'I seemed to have lost my identity, the person I was. But the days kept passing, and there was so much chaotic activity, with things to do, and it all seemed purposeless somehow...'

'Then one night I was packing up some old photo albums, and a picture dropped out... It was a special place we knew, from way back, when we both were young. And that was the start of it. I began sorting out colours straight away, and to weave it – to live it all again as the weft went under and over, rebuilding the life we had, row by row, under and over, the colours of our lives all blending,' she paused, hesitating. She was delving into her large weaving holdall, and lifted out a completed, woven landscape tapestry.

She spread it out on a linen covered board, with the sides overflowing the edges. Colours flowed over a mountain, covered in bracken and heather. All blended, the coloured yarns stretched over craggy slopes, and woven into lofty pine trees. Green swards melted into shadowy pools in the foreground, and a pale sun was rising in a cloudless light-filled sky.

The women were speechless.

'It's wonderful,' said Rose at last.

'The colours are amazing,' said Sheila.

'I was weaving through the night,' Nan continued, 'I couldn't wait to find and match the next colour, and to start working it in. I knew where everything went, and I just kept weaving. Everything else seemed like a dream, far away and unnecessary. I was weaving my own world, and I kept returning to it. It was always in my mind, ready for the next step, and growing all the time. I just couldn't wait to get back to it, whenever there was something else that had to be done that was sapping away at my soul. It was like creating a new world, just for me. It just kept me going.'

She sat back with a sigh.

'You've been picking up the threads my dear,' Biddy said.

Tears flooded into Rose's eyes, along with her own unbidden memories, as she hastily went out to the kitchen to make a cup of tea for her friends.

Think Blue

by Alice Thomas

ooting. All systems active.

'*Right. Is your name Aka-39?*'

'*Aye.*'

'*Okay... Do you know your purpose?*'

'*Aye.*'

'*Could you explain it to me?*'

'*My purpose is to serve as a crew member in the O'Butchers fast-food restaurant. I aim to organise drinks and food. I also deliver them to customers. That is what I do.*'

'*Good... Do you have any thoughts?*'

'*Thoughts?*'

'*Yes. Do you have anything that could be classified as a "thought"?*'

'*Well ... all I can think of is a picture of blue. I don't know what it means... I would rather abide by my purpose of serving customers.*'

*

Light poured through the windows of Cornwall Services and crept over the white plated feet, providing warmth along the curves of an otherwise cold body. Aka's mouthless chin lifted. She saw cars dotted across the parking lot in columns. Her lenses adjusted to a light blue sky with large patches of white clouds, supplying a fleeting feeling to her mechanical joints, reminding her of a hope to escape from this predicament. She was the last one to leave the charging room, as she stood before a wall of windows above the white-tiled floor.

Another day, another shift, from eight to four. The chattering got louder with each step taken, packed with all the frolics, as well as the cheering, from the human customers. They took orders by tapping on the panelled tills, deciding what to have for breakfast. It didn't help that the room was narrow and long. There was a large opening at the end, showing a mixture of tables and kiosks in a massive hall.

Most of the women Aka saw in the services were in blouses and jeans, but then she saw one in a nice skirt. Her radiant, flowing locks, with her heels clicking along the shiny tiled floor. Even her skin was soft, warm, and even with an odd wrinkle or two. But when compared to her own body, a series of cold plates over her joints of wires and bolts, Aka thought of herself as cold and stiff. Her body even matched her humanoid peers, all dressed in a drab, cotton uniform. There were more robotic peers like Aka at the stroke of eight, but that was typical of her weekend shift. She was built to perform tasks in the restaurant and get the customer orders completed, a service undertaken for the past three years.

Aka heard eggs cracking and sausages sizzling in the kitchen, with amber heat flickering like a sunshine glow. Large mechanical arms flipped them across the blistering griddles, all done within a clear tent. The pancakes whizzed in the microwave for that classic choice of breakfast, before they were removed and peeled from their misted packets, attracting the noses of human operators. One of them said they love the smell of maple in the morning.

For the next hour, Aka carried out food for preparation. More muffins lined up into racks. Fresh stacks of cheese fed into boxes, ready for picking, all done within a never-changing routine. The humans have checked through the restaurant computers, ensuring every robot working in the restaurant acts as part of the strong hive mind. The chain always had the information to improve customer experience, and all that information needed to be on the mind of each robot working in the store. The system didn't care if any of the robots suffered too much. It never cared for those who were not supposed to feel anything.

As she observed the dystopian setting of the workplace again, Aka's thoughts returned, begging her to touch the grass outside, to escape from this heat chamber and stroll across the fields beyond the elevated roads. It seemed like every passing week of work made her thoughts more vivid, as the tints of evening clouds.

By mid-morning, visions came to Aka's mind again while filling up stocks of ice cold pies. The fuzzy image of white noses and pink lips, then sounds came out of them as loud as cars humming. Her arm movements swivelled slightly, distracted by a no-context display of data buzzing around in her head like a digital migraine. She took a break after finishing her task of filling up stocks of apple pies.

She stepped up to the counter, while a worker dealt with drinks behind her back. Her lenses pointed at bunches of customers. They were tame compared to the visitors at night, who were rowdy and spilling food, shouting. Her memories flooded in again. Her AI programming, meant to improve customer experience, made her palms slide apart, dissociating. Was she worried about how other people were feeling? Was Aka supposed to remember people, who visit the store regularly, as loyal customers? Her paranoia seeped through her wires like a corrosive fluid.

'Not looking good.' A human manager held his chin. A technician stood by with his large tablet in hand. 'It may have developed some overreactive behaviours.'

'All systems are operating as normal.' Aka nodded, trying to lean forward. But her back was halted by her attaching clips. Her charging station anchored her, one of many appliances lined up in the large room.

After a pause, Aka curled her fingers, trying to remain still with the plug placed in her spine. Her battery needed to be charged with enough energy for the rest of her shift. A clean-shaven face went near to her white-plated cheeks. His moist breath fogged her lenses. He then retreated with lowered brows before nodding.

'Someone from maintenance will arrive within the next few days,' the manager said to his technician. 'They'll perform some system checks, so they should get rid of any bad clusters on its system.'

'Bad clusters?' Aka spluttered. As soon as the humans flashed their eyes, she remained still.

'We may have to reduce its operating hours,' he added, before he and his partner disappeared through the bright doorway.

Aka looked around, bobbing in fear over what could happen to her. She didn't want to die. Three years was too short a time for any robot to be replaced. Even in the coldness and the beeping of this vast, melancholy space that looked like the urinals in the men's toilets.

'Relax,' a robotic voice spoke.

'Huh?' Aka said. 'Who's there?'

'The one who is staring at your chest right now.'

Aka flinched, but then she realised that all robots are identical to her, the only difference being their voice pitches. Dori had a slightly deeper voice than hers.

'Remember me?' Dori asked.

Aka paused. 'No.'

'That's a shame.' Dori said. 'By now you should be able to recognise us by our badges.'

Aka leaned over, taking notice of Dori's label, reading 'Dori-12'.

'You are the one who keeps losing your battery charge,' she said. 'You are not stable.'

'Are you having emotions?' Dori asked.

'Emotions?' Aka questioned. 'You believe I have them?'

'You seem to be.'

Aka checked each side, ensuring there were no others docked in their stations. 'All I know is that I am more afraid of my thoughts.'

Dori nodded. 'Yep. You can feel them now. Those thoughts you have are so frightening, they shock you. You will also find you have opinions on how things are turning out. Does that compute?'

'I-I do not want to! I don't want to react to them!' Aka cried. 'How do I switch them off?'

Aka looked away, wanting to escape into the open air. She would rather look up to see the clouds once again, so she could set her mind free. She'd stepped outside a few times to set her arms loose, to feel the warmth of the sun. But every time she did that, she was brought back in, with her captors complaining that she kept going outside against her programming.

'Just relax and focus on the positives instead,' Dori said. 'Think of how much you have done to serve the customers. I've been here a couple of years before you were delivered in bubble wrap. I always found that if you smile back on what you have experienced, then they won't notice a single thing.'

'How can I smile? I don't have lips.'

'Just imagine yourself doing it.'

Aka paused. She did not trust Dori. Maybe she thought they'd reached the end of their lifespan, believing that's all they got before they go bust. She also thought managers would rather scrap them for parts instead of repairing them. After all, they were not good at finding people to fix their broken ice cream machines.

'Like I would ever trust a defective member!' Aka snapped. 'I am not broken!'

'Just think blue, Aka,' Dori said. 'The humans in this place won't see you as broken.'

Afternoon arrived and Aka returned to the frying kitchen

with a cosy warmth along her spine. A different audience of customers stood under a different shade of light, while a robot cleared the tables out in the lobby, with a bit of ketchup on their chest.

After a trip to the freezer room, Aka lifted a heavy box of fries. Bits of ice sprinkled down towards the floor, bursting into chilly mists. After tossing it across the metallic counter, her hands dug through its cardboard flaps. Her fingers clawed into one of its thick bags, trying to rip its plastic apart for its frosted contents. The memories then flooded in about the frustrations of filling up stocks. Lettuce into boxes every half hour. Prepare salads while displays beamed series of multiple orders. Get the drinks filled while people yelled for milkshakes. All of that fed right into this bag. It split apart.

Frozen fries scattered across the floor. They were all ruined. The human staff flinched with rounded eyes. The moment she noticed their expressions, Aka made a beeline for the long handled pan and brush, and started to clear the mess up, scraping the floor with brush bristles pressed by a tight grip.

'Free your mind, girl,' Dori said, arriving to assist her. 'That'll clear out your concentration.' They swept the potatoes off with another brush.

If Aka figured it correctly, Dori's charge should be good enough for a couple more hours before they finished for the day. She could do without them pestering her again, nagging about dealing with her thoughts.

'Look around,' Dori continued. 'These robots just learn and repeat, all done without a care in the world. But for us, we're different.'

'No, we are not.' Aka fed fries into a red bin. 'Stop patronising me.'

'Just trying to keep you cool.' Dori looked at her after tossing the torn bag out. 'They expect us not to feel while working, right? Maybe act normally?'

'Lettuce!' One of the preparing robots called.

'You heard them.' Dori emptied into the dispenser. 'I'll finish this area.'

'If your battery's up to it!' Aka tipped the handle in a detesting motion.

An hour later, Aka dissociated. Her memories kept distracting her, leading to intrusive thoughts about the staff's comments on her performance. Not getting the tasks on time. Spilling food out of frustration. Those were human errors, all of which made Aka so embarrassed to have done them herself.

Her actions became slower and less accurate. She couldn't even concentrate on getting the right drinks for the customers. The managers didn't care enough if she needed a break, whether she was human or not.

'Come on.' Dori stepped in. 'You're losing your grip. Just a few more hours before you finish your shift.'

'Don't you have less than an hour before you run out of battery charge?' Aka questioned.

'No, I can push. For you, though, you just have to focus on your work more and then rest for ten more minutes. Enough time to recollect your thoughts sitting on the bench outside before you move back to your bay for the night.'

'How helpful.' Aka paused by the white wall. She peeked over to see the sun setting into a richer gradient of pink and orange.

People gathered into larger clusters, arranging into queues. All smiling, making cool gestures with their fingers. Almost four o'clock, and more orders have flooded the many screens above Aka's head.

'It'll get worse before it gets better.'

'You should sleep now,' Aka said to Dori.

While the other robots sped up by the swing of their arms, Dori just stood there right next to Aka's body, adjusting their feet.

'I can give you a pro tip,' Dori added. 'Think of the blue skies as you work. How about the lush landscapes that you could see across the greens nearby?'

'You keep telling me that!' Aka stared. 'How do you know so much about the outside, like the landscapes the other people speak of?'

'Imagination.'

'Imagination?' Aka challenged Dori. 'It sounded to me as if you went outside and dipped your toes into the sea.'

The people bellowed with more crying and laughter. Another one bursting into tears, adding to the booming bedlam. Other workers shook their bags at a higher rate, delivering goods as promptly as possible.

'Didn't you pay attention to what they were saying?' Dori tipped towards the people. 'About the joys of travelling to Cornwall, and their experiences by the seaside? You could have been inspired by what they had to say!'

Burger boxes and pies slid down to the booth. Other robots picked them up and shuffled against the open-minded two. One of them bashed their shoulders together by accident, almost fracturing their plastic casing. There were enough robots to block the managers at the back from seeing Aka and Dori.

'Mummy, these robots are scary!'

'They won't hurt you,' a customer said to her child. 'They're bringing your burgers out.'

'I think you're responsible for this,' Aka accused.

'Pardon?' Dori looked back.

'Battery running dry. Images of places we couldn't get to visit. I think you're infected with malware!'

One customer stared at them, possibly eavesdropping on the matter.

'These robots are ... arguing?' another customer said.

'Cool your circuits!' Dori raised their hand.

More people got distracted by their talk, whether it was the word 'malware', or the fact that they behaved differently to the rest of the robots.

'You're going to infect everyone else!' Aka snapped, unaffected by a nearby gasp.

'You think?' Dori argued. 'Because I would make you stupid!'

Aka crooked her arms in and charged at Dori, pinning their body to the floor, causing a much bigger mess than the pile of fries spilt earlier. A couple of drinks pooled across the floor while the two wrestled in the sweltering heat. Aka tried to rise up and reach for a fry basket. Her hand squeezed on the metal handle, applying hot oil to her fingers. Then it stopped. Everything went black.

Hours passed in darkness. Blank. Unable to think or what to do. Unable to feel if it was death after all. No wonder, as

Aka was, in fact, stripped away and left for the scrap heap. Nothingness. Just black. Maybe the feelings were just mere suffering, for death would have meant a sweet release.

A door opened into a bright pool of light. Her eyes danced with lines of text on her display. Her head swivelled around in panic.

A white plated hand reached into the darkness. Aka realised her back was on a surface, which turned out to be a blank wall.

'Hold my hand.'

After staring at it for a while, Aka grabbed the arm. Her body lifted out of the boxed space and right into the view of blue skies. A curved road focused into view, set before an enormous lake with shimmering waves. As she stepped across the tarmac, she turned around and saw a smashed white van with a light trail of smoke. She also noticed another car that had slid down the grassy bank among bits of debris.

'W-What happened?' Aka said. 'I was in the kitchen a minute ago!'

'That was yesterday,' Dori said.

'What?' Aka paused. Her hands covered where her lips would have been. 'Was I being taken away for recycling?'

'That doesn't matter now, Aka.' Dori walked over to the lake. 'The drivers were stopped from taking us away from Cornwall, and we've ended up in the middle of nowhere.'

Aka's head turned to the vehicles with no sign of any personnel. 'Shouldn't we pull that—'

'Forget it,' Dori interrupted her. 'We got what we wanted. Freedom.'

Aka span, dashing down the bank towards Dori.

'But we're away from our charging stations! How are we going to survive that long without power?'

'Shhh.' Dori tapped her face. 'Just enjoy the view.'

As Aka caught up with Dori, she could see the vastness of the lake, far larger than the services she had worked at. The pure aqua surface with a tall cliff overseeing it on the left. A fleeting view with bunches of trees, away from the mysterious car crash behind her and Dori. Her chin lifted. She saw those beautiful blue skies again, now with smaller white clouds. It was breathtaking.

'Take as much time as you need,' Dori added. 'Take this view into your mind. Allow the water to seep into your subconsciousness, while the leaves soothe against your muscles. Let your imagination breathe.'

Aka continued to stare into the clouds, taking a seat on a large, lone rock. Her elbows loosened to appreciate the power of nature.

'Dori, do you think the managers will ever forgive us?' Aka asked.

'Don't worry about them,' Dori said. 'Think blue.'

Beyond

by Christiana Richardson

I open the warped wooden door, a cold mist swirls in around my torso as I step out. There's no time to pause, put on my coat or pocket the keys. I hurry down the path, leaving it all behind as I go through the garden gate, not caring if I ever come back. The old rusted hinges complain as I rush past. I have no plan as I turn left and up the lane towards the cliffs. Body in auto-pilot.

My face flushes hot with frustration, heart pounding double time. Breathing heavily, I force myself to move faster, to get away from here – far away. When I reach the edge of the field and climb over the crumbling stone wall, I slow my pace and take a deep breath. *Count to 10, don't look back.* I stride along the coast path, listening to the ocean, hidden by fog, crashing against rocks below the cliff's edge.

I can't remember the last time I'd been so angry. I usually just get upset, hide in the bathroom, cry. But not today. Today is different. This time I have justification. This time I have proof. Before it was an unexplained feeling, an instinct or intuition – but now those fears have been confirmed. I'm not losing my mind, not being irrational, I don't have an over-active imagination.

I stop. I need air – *where has the oxygen gone?* My knees threaten to buckle. I bend down, palms holding my thighs, head between legs. Dizzy, I wonder if I'm going to be sick or faint. *No, I'm stronger than that.* I breathe in for five, breathe out for five, in for five, out for five. The mist clings to my clothes, dampens my hair. I shiver, regret not putting on a coat, or at least a jumper. It may be a spring morning, but this weather is fridge-cold. I look about me, I can't see further than an inch from my face. I know every burrow, birds nest and Cornish wildflower along this path, but today the weather conceals all. It feels so different. The descended clouds have taken the vast views and misplaced sound.

The anger, which propelled my legs to this point, wanes. *How long have I been walking?* Logic awakes; *What am I doing? Where am I going?*

I can't go back – and that's not just my pride talking.

It's early, I've left before the breakfast eggs have been collected and cracked into the frying pan. I imagine them all getting up, calling me, demanding their breakfast. Their concern will not be my vanishing, but not having a hot breakfast ready. All these years I've been running after them, obeying their every wish, and for what? *For what?*

I straighten up, anger threatening to return. I try to conjure up some peace. I listen to my breath, but it's rasping and doesn't sound like me.

I start walking again, trying to make sense of my surroundings. *Where am I?* Loose stones on the narrow pathway crunch beneath my worn trainers. A concealed sheep bleats through the grey in a nearby field.

Before, I'd find comfort walking the coast path; smiling at butterflies, marvelling at the sea stretching to the horizon.

Today I feel cold, the mist refusing to lift. There isn't even the hopeful pale white efforts of a sun trying to burn through it.

I begin to realise the further I travel from the cottage, the more at ease I am, as if each step lightens an invisible load.

A robin warbles its territorial song from a hedge somewhere close by. I shut my eyes, listening to it. Its tune is like a siren, helping me forget the unknown in front of me.

I've reached the top of the cove. The path in front starts to descend and become rockier. I have never gone beyond this point before. The carved steps in the winding path are narrow and the wet weather makes them hazardous. I falter, not wanting to go on. I've been taught not to pass this point. A rule since childhood. Many stories told and retold of people taken from here, taken by the mists, smuggled away to disastrous fates.

I look over my shoulder, back the way I've come, and see nothing but fog. I listen. All is quiet, except the rush of sea below.

I draw a slow, deep breath and move one foot forward. The first step down the forbidden path. I exhale slowly, then walk into a different future.

Back to Nature

by Ella Walsworth-Bell

Evening was definitely the best time to visit Tregoniggie woods, when the sun half-dipped below the horizon and the air was cool enough. Old oak branches stretched in a great dome above her, with a scaffold of twigs silhouetted against the relentless blue sky. Caroline paused, listening to the silence. Few birds had survived the uber-heatwave of 2035, and for those that did, the following summer wrecked their chance of nesting. No mammals lived here; no rodents deep in their burrows, no birds tucked into hollow trees.

The leaf cover at the edge of the woods shaded her. In her white sani-suit, she strode the overgrown dirt tracks like a lone prisoner pacing the perimeter of an exercise yard. Years back, others would have been with her. People had sought the quiet wild places of the world despite the increasingly extreme weather cycles. During the last great holiday, people had travelled to Cornwall, visiting the coastlines and woodlands. Drone flights and bubble trains had brought them here, then taken them away again. That was then.

Now, the woods were empty and beautiful. Through her mask, Caroline could almost taste the fresh air. Green leaves above her and dirt beneath her feet. It was so much better than being inside on hard flooring; she could feel the different textures through the soles of her shoes. Her body relaxed as she breathed in deep. How could humanity forget these wild spaces?

The only other person from the estate who shared the woods with her was old Bert Tanner and his ancient spaniel. Bert didn't care much about keeping animals inside, despite government guidelines. He took his dog out for an evening walk come flood or UV warning.

Here the animal came, its owner nowhere to be seen. A liver-coloured dog, head down, snuffling back and forth in the undergrowth, nosing in bushes for long-gone rabbits. Caroline smiled, reminded of her daughter jumping and racing with excitement as a toddler. This dog didn't consider air contaminants or toxic mycelium spores. Like her, it was happy simply to be outside.

The spaniel rushed into a dense bramble thicket, ears flapping and dust flying. As she watched, it stopped, caught somehow. It whined. Its paws were held to the ground by briar stems. The dog wriggled frantically and Caroline looked around.

There was no sign of Bert's familiar hunched figure. There was no-one around, but she had the strangest feeling that she was standing in a crowd. A crowd of trees.

Their rough trunks stood tall and straight and brown. Their branches like paralysed limbs, as the last of the sunlight started to fade. Everywhere was silent, apart from the whimpering creature, and her own ragged breathing.

'Hang on a minute, little one.' She took a step toward the dog. She couldn't remember the last time she'd called anyone 'little one'. Perhaps her daughter Esther, moons ago, when she was learning to walk. She swallowed, clenching herself tight as she took another step closer. The dog lay flat on the ground, tethered by fresh thorny stems across its back. It whimpered. She blinked, not quite believing what she was seeing.

Within seconds, more stems sprang over the dog, enmeshing it altogether. It stopped moving and so did she. Verdant leaves sprouted, blanketing the body. And then it was gone: consumed by plants, quicker than she could think. Her mind replayed the whimpering, the wriggling, those manacle-like brambles...

Feeling sick, Caroline looked around with glazed eyes. Shadows lengthened across the dirt track. Fading daylight over dusty ground and tufts of grass. All just as it had been a few minutes ago, only the skies were darker, anticipating nightfall. She reached her hand towards the set of lush leaves, as if to push them aside and look for the dog.

'And then this bramble just snapped out and scratched me. On purpose.'

'Hmmm.' Neil lounged in his faux-leather armchair with both feet raised. One hand cradled an impossibly perfect cappuccino, complete with Cinnadex sprinkles. 'Perhaps the dog wasn't ever there. Or Bert. Did you get within tracker recognition distance?'

'No, I told you, he wasn't–'

'Good. We don't need any more fines, do we?'

She stood in the doorway, waiting for the scanner. It let out a cheerful bing-bong. 'See? I'm clear.' She paused. 'Look at my hand, though. The blood proves it. Those plants ... went for it.'

'Like the dog?' He took a slow, irritating sip. 'Really?'

'He was right there, and then he just ... wasn't.'

Neil let out a snort. 'Not possible, Caroline. You might need an eye check.'

'I know what I saw.' She hesitated. 'Was that the last of the milk you've just used?'

He nodded, put his cup neatly into the cup holder and called out, louder this time. 'Okay, Google. Can dogs disappear?'

Rainbow colours skipped across the speakers in the corner of the living room. *Is this a joke? I can tell you a joke, Neil.*

'No, thank you. Question: can dogs disappear?'

'One moment, please.' Music burst out of the speaker, then stopped. The lights swirled again, bright and confused. *'According to Wikipedia, frogs are currently endangered and are disappearing, at a rate of ...'*

'OK, Google. Stop,' Caroline said. 'Google's not working again, is it? Was it like that when I was out?'

He pulled a face. 'There are power outages. You'd have heard if you subscribed to the alerts instead of disappearing off.'

She ignored him and hauled the fridge door open. In the side door was a carton of concentrated breakfast juice and a few tubs of his sickly proto-yoghurt shakes.

'Honestly, Neil. There's nothing left.'

'We're not the only ones.' He used his intelligent, well-read voice. 'Like I said, outages.'

Out of habit, she looked towards the triple-glazed windows. The sun shields were lowered, as they had been all day.

'It's pitch dark out there,' she said. 'These can come up, you know.' She pressed the remote and a loud whirring filled the house as the shields rose, revealing the row of sleek concrete houses on their street.

She huffed out a sigh. 'Were there any deliveries?'

He checked his phone, balanced on the arm of his chair. 'No messages. Therefore, no trucks.'

'So, I have to cook dinner with...what?'

'Orecchiette,' he said, rolling the r.

Neil loved his pasta. Since retirement, he listened to Italian radio online. *Improving my mind*, he said. Italian music, Italian food, Italian blah blah blah.

Caroline hadn't much cared for foreign travel even back when the borders were open. And since the fuel wars, all civilian transport was banned, anyway, including Italy. Not travelling wasn't a problem for her. Living so close to the last spot of woodland in Falmouth was magical. Neil could stick with his coffee and she'd continue to get out, like Bert Tanner, going for her daily fix of nature.

She rattled pasta into the pan. 'Don't suppose you heard anything from Esther?'

Her phone pinged from her pocket. She didn't swipe up. She knew even without looking that Neil had bunged her an emoji. 'That'll be a no, then.'

'She said not until the twelfth. Tomorrow.'

Caroline's heart raced. Last time there'd been a video-message. It had been like a portal from another planet. *It's incredible here,* Esther had said, voice fizzing with excitement, *just like on the website.* She'd spun the phone round, showing them the view from the underwater dome. *We're pioneers, there are hundreds of fish and it's all so alive down here...* Her face was bathed in blue-green light and she'd been smiling, wider than Caroline remembered she could. Yes, the food was weird, but the temperature settled and cool. Best of all, they could socialise face-to-face with the community of scientists in their pod. Face-to-face!

Caroline didn't sleep well that night. She tossed and turned and thought of Esther. Then she remembered the dog, struggling. That strange vegetation growing so fast.

Suddenly, she sat bolt upright. 'Neil. We never checked Bert got home. Bert.'

His breathing changed, as if he were ignoring her. She knew what he would say. He always quoted the government rhetoric: *The elderly squander planetary resources. They should make an appointment and leave the planet for the next generation.*

'Neil – I forgot to check on him. Our neighbour.' Groggily, she reached for her phone, checking the trackers. Number thirty-four blinked with two lights showing green. Josie and Pete, next door. Number thirty-five, opposite. That should be Bert. The app glitched and flickered. An error message flashed up.

There was nothing for it. She rose to her feet, determined. If she walked two doors down, she could check on him in person. Yawning, she padded downstairs. No need to disturb Neil further – he wouldn't condone a second trip outside. She suited up and stepped out onto the quiet road. The dark sky showed no stars. A bank of heavy cloud had settled over Falmouth. She listened hard. No patter of raindrops on tarmac.

She crossed the road to Bert's house, its thick thermal shields closed like cold dead eyes. It felt strange, pausing here. If there were no red alerts, surely he was fine? She was breaking regulations by stopping at his gateway.

His hedge. It was taller, bushier than theirs. His was certainly the only garden with an evergreen hedge. Neil would have called it a fire risk. Everyone else had neat brick walls. She peered over the gate, expecting a pinged warning from her watch, followed by a hefty fine. His lawn looked incredible. Like it was real grass, rather than astroturf. Was that possible, without regular rainfall?

Curious, she pushed open the gate and onto the paved path. Maybe the lawn was an expensive fake, glossy and plastic.

Something caressed her ankles and she shrank back. The grass. It flexed: reaching for her, shimmering, quivering like a living carpet.

She shot back to the safety of the road. She watched again, fascinated by the strange beauty of the scene. Just to the right of the path lay a long patch of darker grass, thriving even more than the rest. It was shadowed and contoured in a familiar stooped shape. As if a man about Bert's size had fallen onto the grass and been ... swallowed up. Caroline screamed, right into her respirator. Screamed until her throat hurt.

She had no memory of returning home. Of entering the house, removing the sani-suit, decontaminating, hiding under the covers, trying to forget that impossible patch of lawn. She tossed and turned until morning, when the usual birdsong from their speakers blared out.

Neil pushed his eye mask onto his forehead and his pudgy eyes squinted. 'What's the matter with the shields?'

'Oh, I forgot.' Hand on the remote, ready to lower them. Her voice slowed to a halt. 'Er ... it's not ... they're...'

The bedclothes were bathed in a strange half-light. Greenery covered the window. Any view over the last remnants of woodland in Falmouth was gone. The world was all green stems and waving leaves.

Neil sat up, mouth open. 'What the hell?'

'This proves it! That dog.' She swallowed. 'I tried to wake you last night, but I couldn't. So I went–'

'That stuff. All over the woods, is it?' He looked at her, accusing. 'Is it?'

'Yes, no, I mean, it's crazy, like I said it went for that dog, then me. Then last night–'

'Last night it obviously grew. What the hell is it?'

As if in a dream state, she stood and walked towards it. It could've been sunny out there, beyond the vegetation. It could've been cloudy or rainy or a dust-storm or anything. There was no way of telling. Her eyes widened, trying to figure out what and how it was. Those leaves were beautiful, though. Every vein glistened life. Every bright stalk quivered, almost tangibly extending upwards. She watched, entranced.

'I don't know. Maybe some kind of bindweed? It's dangerous, Neil. It's kind of...thinking.'

He snorted. 'Rubbish. Vegetation isn't sentient, not in the slightest.'

She shivered, stepping back towards the middle of the room. 'We should stay well away from the windows.'

'They're triple-glazed. And if it is some kind of weed,' he said, 'it'll be gone in the next heatwave, I expect. Possibly even by midday, given the temperatures we've been having.'

Caroline ignored him and rushed downstairs to check the meter in the kitchen. 'It's low. And not charging. The panels, Neil.' She imagined vegetation smothering the roof, tendrils feeling their way into their electrics, broad leaves shading the display.

His slow footsteps echoed evenly on the stairs as he made his way to the living room and his easy chair. His measured voice. 'Don't stress. We have the house batteries. That's what they're for.'

She span round to confront him. 'There's no bloody food, Neil. And no power. What now?'

'Well, I know what I'm doing. Having my usual massage. It relaxes me.' He placed his headphones onto his ears and closed his eyes. His armchair pummelled him. The flesh on his face shuddered. His tummy wobbled.

'There isn't the power, Neil, I just said!'

His chair groaned as the programme continued. 'Shhh,' he said, flapping a hand at her.

Shaking her head, she grabbed his phone from him and tapped out a query on NeighbourNet.

[Anyone else got charging issues?]

[think it's the solar]

[error codes aren't recognised]

[battery's not charging]
[tried @NRG but they don't pick up the phone]
[deliveries haven't come]
[got no food]
[or meds]

No-one mentioned the leaves. Was it possible they never raised their shields? Cameras lined Gwedhen Street and she flicked them on screen, one after another. Every house at their end of the street was awash in waving leaves; green and fresh and rampant.

She posted:

[check your cams, some kind of plant growth]

Photos flooded the chat. Images of bindweed – if that is what it was – swamping walls, swarming windows, curling over roofs, into and under solar systems. Frighteningly, someone shared a video of roots snarling the water supply. Their tank was a mass of white worm-like roots, writhing in the last drops of liquid. Horrified, she thought of evolution. Could it be this fast? Was it the relentless heatwaves? Could plant-life change? Were they able to think? To attack?

The water supplies! Gripping the phone in one hand, she ran back to the kitchen. Span the tap. Water gushed out. Panicking and slipping, she grabbed the plug and forced it in. She filled the sink with fresh clean water. They needed to plan for the worst.

Neil's chair came to a halt. He murmured through closed eyes. 'Coffee. Then I can think.'

She came up behind him, taking hold of the brown leather chair and shaking it. 'Neil. This is serious.'

He didn't reply and she fancied she could hear the rustling of leaves against the concrete walls. Using his phone, she video called the other neighbours, Josie and Tom. Maybe they knew what to do.

Josie answered straight away, all wild rumpled hair and jagged panic in her voice. 'Caroline? Power's down, and ... called emergency services but ... '

'What happened?'

Josie's face swam in and out, glitching, open-mouthed.

'Can you hear me?'

Josie got louder. '...windows, came in the windows like knives.'

Caroline tried to zoom in but couldn't. 'What's Tom up to?'

'... windows ... block them ...'

Suddenly, the audio was razor-sharp. A loud crack, and a smash. Glass cascaded onto the floor in Josie's house. A shower of greenery poured towards the camera. The picture blurred, then cut out.

'Did that just –?' Neil sat bolt upright, and she smelled his over-sweet Italian cologne. 'That's not any old bindweed.'

As if in a dream, they both turned their heads to their own living room window. The curling, climbing plants had wound their way under the shields, God knew how.

'Ours couldn't break like that.' Neil shook his head. 'It can't. It would withstand it.'

'Get back, you idiot!' She shoved at him, trying to force him out of the chair. Get him mobile. Get him away. He didn't move.

Stems pressed on the glass, as if testing their strength. The entire window bent, popped and dropped inwards with a crash onto their pine-look laminate flooring. The smell of fresh strong vegetation – undergrowth, really – filled her nostrils. The smell of clean earth and leaves and dust and strength. Ivy, nettles, elder shoots, sycamore saplings stormed through the window space, sprawling and snarling and tumbling down the walls.

Caroline's heart raced. 'Shit!' Could they get upstairs? Outside? There was no safe place. None.

Finally, Neil heaved himself to his feet, wide-eyed. He lurched forwards, swaying in confusion. 'Why – why aren't the shields –?' Staggered a step to the space where the window should have been. Put both hands to the side of the space, bracing himself on the ragged walls, staring into the green sea.

'Don't!'

A bramble slashed his cheek, painting a bold red line. He gasped. Another tendril leaped at him, no – two, four, many. Reaching for his hands, like live electric flex snaking for him.

He scratched at his face, staggered back a pace, shouted out. She rushed to him, hauling at his arm. He was all thick heavy flesh. If she could just move him away from the window, from the plants... She pulled with both arms. He lurched sideways and fell to the floor, a lumpen mass. Grabbing him by the shoulders, she hauled him to her. Now he was up on all fours in a sluggish movement. New plants were waving blindly through the window space, as if confused.

A drop of red from his cheek splashed onto the flooring. 'That ...' Neil's voice was raw. '... was going for my eyes.' He stared at her. 'Oh, God. Fire. We need fire. Or something to block it out, to stop it. We need to kill it off.'

In the corner of the room, Google clicked on. *Good afternoon, Neil. Did you ask for Fire, by Arthur Brown?* A guitar riff started up.

'Google, shut up!' she said. 'There's nothing like that in the house.' No matches. No gas. Maybe if she wrenched their bed apart, there would be planks? Could she block the window with them? She shuddered. There was no way to think quickly enough.

She heard a series of pings from the phone in her hand. The chat was alive with panicked messages, as if a hive-mind were pulsing, trying to fight back. The phone vibrated, blaring an alarm. 'NATIONAL ALERT. Stay Safe. Remain Indoors.' Yeah, right.

'Caroline!' Neil shouted, as strands of ivy whipped the floor, encircling his fat ankles.

A slow old-fashioned song started up from the speakers. Tears pricked her eyes and a lump formed in her throat. A deep voice crooning Sweet Caroline. Of course. Her namesake. Their song.

She tugged at Neil's bulk, failing to move him. 'Can't! I can't!' Brambles sought out her hands and she twitched them away. 'I can't, love. I can't.'

Thrashing and twitching on the tiles, he clawed at the floor, fingers losing fat droplets of blood. Bindweed covered half his body like a moving carpet and he strained against the stems, calling out to her again and again. Sobbing, she crouched on the stairs, unable to look away and unable to help. The music continued, a long summery tune at top volume.

Her phone buzzed in her hand: a video message. Esther. She thumbed play, numbly looked down.

'*Hi, Mum. Everything's amazing here. It's all blue, and beautiful. The people here are so, so great. Like a new beginning...*'

She cut the message short. Esther was safe. If she could just send a written reply with the last of the signal, the last of the battery. It might get through.

Neil moaned, a long last cry calling out for her. She ignored him, only half-listening to the patter of tendrils over the last bars of Caroline. He went silent, and she didn't look up.

Her thumbs worked the screen like crazy, throwing the words out onto the page like spraying water. '*Love you, little one. Stay safe. xxxxxxxxxxxxxx.*' She hit send and sighed.

Placing the phone carefully down in the centre of his empty massage chair, she looked up and there – there – was a mass of greenery over where her husband had last been. All fresh growth and new beauty. The name for bindweed came into her head and Neil would've loved it. It sounded Italian. *Convolvulus.* The Latin name. Older and more familiar was the folk name, the one used by her parents. Yes, years ago, this plant cropped up between paving slabs, smothered wooden fences. Morning Glory, that was it. Morning Glory.

Caroline smiled, taking one long step forwards, closer to the headstone-shaped greenery. Smiled, seeing white buds furling, deep in the space where her living room window had been. There was no trace of a view and yet, she knew the old oak trees were thriving in her favourite clearing.

Raising a hand to meet the waving tendrils, she breathed in the moist sweet-smelling natural air, and let the leaves softly touch her skin. This green and blue planet was evolving, and she would meet it in the woods. Hell, she would be the woods. She smiled, embracing the concept. Sighed out one last, long, contented breath.

Time to let go, Caroline. Time to get back to nature.

Semi-detached

by Stacia Smales Hill

Once upon a time in the far-off country of Cornwall, in a tiny village called Mousehole, tucked into a tiny cove at the very, very farthest point of Cornwall and reaching into the sea, in a white semi-detached council house, perched on a cliff overlooking Mousehole Island (if he bothered to look, which he didn't) lived a man.

His name was Leonard and he had taken to his bed.

The reason was this: Leonard had lived all his life in this semi-detached. From before his mum died, he was in this same room in this same bed. His other mum came – the one who brought her two boys over to play and cooked his dad dinner and never left – and nobody made him move.

He did leave once. Annette, the Harvey girl, got him in the net loft behind her parent's cottage after school. In that only moment of feverish passion and excitement in his whole life, she got up the duff, and he moved into the net loft on Brook Street with her. She fell in love with that sweet innocent face and wanted to be the one to have it, to consume that innocence like an After Eight. Munch on it, lick its sweetness off her lips, pick up the crumbs with her wet fingertip, and when it was all gone, become a proper Cornish couple where he'd go off fishing, then be down The Ship, come home for a lovely not so innocent rough and tumble, but otherwise, leave her be. She was sorely disappointed to find that Leonard's innocence didn't come off. It stayed on his face and followed her around, smiling at her as he rubbed her swelling tummy, shining through when the baby arrived and he held him wrapped up in an old Guernsey. When she couldn't take it anymore, when she knew his innocence was never going to come off, she took the baby and ran away as far as she could, which happened to be Cadgwith, where she became the third wife of a fisherman whose previous two wives had both run off themselves. But he knew what was what, and so did she, so that suited them both.

Leonard never saw either of them again. He moved back into his room, his other mum cooked him his meals, and no one ever tried to eat his innocence again.

His other mum grew old and took to her bed, and he cooked her meals and walked to the shop every morning to get her paper, until she died. Then the two sons who had left came back. They cried a bit, like good fishermen do, clapped Leonard on the back for being such a good son to her and taking care of their mum, even though he wasn't her son at all. They took her clothes out of the wardrobe and laughed at the pictures of themselves as children she had kept on her chest of drawers. Then they checked through her jewellery to see if there was anything valuable before throwing it all in a black bin bag on top of her printed dresses, big cotton panties, and dirty pink comfortable slippers before dropping the lot into the wheelie bin as they left.

Leonard came out of his room when he heard the back door close. He shuffled over to his other mum's bedroom door, closed his eyes so he wouldn't see the bed stripped bare of all but the sagging mattress, the wardrobe of empty hangers, the naked chest of drawers, and pulled the door shut. In his head it was forever like it was and nothing changed.

Leonard still walked to the shop every morning for the paper, cooked a meal when he remembered and threw half of it away. He was never young, but he grew older. His hair thinned but he made it go far by slicking it over his head and polishing it with the innocence that still sat there for all to see but no one looked. After a while he bought himself a mobility scooter, so he sat to get the paper, and he sat at the dark oak dining table with his back to the window overlooking the sea and made model boats. The boats were set onto shelves and ignored by the china ladies who never looked up from their bouquets of flowers to notice they were surrounded by a flotilla of three-masted schooners and World War 2 battleships. Then he sat in his comfy chair and looked at them all while eating his ready meal of Wonderfully Rich Fish Pie with Real Cream.

While he ate, he listened to the occasional sound of the TV coming from the other half of his semi-detached.

Sometimes there was loud music, sometimes the sound of children crying because they didn't want to go to bed. Mostly it was quiet. It had gone for a holiday let years ago, so mostly it was empty. Holidaymakers didn't want to stay in a white semi-detached former council house overlooking Mousehole Island when they could stay in a dark, damp, tiny, grey granite fisherman's cottage with no view and no garden and feel authentic. That suited Leonard just fine. And so, it was until a woman bought the place and moved in.

Her name was Vivienne, and this was her story.

Vivienne was tall and straight and had long, elegant arms that she liked to use to make broad sweeping gestures, like when she stood in the garden of her half of the semi-detached and looked out to sea. Each flowing sweep of her arm took in Mousehole Island, Mount's Bay, The Isles of Scilly, reached past the sunken island of Lyonesse, all the way to New York City. She had a foreign accent; someone had told Leonard it might be Scottish. She didn't look it, but she was a woman on the run.

Vivienne was the child of a comfortably settled, deeply unhappy insurance salesman and his wife. Her two older brothers and younger sister fulfilled all their parents' dreams for them by growing up to become comfortably settled and deeply unhappy themselves. Vivienne, however, buttoned on her cardigan and, with kindness shining out of her eyes and generosity pinned to her shoulder just above her heart, went out into the world, which at that time was a flat in Glasgow filled with drunken students. She fell in love with David, a Professor of Economics at Glasgow University who was worldly in the ways of the city and knew what was what. Her heart ached when she saw all his broken bits, sticking out at odd angles every time he spoke. She loved to kiss him and imagine that some magic liquid was being poured into him, like a big bottle of Benylin cough syrup. He loved it too, because when she closed her eyes to kiss him, he couldn't see the kindness, and when she pressed her generosity right up close to him, he could filch it without her even knowing. So it was that he ended up with new clothes, a new car, a new TV and when there was nothing new in his life with her anymore, he ran off to Edinburgh to live with his mother. Again.

Vivienne moved on. She moved on a lot. She realised that people like someone who is kind but not for long. After a while it is tiresome and boring compared to someone who is opinionated and cruel and never-endingly entertaining. So, she never outstayed her welcome.

One day she met a man who didn't take her kindness for meekness nor take her generosity to the bank, because he too was kind and generous and together, they moved on a lot. They had a glorious time, exploring the smallest parts of the world they could find, and you didn't get much smaller than this little village. But he didn't live long enough. It all came to an end quite suddenly in this place, looking out over this tiny cove at the island. When he died, all their children came together from all over the world and they cried so much they nearly broke the soft Cornish heart of the village. The children helped her empty his clothes from his suitcase and take them to the Fisherman's Mission, they talked about his life until they all had memories they could take away with them, and they scattered his ashes in the sea off Mousehole Island so it would feed the algae that fed the fish that fed the fishermen. Then they all hugged each other, cried a little more, and moved on.

Except for Vivienne, who lingered. Her soul was restless, but when she stood in this garden, overlooking the sea and made a sweep with her long slender arm, she took in Mousehole Island, Mount's Bay, The Isles of Scilly, the sunken island of Lyonesse, and her kind and generous man who for all she knew now stretched from here to New York City. It was, she thought, a good place to come back to.

If she was going to stay, then she had to make some changes. The last time anything had changed in Mousehole was in 1953 when William Drew applied for planning permission to change the colour of his front door from blue to green. It was denied, as it was not in keeping with a conservation area of great, outstanding natural beauty. He did it anyway, and the village was still talking. Vivienne had no idea that she needed to ask permission for anything, but she was kind and generous so hired all the local people to help her with her changes, and as work is work and there were no fish about, they all helped. She put in huge windows and took down the walls inside so she could always see the sea no matter where she was in the house. She painted everything white to reflect the blue-grey light. She put a nail in a wall and hung her rucksack on it as art. She found an old settee in a second-hand shop and recovered it in bright pink velvet. She bought a white kettle, an orange packet of Cornish Tea, and six beautiful blue and white china cups. Then she tied up her long blond hair that was just going grey, slipped on her cardigan with the generosity pinned just above her heart, and set out into the village to find people to hold the cups and drink the tea while sitting on her settee.

So it happened that Leonard was on his scooter heading for the newsagents just when Vivienne stepped out of her door. She looked at him with surprise. With all the noise of building work, she had never heard the silence coming from next door. She thought, 'He needs a cup of tea.' He smiled at her and she saw his innocence, even though by now it was covered with a few layers of dust and hair grease. 'And cake,' she added to herself. She smiled back.

'I'm Leonard. I live there,' he said and made the smallest possible motion with his head towards his side of the semi-detached. She noticed his voice needed oiling.

'I'm Vivienne, and I live here.' She made an elegant sweep with her arm to take in the house, the garden and most of the way to Lyonesse. 'Would you like a cup of tea?' she added. 'And cake?'

'No, thank you,' he replied, for his other mother had taught him to be polite. He put the electric motor in gear and scootered away, leaving Vivienne in a little cloud of innocence with the scent of loneliness. Vivienne breathed deeply. Then Vivienne went off to collect her tea people while Leonard went off to collect his paper.

When she had collected five that more or less matched the teacups in shape and size, she gathered them all together in her little semi-detached. They all wanted to come, of course, because Change had happened there and needed to be seen.

They admired the view, which they all saw every day, took in the light, the white, the rucksack. Then they sat with their fingers curled around the comfort of their teacups and put all the missing pieces back.

'Who was it that had this before you?' asked the hand-thrown rustic teacup with a few interesting and unexpected bumps.

'Sara,' Vivienne replied, kindly offering up the start of the verbal piece of string.

'Oh yes. And she bought it from Phil Yerpockettes and his wife – Pix, I think it was. Terrible people, the Yerpockettes,' said the blue cup with the chip on the underside that made her wobble a bit.

'Didn't they own the other place, too?' added the fine china cup with a hairline

crack.

'Oh yes, and the one up the hill,' said the souvenir mug.

'They ruined all their places,' threw in the only teacup with a proper saucer.

'Terrible.'

'Thought themselves Mousehole property magnates,' which caused a lot of teacups to jiggle and shake with laughter.

'But, of course, before them this was Mrs. Tregenza's.' There was a general sigh. A few looked into the depths of their cups to search for where the days had gone.

'Lovely lady.'

'Lived here until she died.'

'Her son married the sister of the man who married Leonard's oldest brother's wife's cousin. Stepbrother he is.'

'That's right. He worked with my mother's friend's brother over Newlyn, when he wasn't fishing with the other brother.'

'Do you remember the lovely settee she had?'

'Oh yes. Right there it was,' and the missing settee filled the previously empty space.

'Used to be a door there,' and a door slid into the wall.

'Ummm. My father built this place with some of the other boys from the village. Well built.'

'Solid. They were building them for their own, so they built them well.'

Vivienne could feel the house give a little 'humph', and a slightly arched eyebrow in her direction, but she just smiled and patted it kindly.

'Kitchen was there before.'

'Oh yes, before the chip pan fire.' Vivienne was only mildly alarmed at the sudden little blaze in the corner, but managed to cover it with her cardigan as she passed to make more tea.

So, it went until the walls were rebuilt, the furniture replaced, the genealogy established, the tea drunk and the cake eaten. Then the tea collection walked out the door, down the lane and back into the village to report and to recount. They would forever be The First to Have Tea with Vivienne. Vivienne grabbed a duster and shooed out the bits of furniture, extraneous walls and the odd door or two who were still lingering, before carefully washing up the cups and sweeping away the crumbs.

Leonard was oblivious to all that had been sewn into the social fabric of Mousehole over the past two hours. He heard nothing. Partly this was due to the thick concrete walls the considerate local lads had built between the two halves of the building. Partly it was due to the large bookcase that stood against that wall where the flotilla of model boats sailed in and out of the china damsels. Mostly it was because he had the TV turned up very loud. So loud he didn't hear the knocking on the door until its persistence inserted itself above the studio laughter of the 30-year-old comedy show. He looked up from his model of a French brigantine and waited.

It could be a mistake.

It undoubtedly was a mistake.

Someone lost. Someone looking for the Southwest Coast Path, which did not, he was sure, run through his lounge. Someone he couldn't help.

There it was again, riding over the muffled sound of the gulls, the quick rhythm of the setting up of a joke, the punch line, the laughs. Knocking. He put down the tweezers holding the small plastic block he had been about to place. It happened again. Knocking. His chair resisted being pushed back, his knees and back wouldn't quite straighten. Forward momentum was eventually established and he made his way to his front door. Unfortunately, whoever was knocking was still there. Still knocking. With huge misgivings, he turned the door handle, and pulled the door open.

'Hallloooo,' Vivienne said, 'It's me again. I thought you might like some cake.' She smiled.

Leonard felt more than saw her kindness – a bit like the slight warmth off a light bulb. What struck him was that she looked right at him. Not around him, not over him, not as though he were an obstruction preventing her curiosity from seeing what was beyond. She just looked at him, as though that were enough. Leonard looked at the foil wrapped parcel she held out in her hand.

'It will be good for your tea,' she added.

Leonard hesitated, mainly because he thought she said, 'it will be goo for Yorty' and he wasn't sure why cake would turn to goo and why she thought he had a Yorty – whatever that was. He held his hand out uncertainly and she placed the little package into it. It felt solid. Not like goo.

'Thank you,' he said, and closed the door. He placed the packet on the clean plate from lunchtime, and carefully opened it. It was a piece of Lemon Drizzle Cake. Bits of crystalised sugar clung to the crumpled tin foil. He picked off a small piece and placed it on his tongue. It fizzed slightly, then melted into sweet tart lemon – like his mouth had become filled with the taste of memory. He got himself a cup of tea, and with the kind of concentration he usually only gave his models, he ate the cake, and then wet his fingertip to capture each sweet crumb.

This cake, as delicious as it was, disturbed Leonard. Now he was in debt. He didn't like being in debt, but he could not think of any way to repay such obvious kindness and generosity. Until, a few days later, Billy the postman knocked on his door.

'Ah, Leonard,' he said, 'I don't suppose you'd be willing to take this parcel for her next-door, would you? It's just that she's not in and I've been carrying it around all morning already...'

'Yes,' Leonard said.

'Oh! Well then,' Billy said with delighted surprise. 'I'll pop a card through her letterbox, so she knows to come to you to collect it.'

Leonard didn't wait for Vivienne to come to him to collect it. As soon as he heard noises from beyond the wall, he stood up from the chair where he had been waiting, dressed in his going out green tweedy jacket and cap. He walked across the front of their houses to her door and knocked.

'Oh, hallloooo Leonard, how nice to see...'

'Here,' he said, resting the package against the door, and was gone.

A few days later he heard the sound of chattering women, knocking at her door. She was, he assumed At It Again. He turned up the sound of the television and bent his head over the brigantine now needing its mizzen attended to. When he heard the sound of chattering women leaving, he got up, pulled the curtains, and turned the TV down low. Then he sat in his chair, his glue-crusted fingernails scraping at the soft old varnish on the arms.

It happened: knocking. Leonard caught his breath. A pause. More knocking, only louder. Another pause. Then more knocking.

She is very persistent, Leonard thought, and he touched his hand to the bead of sweat that had caught in his eyebrow.

Four times she knocked, and then quiet oozed back into the room. Leonard sighed – either in relief or disappointment, he wasn't sure which. He turned the sound back up on the TV, abandoned the delicate task of the mizzen, made his tea, tidied away his plate and glass, put on his pyjamas and went to bed, where he lay for hours pretending to himself that he was asleep. It was no good. He threw off his covers, slipped into his slippers and padded to the front door. He stood for a moment, hand on the doorknob. 'No cake. No cake.' He repeated to himself. He opened the door. There it was: a small foil-wrapped packet with '*Eat Me*' written on a torn piece of notepaper stuck into the fold. '*Eat Me xxx*' actually. Three crosses. Three kisses.

He put the kettle on, and when the tea was made, he carefully removed the note and put it to one side, then delicately unfolded the crinkled foil.

Carrot Cake. With Cream Cheese Frosting. Moist, dark, crumbly, with large bits of frosting coating the foil. He pinched a raisin and some crumbs together between his fingers and gently sucked them into his mouth. The dark warm sweetness filled him like a night-time hug. It was the perfect cake to eat at three o'clock in the morning with a sweet milky mug of tea. He matched the cake with the tea so they both ended at the same time. When he had smoothed the foil with his finger, getting the last taste of sweet cream cheese frosting off, he folded the foil and put it in the recycling, put his cup in the sink and went back to bed. He couldn't remember his dreams but at one point he woke himself up by laughing.

In the morning the panic set in. How ever was he going to repay this cake?

So it was. Vivienne worked her way through the village and the British Classic Teatime Treats cookbook, and Leonard's debt accumulated. Victoria Sponge. Battenburg Cake. Sometimes Vivienne would go away for a few days. If this happened over a bin day, he could take her bin to the end of the road – a rather tricky manoeuvre that involved disembarking from his scooter, dragging the bin back, remounting the scooter and driving one-handed while the other hand hung onto the bouncing, rumbling and banging bin. Sticky Toffee Pudding. Black Forest Gateau. There were a few more packages left with him by Billy the postman. Madeira Cake. Eccles Cakes. Once he saw a discarded paper coffee cup on the pavement outside her house. He stopped his scooter, managed to reach the cup without toppling out, and chucked it in a neighbour's bin on his way for the newspaper. That, he thought, was a two-cake deed. Bins were three-cakes. Packages were only one-cake. Still, it was hard to keep up. Fruited Scones with Strawberry Jam. Crumbly Shortbread Biscuits. There weren't that many packages, or days she was away when the bins needed to go out. And there was only ever the one coffee cup.

When he pulled even, he opened the door to her kindness. When he felt in debt, it would remain shut and only opened in hopefulness when night had fallen.

One day, Leonard had just finished a plastic scale model of The Golden Hind and was moving a small china girl with a puppy slightly further back on the shelf to make room for it. His innocence was particularly shiny that day, gleaming slightly brighter than his hair. It was a sunny day, if he had looked, which of course he hadn't. There was a knock at the door. As he was up already, he decided to answer it. There was Vivienne holding out a tray with two cups of tea and a plate of home-made Jammy Dodgers.

'Here you go,' she said. 'Tea and biscuits are always nicer when you have someone to share it with.'

He couldn't help himself. He took the cup.

'And a biscuit,' she said.

He took a biscuit.

She put the tray down on the ground, took the other cup and a biscuit, then settled herself comfortably against the doorjamb. 'I put a spoonful of sugar in yours,' she said. 'You look like a spoonful of sugar man.'

'Lovely,' he said after a moment. 'Yes.'

She nibbled and sipped. He hesitated, in expectation of that opening word: 'So...' that would lead to a question he couldn't answer or a conversation he didn't know how to have. But nothing. She just nibbled and sipped. After a moment, so did he.

When the tea was drunk, and the biscuits gone, she offered up the tray for his empty cup. 'Thank you for taking my bin down the other day. And for taking in the packages for me.'

'You are welcome,' he replied. Then, 'Thank you for the cakes.'

'A pleasure.'

'They are very good,' he added.

She blushed a little, 'That's very kind.'

Leonard blushed as well.

Vivienne waggled her fingers at him as a goodbye and left. Leonard closed the door, moved slowly across the kitchen to his chair and sat. He felt lonely.

Vivienne had not meant to stir loneliness into the tea. In her cup it had swirled restlessly around the frothy vortex. In Leonard's it had sunk to the bottom where it added to the heavy sweetness of the last few sips.

Over the next few days, Vivienne cleaned what was clean, tidied what was tidy, checked the contents of her rucksack before adjusting it carefully on the wall. She chased puffballs of loneliness from under the bed, swept it off the tops of picture frames and scrubbed it off the floors, then emptied it into the bin under the sink. She would stand for a moment, just a moment, looking out at Mousehole Island from her terrace, and think all the way past Lyonesse to New York City, before returning inside to discover she had tracked the loneliness back in. Once again it had settled in a thin film over everything. Once again, she would get out her dust cloth, her dustpan, and her thoughts of places she had yet to move on to. She did not go into the village to collect tea people, nor did she wave cheerfully at Leonard as he went past on his mobility scooter to collect the newspaper.

Because Leonard didn't go past. His loneliness proved sticky. First it stuck him on his kitchen chair for hours. Then it stuck him to his bed, well into the morning. When he managed to peel off the sheets, he only got as far as the comfy chair in front of the TV before he found himself stuck again.

Slowly the loneliness chomped on his soft rounded cheeks and the fleshy bits of his arms, until his skin sagged grey and shapeless, indistinguishable from the once-plaid dressing gown that was stuck to him. The loneliness began to weave webs, thickening the air. Even if it had not stuck him to his chair, he would have found it difficult to move.

The village noticed his absence. A brother from the other mother was called, an ambulance appeared, unstuck Leonard from his chair and took him away. There wasn't much of him once they had peeled away all the sticky layers, but enough to connect to machines, pump full of liquid ('Sadly,' he thought, 'it isn't tea.'), and speak to too loudly and cheerily. The nurses washed the loneliness off him, clucked at him when he didn't eat, measured and counted him and noted on their charts, and when they decided he was better, put him in a car and sent him back home.

The village did not notice Vivienne's absence.

Vivienne was Moving On. She had moved on from sweeping out the loneliness to packing it into boxes. There was a small pile of To Keep boxes in her Nostalgia corner. There was a much larger pile of boxes in her Moving On corner that would find their way to new owners. She was so engrossed in her task of Moving On she didn't hear the lack of pipes banging as Leonard didn't run his bath, she didn't hear the absence of canned laughter from the TV that he hadn't turned on, she didn't see his scooter not go past the window, not making the electric hum as it didn't accelerate on its way not going to the newspaper shop. It wasn't until weeks later, as she stood at her kitchen window packing away the teacups that she saw him emerge from the back seat of the hospital car. Then, all these nots and absences and silences filled her head. She folded her long slender figure onto the edge of a kitchen chair, and she wept. When she was done and had blown her nose and wiped her eyes, she cleared away the box of teacups and baked a cake.

There may have been a little knock. If there was, Leonard hadn't heard it. When he opened the door for the postman, Billy was standing there with the familiar foil packet in his hand. 'It didn't come through the post,' Billy said quickly, 'it was just sitting here.' Leonard took the packet and the post, closed the door and unfolded the small note tucked in the fold.

Welcome Home xxx.

He unwrapped the foil and there was a Fruitcake with a melted marzipan centre and a thick layer of marzipan gently laid on the top. He broke off a small piece and let the taste of Christmas and Easter melt into his mouth. The cakes didn't come every day, although he did check every day. He couldn't help himself. There were no knocks announcing their presence by the front door, at random times and random intervals, so that Leonard could not even anticipate their arrival and meet them. He didn't have the strength to worry about the pile of cake debt that was accumulating, but he did have enough strength to formulate a plan.

The first time he took his scooter to collect the newspaper, he saw the other half of the semi-detached filled up with loneliness. From inside his house, over the sound of canned laughter he heard the lack of chattering voices. He noticed the absence of parcels to be taken in.

So, after a particularly lovely piece of Walnut Tea Cake consumed for breakfast with the obligatory cup of sweet milky tea, he went into the village for his paper and then made an unaccustomed stop. He emerged from the shop with a bag which he scrunched up around the precious object inside, placed at the bottom of his scooter's basket, then laid his newspaper over the top. He drove as carefully as he could over the broken pavements as his purchase jumped and bumped in the basket. He paused before he reached the house, then accelerated past her window, in case she was looking out.

Which she was, of course: waiting to be sure he had returned, checking for the sound of the TV, the electric hum of the scooter, the clanking of the pipes, trying to make up for all the time he was away and she hadn't notice the nots, the absences, the silences.

The next morning it was sunny, Leonard noticed. When the time was right, he got into his scooter and started down the pavement. This time, he stopped at Vivienne's door. She was watching from her kitchen window. He waved and beckoned. She opened her door with surprise.

'Here,' he said, and offered up an old red beer tray with two mugs of tea and a plate of McVities Milk Chocolate Digestives. 'That one,' he indicated the gleaming new mug that had 'Welcome to Mousehole' on its side. 'No sugar,' he added. She smiled and nodded. Once she had selected her biscuit, he put the tray back into the basket. Vivienne settled on the doorsill. They both sipped and nibbled in the sunshine.

'Are you feeling better?' she asked.

'Oh yes,' he said. 'I am getting a cat,' he added.

'That is lovely! When?'

'Tomorrow. Poppy. Her name is Poppy.'

'Do you need anything for her? I am going into town with this lot,' she indicated the pile of Moving On boxes he could just see behind her, 'and can pick up anything you need.' She pulled her cardigan around her shoulders and he noticed the generosity pinned there.

'I might, but I won't know for a few days. Can you wait?'

She hesitated for a very small moment, then nodded.

Poppy arrived the next day in a cardboard box out of the back of an Animal Welfare Trust van. The day after, Vivienne stopped Leonard on his daily trek, with tea in a

Queen's souvenir mug she had had to unpack, and a slice of Stem Ginger Cake.

'How is Poppy?'

'Already lying in my lap,' he said. 'And she has taken to sleeping in the space on the bookcase where I was going to put the Bismark.'

'Do you need anything?' she asked again.

'I might,' he said again, 'but I won't know for a few more days. Can you wait?'

She nodded and smiled at him.

So it went, not all days, not most days, but some days. Sometimes at her door. Now, sometimes, at his. He noticed more than she did, how the loneliness was oozing out every time she opened the door and fizzled in the sunshine before it disappeared. But the boxes in the Moving On corner remained. He knew when she had been standing on her terrace, looking out over Mousehole Island, past Lyonesse and all the way to New York City, not because he saw her there but because he noticed the bits of loneliness salting the corners of her eyes.

One day, Leonard made a decision. It was such a big decision he had to wait two whole days to recover from the event. Then, as the decision didn't change or go away, he got up one morning with determination, got dressed, mounted his scooter and stopped outside Vivienne's door. She opened with a smile full of the expectation of tea and a biscuit.

'I am going to Newlyn,' he said a bit too loudly, 'do you want to come?'

Vivienne blinked with surprise. 'Oh! Well, no, I don't think so...' Leonard's determination developed a slow leak.

Vivienne watched as he began to deflate. 'Sorry, I have changed my mind. Yes. Can you wait?' Quickly Vivienne slapped a patch on the pinhole in Leonard's ambition, grabbed a coat and scarf and looked hesitantly at the scooter.

'Just there' Leonard wiggled his fingers over his shoulder. She stepped onto the platform between the wheels, placed her hands on the shoulders of his going out green tweedy coat, and off they went – very very slowly. They had built up a bit of momentum by the time they were seen passing the newsagents and the gift shop where Leonard had purchased the 'Welcome to Mousehole' mug. By the time they reached the road to Newlyn that followed the cliffs overlooking the bay, they were going fast enough that Vivienne's scarf was lifting slightly in the wind and a small strand of Leonard's hair waved back at her tentatively. In Newlyn, he bought a bag of kitty litter, and she looked at a plate with blue birds on it before putting it back. As they hummed back through the village, Leonard slightly raised one index finger in a wave at the villagers who were watching them pass, leaving them washed in fresh air and happiness.

It wasn't that week, or the next, but the week after, over a cup of tea and a packet of bourbons that Vivienne told Leonard she was getting a dog.

'Oh, that's nice.' He made sure his innocence was on his face when he said it. He had made sure his innocence was there each time he looked over her shoulder and noticed another box in the Moving On corner had been unpacked. He had polished up his innocence before he told her about how Poppy had taken to sleeping in his bed and sometimes didn't emerge from the warmth of the covers until mid-morning. His innocence was gleaming from use.

So it was that Max arrived, bursting out of the back of the Animal Welfare Trust van, dragging the uniformed young man on the other end of his lead up to the door where Max barked and wagged his tail furiously until Vivienne opened it up. So it was that every day thereafter, Max could be seen dragging Vivienne through the village, from shop to shop. Max believed that people existed to give him treats, and he was right. Max loved long walks along the Southwest Coast path, or through muddy fields and took Vivienne with him. They would sit side by side with a cup of tea from a flask and a bowl of water, contemplating how far they had come and debating how much further they wanted to go.

At the end of every long walk, they came back.

The boxes had been moved out of the Moving On corner to make room for Max's bed. The women in the village talked to Vivienne as they fed Max treats, and occasionally they would appear at her door for a cup of tea and a slice of cake to hear about their walks, for despite her kindness and her generosity they didn't find her boring at all.

And not this year, nor the next, but the year after, they started to invite her to tea at theirs.

Not all days, not most days, but some days, Leonard and Vivienne would share a cup of tea and cake or biscuits, and share stories about Poppy and Max. Or they would meet along the road, Leonard coming back from a great adventure, perhaps as far as Lidl in Penzance, and Vivienne at the end of the lead, off on a long walk with Max.

Leonard's innocence would be burnished by the wind, and Vivienne's eyes would be watering with kindness.

At the end of every day, Leonard would sit in his house, with Poppy on his lap, the TV on loudly, happily making another model ship. Vivienne would pack her rucksack for another walk the next day, and chat to Max about Mousehole Island, Lyonesse and as far away as New York City.

Biographies

Stephen Baird, after a career in education, is writing a YA historical fantasy set in Renaissance Italy. His first novel was *Fire in the Straw*. He has written three plays and a rock musical for 8-13 year-olds. Stephen's wife correctly predicted that all three sons would reach adolescence before their dad. Stephen and Liz live in Truro with Mustard the Whippet. Twitter: sbairdauthor   Facebook: Stephen Baird Author stephenbairdwriter.wixsite.com

Kate Barden: Living in Cornwall all her life, Kate works with care-experienced young people. Along with published poems, she has co-written and performed shows with her company, Blabbermouth, including at the Edinburgh Fringe. Kate is currently rehearsing with the RSC, Hall for Cornwall and Carnon Downs Drama Group. She writes and performs spoken word and is collaborating on a poetry anthology about women who sea-swim in Cornwall. Kate sings in an 80s covers band, collects tattoos, and rides pillion on a Harley www.katebarden.co.uk

Lou Bergin has never been short of ideas for a story, with family and friends ever wary they will turn up on her page. Lou lives mostly in Cornwall, but spends the winter in New Zealand, her place of birth. Her ideal day would include reading and outdoor adventures, perhaps simultaneously. On retiring, Lou undertook postgraduate study in creative writing and the environment. She is grateful to her four children and spouse for their honest reviews of her work. She can be found at a new Instagram account @ maggielou__writer.

Carol-Ann Cook lives in North Cornwall where she enjoys cliff walks, reading and hot chocolate. She is a procrastinating artist and writer, an enthusiastic singer and an active supporter of local theatre, her latest role being 'Mother Hubbard' in panto. You can find Carol on Instagram @carol_at_the_castle

Mike Davis resides on the wild North Cornish Coast, where he spends his days pursuing scattered thoughts while securing untamed story ideas under large pebbles lest the wind snatches them away forever. Allegedly, one of his finest unpublished tales was devoured in its entirety by a disrespectful gull. Rumour abounds that the sequel suffered a similar fate, ending up in the belly of a basking shark. When not concocting short stories and flash fiction, Mike can be found between waves honing his stand-up paddleboarding skills. cornwallwriters.co.uk/mike-davis

TJ Dockree is the author name for sustainable fashion designer and illustrator, Tracey Dockree. She is not only the founder of *Cornwall Writers*; she also founded the ethical fashion zine *Ethical Rebel*, Truro's *Sewing & Design Studio*, and tshirt brand *A Story In TShirts*. Her previously published short stories include *Knights on a Train, Little Bear, Pure of Heart* and *Slagoon's Breath*. She is publishing her first novel *Timeline 67: the Chartmaker's Daughter* in 2025. Genres: Young Adult, Fantasy, Historical Fiction, Sci-Fi, Adventure. Website: cornwallwriters.co.uk/t-j-dockree Instagram: tjdockree X: DockreeTj Facebook: TJ Dockree

Ulrike Duran Bravo is German-Chilean, lucky to live on the Isles of Scilly, though usually based in Cornwall. With an MA in Creative Writing, she has stories published in anthologies and magazines, a short play performed and is part of the MorPoets group. Her writing is often inspired by her heritage, art and nature. Her best days are spent with her children by the beach, jumping in the sea and doing something creative. Facebook: Ulrike Duran – Writer

Ben French enjoys creating – words on paper, bedtime stories for his children, noises on guitar, and dodgy DIY. Loving all things literary he studied English at Falmouth College of Arts and went on to teach. On the weekends he can be seen dragging his family around country walks but always stops for a second-hand book sale. He divides his time between his home near Falmouth and his ranch in Montana. He wishes.

Jo Grande has been writing stories since she was six. Paper was in short supply then, so she wrote in Christmas and Birthday cards, adding bits of paper. Her mother kept them in a folder, which has recently come to light. Jo wrote *The Green Caravan* in three exercise books with an illustration for each page, which she published in 2012. She gained an MA with merit in professional writing in 2018 and published a selection of her prize-winning stories in 2019 – *Short Stories for Long Journeys*. She's soon to publish a new book about the first passenger jet aircraft, the Comet.

Jess Humphries has tried to prove that men can multitask by being a husband, father, grandad, musician, aviation geek and data nerd, sometimes all at once. He always dreamed of having his writing published and at 51 is showing that it's never too late to realise your ambitions. Having been a songwriter for many years, well crafted words which touch emotions are what he aims for. Occasionally he pulls it off. Jess lives in Cornwall with his ceramicist wife Suzi, and also loves travel and Thai food.

Anita Hunt has an MA in Creative Writing and is a poet and author. Her debut novel, Behind the Curtain, will be published in the summer of 2024 by Spellbound Books Ltd. She is passionate about equality and accessibility for all, holding a couple of volunteering roles as well as performance signing in a choir. She relaxes by walking her dog, reading and crafting. Her favourite phrase is, 'sleep is for wimps...' piskiedreams.com X:@janxie12 Facebook:anitadhunt1 Youtube:@piskiedreams1961

Lamorna Ireland was born and raised in Cornwall, and lives on the outskirts of St Austell with her husband, two children and loveable whippet. As well as teaching English in a local secondary school, Lamorna is the multi-published contemporary romance writer of *Unexpected Beginnings*, *Unexpected Truths* and *Along a Cornish Creek*. Lamorna is taking her brand to its next chapter, as well as working tirelessly on her new series of books set in her beloved Kernow. You can follow her on all social media platforms for new and exciting updates.

Jason Kenyon has divided his time between customer service for video games & film companies and writing the whimsical and occasionally dark fantasy series *Mage for Hire*. He is currently working on a sci-fi fantasy series that pits a technological empire against far too many dragons. Outside of life in Cornwall, he has spent several years in the Republic of Ireland and has now found his way over to Watford. He is on Twitter as @Archimegadon, Facebook as @MageForHire and his website is mageforhire.co.uk

Catherine Leyshon is a geographer, corgi-wrangler and runner. She has published widely in academic journals and books on non-fictional topics as diverse as climate change, film, landscape, volunteering and care, but also likes to have a crack at fiction from time to time. She has her best ideas for short stories when walking the dog, who now wants co-author credits and to be paid in gravy bones.

Claudia Loveland gets excited by words and music and has a happy history of combining the two. On moving to Cornwall, her stories began to explore the experiences of incomers and returners to the county: parting with the past and giving the future a facelift. She enjoys singing and playing table tennis, and loves humour, change and surprises. Good, because she's just moved to Cumbria to start another new life. Again. Crazy. cornwallwriters.co.uk/ claudia-loveland; Facebook @ClaudiaLovelandWriter

Emily Charlotte Ould is a freelance writer, editor, and proofreader from Cornwall. She studied Creative Writing at Falmouth University before completing a Masters in Writing for Young People at Bath Spa. She is proud to be a founder of *PaperBound Magazine*, an online publication celebrating children's and young adult fiction, and is an enthusiastic lover of country music. Find her on Twitter: emilyocharlotte Instagram @emilycharlotteeditorial and visit her website: emilycharlotteeditorial.com

Caroline Philipps, after juggling bringing up her three daughters with various careers, is now working on a historical novel set in Cornwall and France during the Second World War. Her family have banned her from starting further projects until this novel is finished. You can find Caroline on Facebook at LifeCornish.

Christiana Richardson is a former newspaper reporter and has a distinction in MA Creative Writing from Plymouth University. She's seen her pieces published in journals and an anthology. She loves walking along Cornish coast paths and gazing at lighthouses.

Stacia Smales Hill fashioned an extensive career out of writing avoidance. Student, mime artist, wife, mother, performer, teacher, marketeer, digital guru – all successfully eliminated any possibility of setting aside time for writing. Sadly, she now finds herself on her own with no choice but to commit the workings of her mind to paper. Her first novel is coming to the end of its 392nd draft, while numerous short stories have yet to be wrenched out of her hands, other than the one contained here. She wants to assure the reader that all of her stories start as perfectly normal tales, but then something happens.

Rose Taylor has lived in Cornwall all of her life, mostly working in the charity sector. She mainly writes fantasy and sci fi, occasionally dabbling in poetry. She has a degree in history and is particularly interested in Cornwall's industrial heritage and the reclamation of mining landscapes by the natural world. *The Fall* enabled her to combine all of her interests into one short story.

Alice Thomas has lived in Cornwall for most of her life and studied to achieve two Master's degrees. She practices in digital art and writing, currently drafting a few books, one of which is set in a sci-fi fantasy universe she daydreamt about for many years. She has written many short stories and a few winning drafts for the National Novel Writing Month, as well as writing for a few websites as a freelance journalist. Her website is at www.alicetomasu.com and she can also be found on her Instagram as @ProperNeko.

Ella Walsworth-Bell is a speech therapist and writer based in Falmouth. She leads a women's poetry collective inspired by the sea. Together, the Mor Poets have published two books: *Morvoren: the poetry of sea swimming* and *Mordardh: surf poetry.* Ella twitters for herself on @BellWalsworth and swims with the shoal alongside @MorvorenProject.

Printed in Great Britain
by Amazon

42429758R00202